Palace of Betrayal
WOMEN OF DECEPTION: BOOK ONE

MADDIE WADE

Palace of Betrayal
Women of Deception Book One
By Maddie Wade

Published by Maddie Wade
Copyright © September 2022

Cover: Clem Parsons-Metatec
Editing: Black Opal Editing
Formatting: Black Opal Editing

This is a work of fiction. Names characters places and incidents are a product of the author's imagination or are used fictitiously and are not to be construed as fact. Any resemblance to actual events organisations or persons—living or dead—is entirely coincidental.

All rights reserved. By payment of the required fees, you have been granted the non-exclusive non-transferable right to access and read the text of this eBook on a screen. Except for use in reviews promotional posts or similar uses no part of this text may be reproduced transmitted downloaded decompiled reverse-engineered or stored in or introduced into any information storage and retrieval system in any form or by any means whether electronic or mechanical now known or hereafter invented without the express written permission of the author.

First edition September 2022 ©Maddie Wade

Acknowledgments

I am so lucky to have such an amazing team around me without which I could never bring my books to life. I am so grateful to have you in my life, you are more than friends you are so essential to my life.

My wonderful beta team, Greta, and Deanna who are brutally honest and beautifully kind. If it is rubbish you tell me, it is and if you love it you are effusive. Your support means so much to me.

My editor—Linda at Black Opal Editing, who is so patient. She is so much more than an editor, she is a teacher and a friend.

Thank you to my group Maddie's Minxes, your support and love for Fortis, Eidolon, Ryoshi and now Shadow Elite you are so important to me. Special thanks to Rowena, Tracey, Faith, Rachel, Carolyn, Kellie, Maria, Rochelle, Becky, Vicky, Greta, Deanna, Sharon and Linda L for making the group such a friendly place to be.

My UK PA Clem Parsons who listens to all my ramblings and helps me every single day.

My ARC Team for not keeping me on edge too long while I wait for feedback.

Lastly and most importantly thank you to my readers who have embraced my books so wholeheartedly and shown a love for the stories in my head. To hear you say that you see my characters as family makes me so humble and proud. I hope you enjoy Bebe and León's love story as much as I did.

Cover: Clem Parsons @Metatec
Editing: Black Opal Editing

Prologue

"BELLADONNA, DUCK!"

Bebe reacted, dropping to her haunches as the fourth man she was fighting threw a blade straight for her heart. Then, spinning on the balls of her feet, she swung low and took out the legs of the third man with a sweep of her leg. He hit the ground hard; the wind knocked from his lungs with the force.

With no time to think, she reacted on instinct, jumping lithely to her feet and blocking a strike coming from the man who'd missed with the knife. Her forearms took the brunt of the blow as she spun underneath his arm, landing an elbow strike to the back of his head. He fell, his face hitting the side of the coffee table as he went down.

"Stay the fuck down." Her breathing heaved, her blood pumping adrenalin through her body and it felt damn good.

Finally having a second, she drew her weapon, a 9mm Glock 19 and her personal favourite, on the two men on the ground at her feet and turned to Lili with a smile. "Thanks, Wolfbane."

Lili, her dark hair wild around her face, grinned as she pushed the man at her feet back to the ground with her scuffed biker boot. "No problem, this felt good."

Bebe nodded in agreement, flicking her ponytail out of her face. "Yeah, it's always good to take out assholes like these."

Walking around the four men groaning in pain from the beating they'd just taken, she searched them for weapons, checked their pockets for any surprises, and when she found none, cuffed them with cable ties. Lying on their bellies with their arms behind them, they looked like the weak and pathetic men they were. It would do them good to feel as vulnerable as the girls they'd victimised.

"You got this while I call it in?"

Bebe waved a hand for Lili to go ahead. "Sure."

Lili left the living room of the grand house in Surrey to call in their location to their boss, Roz. Bebe looked at the four men on the expensive cream carpet who'd been grooming young girls and selling them to the highest bidder. Her disgust for men like these was only surpassed by her anger that they'd gotten away with it for so long.

Asaf, the leader, looked at her from the ground where he lay, hatred in his cold, dark eyes.

"You'll die for this."

His accent was thick from his pain, and Bebe didn't feel an ounce of sympathy for him. She crouched beside him and grabbed a handful of his hair, pulling it back until he hissed in pain, hatred on every muscle of his face. "You know, Asaf, bigger, and I must say better, men have tried and yet here I am and there you are. So, stop embarrassing yourself and shut up. You're going to jail where I'll make sure they know exactly what kind of man you are. We both know men like you don't do well in prison."

Watching him pale almost made her smile. What stopped her was the thought of these men's victims and the very real battle they faced to have a somewhat normal life after what these animals had done to them.

Lili stepped back inside. "Authorities are on their way."

Bebe heard sirens in the distance at the announcement. The police had been hunting these guys for a while. Now they had them and the evidence to put them away for a very long time. "Time to go, boys. Enjoy prison."

Lili and Bebe left by the back door and slipped through the garden and onto the street behind. Her head was on a swivel as they weaved through the cars until they found the Mini Cooper Roz had left for them, the keys under the front driver's fender as always.

As Bebe drove, Lili offered her a Bounty chocolate bar she'd found in the glovebox.

"And this is why I love Roz."

"Yeah, always chocolate left in the getaway cars."

"We headed back to the safe house?" Bebe asked around the sweet, coconut goodness in her mouth.

Lili shook her head around a mouthful of Cadburys Caramel, her favourite. "No. Boss lady wants us home. She has a big job for five of us and we have to meet her at midnight at Athena."

Bebe frowned at the news wondering what it could be, then shrugged. She'd find out soon enough.

Talia, the woman who'd saved and then taught Roz everything she knew, had been the last of the line of warrior women until then. She'd taught Roz about fighting, killing, and surviving, making her stronger both in body and mind. Roz had then recruited each of the ten-woman team and had done the same with them.

Roz was hard, strict, and didn't tolerate weakness, especially in herself. But she was fair and loved them all like family. She never let any of them give up or give in to the emotions that warred in their minds, making them feel weak. The chocolate was just one way she showed she cared without being overly emotional, which wasn't her style.

It was funny how things worked out. Once an insular force, they didn't operate alone all the time now. They did joint missions with other organisations, and her family had become significantly more extensive than she'd ever expected it would be. It was almost enough to eradicate the pain and rejection from her own blood family.

Shaking the thoughts away, she turned on her favourite playlist. She and Lili sang most of the way home, letting the adrenalin of the fight leave their bodies as they belted out tune after tune, much to the amusement of the people who drove past.

Dropping Lili off at her home, she headed into her apartment on the ground floor of an old Victorian house owned by two of her friends, Mitch and his wife, Autumn. Mitch worked for Eidolon, one of the companies they partnered with on occasion. The property had been converted into four gorgeous apartments. Mitch and his wife had the top two, and Waggs, his wife, and their son had the apartment opposite hers on the ground floor. She loved living there and making the space her own while still having people she cared about, and who she knew cared about her, close.

Bending, she picked up Mountbatten, her white Persian cat and tried to give him some love. He fought to get free from her hold in punishment for leaving him. "Seriously, Monty, if I don't work, you don't eat."

Her cat flicked his tail in the air in evident disgust and walked toward her bedroom, where she knew he'd lie in the middle of her bed, ignoring her for the rest of the night.

Taking a quick shower and changing into skin-tight jeans and a white tee, she spotted her wolf tattoo in the mirror as she pulled the tee over her belly. The small tattoo was the same one all the Zenobi girls had, although they had them in different places. Hers was on her left rib cage and had hurt like hell, but she liked it. It represented the spirit of the wolf and the pack mentality. Zenobi was a pack, a family, and they looked after the weakest when needed.

Heading into the kitchen, she grabbed an apple and moved to the fridge for some water. Eyeing the medication sitting on the middle shelf, she sighed. Bebe had been taking the drugs for a month in preparation. Now it looked like it wouldn't happen if she was out of the country. Grabbing a mineral water from the fridge, she wondered if there would ever be a time when she had a family of her own. Roz made it work with her gorgeous girls and that adorable baby boy, but she had the love and support of a man who thought she hung the moon.

A pang of envy twisted in her belly, not because she begrudged Roz that happiness. God knew she deserved it more than anyone after the hell she'd been through, but Bebe wanted that too. Going it alone was her only option right now as the clock kept ticking and that elusive man stayed hidden from her. If he even existed.

Closing the fridge, she headed out the door to the meeting Roz had requested, driving the Mini, which was a gorgeous grey and so much fun, to the Athena offices. When she pulled into the car park at the front, the lights were out, but she knew they'd be using the room at the back, which had no windows to give away a mission. Secrecy was crucial to everything they did.

Laughter moved through the building as she entered, closing the door and reactivating the alarms as she went. The sound of Mercy laughing, after everything she'd been through, made her lips tip into a wide grin, a sense of pride and love for her friend filling her heart.

Zenobi had come close to losing her. First physically from the wounds she'd received, then from the mental torture she'd been through at the hands of those animals, but now she was out the other side. She'd had her cover blown during a mission involving Zack, the leader of Fortis Security, the other group of Black Ops guys they worked with on occasion. Mercy had been raped, beaten, and left for dead. She still had bad days, and when she did, they all rallied around her, making sure one of them was there for her.

"Hey, Mercy."

Mercy smiled, her honey blonde hair swinging in the ponytail she wore. "Bebe." The younger woman crossed to her, hugging her tight. "God, I feel like I haven't seen you in ages."

Bebe pulled back to look at her and get a feel for how she was doing. Satisfied her friend was okay, she squeezed her arm gently. "Yeah, we've crossed over a bit, but it's good to see you now."

Mercy shrugged. "Nature of the job."

"Bebe!"

She twisted to see Lorna, Laverne, and Lili walk into the room. The three women were all wildly different to look at but all stunningly beautiful. Lili was medium height with dark hair and big blue eyes and looked as innocent as the purest snow. Laverne was blonde, with long hair and hazel eyes with long lashes, and at nearly six feet in height was model tall for a woman. Then there was Lorna, who looked like she ran an empire and dripped class from every pore with her sleek blonde hair and intelligent hazel eyes.

Lastly, there was Roz, who was the epitome of badass in her book. She had short dark hair, full lips, wide, pale green eyes, and a body men had, and would, die for if she were still in the field. Her own colouring had become something that she hardly recognised as different to these women. Her copper skin and dark hair were typical for South Asian women and yet here she was, just Bebe, the sister they loved for her heart. That didn't mean she didn't endure the hatred her Pakistani heritage could elicit in some ignorant people. The hate towards people with her skin tone could be exhausting but she'd learned to roll with the punches and only educate those worth educating.

"Hey, Roz."

The woman assessed her and Lili before, seemingly satisfied, she spoke. "Good work on that last job, you two."

The compliment was as good as they'd get from Roz, but it meant a lot.

Bebe winked at Lili, who smiled. "Thanks."

Roz had a handful of files in her hand as she moved behind her desk and took a seat. The desk was glass and chrome and had several pictures of her family proudly displayed. The room was large, leaving plenty of room for them to sit in the easy chairs or on the couch as the meeting began.

Leaning forward, Roz clasped her hands, and the anticipation in the room rose. There was an electric current in the air increasing the feeling that something big was about to happen.

The thrill of a new target, a new mission, was revving through her blood.

"I know I don't have to say this, but I want to reiterate that the job I'm about to give you is top secret. Nobody but the people I'm talking with and those of us in this room are to know about it unless I say so. Do you all understand?"

Bebe felt her blood run hot. Her heart rate increased just a fraction at the serious tone and the fact Roz was reiterating the secrecy they worked under when each of them knew the importance already. "Yes, of course."

Murmurs of agreement came from the others, and she saw Mercy cast her a glance.

"Good." Roz nodded and opened the file on the top. "We have reason to believe that five underground auctions will take place over the next six months. We don't know where or exactly when, or what the product will be, but we do know that the buy-in for even entering the auction is a priceless object."

"Do we know who?" Bebe asked, feeling her skin itch with the need to get started already.

"We believe The Collector is behind it."

Laverne crossed her long legs; the denim shorts she wore made them look even longer. "Damn, no wonder they called us. The entire world has been hunting that bastard for years and hasn't had any luck."

"Which is why they brought us in to handle this. We believe the items for auction are projects stolen by The Collector and his people from different government agencies around the world. Not just projects but software and hardware that, if allowed into the hands of terrorists or even garden variety assholes, could bring the world to its very knees. The agencies involved haven't come up with anything, and as they don't trust each other not to lie, they decided as a group to bring in an independent to chase this down."

Bebe cocked her head, a frown marring her brow as her lips pursed in thought. "I agree it's a good solution. Although I'm shocked they went for it. Multiple government agencies agreeing is almost unheard of, but why us? Surely Shadow would be the obvious choice."

Shadow Elite was a secret group that handled this kind of thing, and although they were just as good, Zenobi was more independent. Shadow answered indirectly to the Queen of England and came under Eidolon as their parent company.

"I'm glad you asked." Roz flipped the folder and spread out five pictures on the desk in front of her.

Bebe and the other women moved closer to get a good look. Lined up were five images of priceless gemstones. The Blue Water Diamond, the Blood Ruby, the Tanzanite Tears, the Mystic Alexandrite, and the Evergreen Emerald. All were unique and invaluable pieces.

Her eyes flew to Roz before looking around to see similar looks of surprise on the faces of her friends. "The Collector wants them?"

"Yes, and they've been pledged as bids for entry into the auctions. These gemstones were gifts to the monarchs of these five countries by Queen Lydia. As you can imagine, we don't want them falling into the hands of this thief."

"So, what's the mission?"

"Each of you will go undercover in the Palaces of these countries and find out who's entering the bid. The ultimate goal is to find each auction location and bid item and stop whatever it is from falling into the wrong hands. Identify the person involved and find The Collector. Each auction will trigger the next one. Bebe, that means you have the least amount of time."

Bebe shrugged. "How long?"

"We think a month, six weeks tops. Here, read your dossier and if you have any questions, ask them now or see me later."

Bebe opened the file and saw the image of a man who screamed power and wealth. Not just that, he also screamed secrets, and she'd bet her favourite throwing star he had military training. He was incredibly handsome, with just the right amount of arrogance in his bearing. He was also the Crown Prince of a country known as Soflye. Soflye was an island in the Mediterranean that had managed to keep its independent status, despite European nations trying to take it over multiple times over the years. They were a small, proud, and prosperous nation known as a tax haven, and therefore frequented by the rich and famous. "What's my cover?"

"Prince León Cataleya is your contact, and you'll be going into the Palace as his flavour of the month."

"Urgh, a playboy."

"Indeed, the prince is somewhat of a playboy if you can believe the press. But he's also a veteran, so he has some training."

"We know the press can't be relied upon, but let's assume they're correct. How are we selling me being there so long?"

"You're going to fake falling in love and turning the prince into a love-struck puppy."

Bebe rolled her eyes. "And they're going to buy it?"

"Yes, because you're going to make sure they do. Prince León is on board as he doesn't want the good name of his country embroiled in this shit show."

"Who's my handler on this?"

"I'll be available to all of you, day or night. Back-up is available when and if we get actionable intelligence, but you can't break cover unless it's irrefutable. You also can't contact each other unless I authorise it or it will compromise the others."

Bebe looked up from the piercing green eyes of the man she'd need to pretend to be in love with. "When do I leave?"

"Plane is ready to go wheels up in an hour. A helo will collect you from the usual pick-up point in thirty minutes. Clothes etcetera will be provided for you at the destination hotel when you land. Details are in the file, but you can't take the file out of the helo as we can't risk someone finding it. So, grab your personal weapons and toys before you go. A burner phone will be given to you at the location when you land. I'll feed your cat while you're away."

Bebe smiled at that detail, more proof of who Roz really was inside.

Roz stood and came toward her, gripping her upper arms. "Be safe, Bebe."

Bebe knew this mission was different somehow. The entire world's security was now in the hands of five women who'd been rejected and shunned by those same people.

"I won't let you down."

"You never could, my *volchitsa*."

Bebe swallowed at the term of endearment Roz rarely used on them, calling them her little she-wolves in her native Russian tongue.

Bebe hugged the others and wished them luck before she turned and left for what she knew might be the most challenging mission of her life.

One

"Come on, León, this party is boring. Why don't we find a couple of girls and take them back to the room for a private party?"

León glanced at his cousin, Alain, who was a year younger than his thirty-four and wondered if the man would ever grow up and become a responsible adult. "I told you, Alain, I'm not interested."

Alain pouted, his eyes having a glazed look, the pupils almost blowing out the colour of his irises. León knew he'd been on coke or whatever party drug he was into now.

León wasn't an angel, but drugs were where he drew the line. Sex and booze had been his vices. León had played hard in his youth, although not as hard as the press liked to make out. According to the papers, he only had to hold a door for a woman and she was pregnant.

"You know, cousin, you're no fun these days. You're becoming boring."

In truth, León *was* bored. Bored with parties, bored with the continued social gatherings and the same faces, the same women throwing themselves at him in the hope he'd suddenly fall in love and marry them.

Then there were the married ones who just wanted to fuck a prince. Little did they know that would never happen, which was why the idea of going undercover made his body hum with excitement. He missed his days in the Special Forces, running missions with his brothers in arms. His time in the military had given him purpose. Coming back to this life and trying to settle into it was more complicated than he'd expected. He felt displaced, unsettled in his own skin. "If I'm so boring, why do you insist on dragging me to parties?"

At one time, Alain had been his best friend, but now they'd changed so much. Or rather he had, and Alain had stayed the same.

"Because the chicks dig it. Not all of us carry the title of Crown Prince."

More sulky behaviour from his cousin made his head ache. He didn't have time for this. He should be meeting his contact to begin their façade of being in love. Learning some unknown person was dragging his beloved country into an illegal auction, potentially damaging relations with other countries, had made him seethe with anger. Not forgetting the damage it would do to the economy if tourism died. "Listen, why don't you borrow the yacht for a few days and have a private party? I hear Porcha is in town with her friends, and I know she loves the yacht."

Alain's eyes lit up. "Really?"

"Yes, of course." León just wanted him gone so he could meet this mystery person. He'd intended to come alone, but Alain had cornered him and followed when he found out where he was going.

"Thanks, cousin."

"My pleasure."

León watched his cousin walk away and knew the crew of the yacht would hate him for this. He'd need to add a generous bonus to their pay for this excursion. Along with a cleaning crew to get all the drugs and God knew what else from his yacht.

Taking a seat at the bar, he ordered a whiskey neat and watched the door, ignoring the looks of the women around him who were trying to catch his eye. He was to meet his contact here; a woman León had no idea about. They were to pretend to fall in love so he could move her into the apartment within the Palace where he resided. The thought made him roll his eyes at the ridiculousness of the notion.

He had no idea what she looked like, just that she'd know him and make the first move. He assumed she'd be beautiful if she did this femme fatale gig for a living, but beautiful women were ten a penny on this island.

"Is this seat taken? My feet are killing me."

Hearing the words that were to introduce him to his accomplice in this charade, he turned, a fake smile of seduction on his face. His breath suddenly felt like it was frozen in his chest when he saw her. Air seemed to expand until he could hardly catch his breath, and he had to consciously exhale and respond. "Yes, of course."

The woman smiled at him, and it was like being sucker-punched in the gut, feelings he'd never experienced before pummelling his midsection. She was medium height, probably five feet seven in her heels and had curves to die for. This woman wasn't a stick. She was voluptuous with an ass that made him grit his teeth as she hitched her long dress up so she could take the seat beside him on the bar stools. Her copper-coloured skin was utterly flawless as he gazed at her. The split in the silver dress shimmered and slid off her toned thigh, giving him a glimpse of utter perfection before she chuckled, a low husky sound that made his dick sit up in his dress pants.

Lifting his head, he could see she'd caught him in the act of checking her out, and his head tilted to acknowledge it. Her long, dark hair was thick and waved down her back, giving him an uninterrupted view of the deep V in her dress, which landed just north of modest.

"My name is León." He offered his hand, which she took, the silky skin of her palm at odds with the slight callouses he could feel on her finger joints. She was used to handling weapons or using weights, he guessed. Which made sense, he had the same ones on his own palm. "And you are?"

"You can call me Bebe."

León bent his head and dropped a light kiss on her knuckles, the movement taking him that much closer, and he could smell the scent of her perfume. Something spicy and seductive, which made him think of moonlit nights and her spread naked over his bed. He pulled away, dropping her hand, not liking the direction his thoughts were taking.

In the space of minutes, this woman had snared him in her trap with barely a word or action. She was good. Pretending to become enamoured with her would be easy because he could already sense the chemistry between them. He just needed to keep it to acting and not fall for her wicked charms. She was, after all, a professional at this and trained to make men fall for her considerable attributes.

"So, León, what do you like to do for fun?"

León considered her question as he called the bartender over. "Drink?"

Bebe smiled at the bartender, and it made León scowl at the man who was grinning like an idiot at the woman he was seated beside. "Yes, please. I'll have an old fashioned."

The bartender disappeared to make the cocktail, and León wondered if he could make the man disappear permanently. Shaking the ridiculous thought away, he tried to focus on the question and get into the role of the lovesick fool he'd be playing for the next however long this took. Glancing at Bebe, he realised that it certainly wouldn't be a hardship being close to her and having to pretend to be in love.

The woman was stunning, but it was more than that; he could feel it. The pulse in her neck was pounding. His eyes moved up her throat, over her face to her russet brown eyes, and found them almost slumberous with desire. Smokey eye make-up with long dark lashes and full red lips made him jump to very inappropriate places in his mind.

"I love sports, particularly rock climbing and deep-sea diving." His voice was husky, deep, and he coughed lightly to clear it.

Bebe ran her finger around the rim of the glass as if she was totally unaware of the seductive picture she made. "You certainly have a beautiful canvas available to you for both here. Your country is stunning."

Pride filled León's chest at the compliment he knew was genuine. "Thank you. Have you visited before?"

"Many years ago, but it was brief, and I never got a chance to explore."

"Are you here for long? I'd be delighted to show you my country."

"As long as I need to be, and that would be lovely. Thank you, León."

She took a sip of her drink, the red of her lips leaving a smudge on the glass and his body responded to the sensual visual. He knew her words were a reminder, whether intended or not, that this was a job, but he wasn't sure who it was for—him or her.

León noticed a group of people he knew come up behind him, his instincts as sharp as ever from years in the military. Hearing the alcohol-fuelled voices through the music playing, he almost groaned at the sudden interruption, but it was the perfect chance for him to put on a show for their cover.

"Leo, old boy."

Atticus, with whom he'd gone to school and later college, was an old friend. But he was like Alain, obsessed with stature and social status and never satisfied with what he had in life. He'd never had a real job, living off his trust fund and León wondered how he could go through life with so little purpose.

Twisting in his seat, he kept Bebe in his sights as he addressed his friend. "Atticus."

The man was tall with blond hair and blue eyes and was always in the gym when he wasn't partying. So, it wasn't a surprise for Leo to see his ex-girlfriend Chelsea hanging off his arm, her irritated pout aimed at Bebe. It was laughable. As he looked between the two women, he realised he couldn't compare them. Bebe was something Chelsea would never be—a natural beauty with an aura about her that screamed class. Chelsea might be rich because of her family's money but she was spoiled and pampered with no thoughts of her own. Even knowing Bebe for such a short time, he guessed she probably had an opinion on everything.

"And who's this little doll?"

León gritted his teeth at the subtle way Atticus reduced Bebe from a flesh and blood person to a piece of meat. As if sensing his sudden mood change, Bebe laid her hand on his arm. Moving his head to look at her, he saw the warning not to react in her expression as if they'd known each other for years not minutes.

Consciously relaxing his jaw, he winked at her and directed his attention to Atticus, feeling the loss as her hand left his arm. "This is

Bebe, and we were about to dance. So if you'll excuse us, Atticus, Chelsea."

He nodded at them and slid from his stool, turning to take Bebe's hand, and leading her to the crowded dance floor.

Taking Bebe in his arms, he drew her close until her body touched his own and looked into her eyes. They fit like they'd been doing this dance for years, her soft curves and his hard muscle. He was dying to talk to her about the mission, to find out more of who she really was but they were too close to other people. He couldn't risk an ill-advised comment getting back to whoever was using his family name and gems though.

"What brings you to Soflye, Bebe?"

Her lips curved into a subtle smile that made his cock twitch in his pants, causing him to grind his teeth as her body brushed against his.

"Work."

"And what is it you do?" León hoped the conversation would help him to ignore the chemistry between them.

"I'm a buyer for a well-known perfume brand and I know you have the best orchids in the world here."

Her answer was both intriguing and drew him to respond naturally. "Did you know my surname is Cataleya?"

"I didn't know that."

León nodded. "Yes, and the Cataleya Orchid is the most fragrant of them all. Did you also know the name orchid comes from the Greek 'órkhis', which literally means 'testicle', thanks to the shape of the root?"

Bebe's eyebrows rose, her lips twitching with delight. He could tell it was a genuine reaction to his words before she chuckled, the lyrical sound making her breasts brush against his chest.

"I know, not exactly romantic. It comes from the Greek myth of Orchis. The legend goes, Orchis, the son of a satyr and a nymph, stumbled upon a festival of Dionysus in a forest. As tended to happen at 'bacchanales', he drank too much and became over-amorous towards a priestess. The Bacchanalians tore him apart for the slight. His father

Bebe fought the gulp at the visual of this man between her thighs using the bullet on her as his wickedly seductive eyes wandered over her body.

Before she could respond, León left the bathroom with her trailing after him as he scanned the room. His face lost its confident smirk when the scanner alerted him to a device in the lamp beside the bed. He glanced at her, and she shook her head, indicating he should leave it for now. His countenance darkened further as he found five more bugs planted throughout the apartment.

Beckoning him back to the bathroom, Bebe closed the door behind them.

"Fucking bastards bugged my personal space."

"Which says it's someone with full access to this room. But let's put a pin in that for now. We need to leave the bugs in situ. If we take them out, it will tip them off that we know or suspect something."

León's demeanour grew cold, his teeth gritting, accentuating the strong jawline, and giving her a glimpse of the soldier beneath the bespoke suit. "I'll leave the others, but I won't tolerate one in my bedroom."

Bebe nibbled on her bottom lip as she thought it over. "Okay. We can find a way to get rid of that one, but it means this has to be believable, even behind closed doors, unless we're in the bedroom or bathroom."

"So, we have to share a bed?"

Bebe cocked her head. "I can take the couch in your room."

"Absolutely not. My mother would turn in her grave if I made a lady sleep on the couch. You take the bed. I'll take the couch."

"Hate to break it to you, but I'm not exactly a lady. I kill people for a living."

León looked her over as if trying to see if what she was telling him was the truth. She knew her appearance made it difficult for people to believe she was as dangerous as she was, and that always played to her advantage. This time though, she found it irritated her. She needed this man to see her, to see who she really was.

"You may be a killer, but you're still a lady in my book. The two things aren't mutually exclusive. You take the bed and I'll take the couch."

Bebe shrugged, not wanting to give away how much his words affected her. "Fine. Let's go deal with this bug in the bedroom because I'm exhausted."

León walked behind her as she stepped into the bedroom.

A moan erupted from her mouth, and she watched his face go from cool and composed to the muscle in his cheek twitching as each loud, over-exaggerated moan and whimper slipped from her lips.

"Yes, Leo. Oh God, yes. Just there."

Bebe faked her breathing becoming rapid as she held the eyes of the man opposite her, her idea suddenly backfiring as the room became drenched in the heady feel of desire. Stuck in her own web, she had no choice but to continue as breathy sounds came out of her mouth.

León let his eyes wander over her body and her nipples beaded in response. Her womb tightened and her pussy ached as she imagined what it would feel like to have this man inside her for real instead of the performance she was putting on. His fists clenched at his sides. She could see the hard ridge of his cock in the dress pants he wore as she continued like this was just for him and not a ploy to knock the lamp over and have it removed.

"Fuck me, Leo, harder."

His eyes darkened and he stepped forward as she moved closer to the bed and the expensive lamp she was about to destroy.

"Harder. Oh, God, I'm going to come."

"Not until I say so."

Bebe felt her breath hitch as he spoke, his deep, rugged voice made her thighs clench. His hand snapped out to cinch her waist as her heart beat so hard she thought she might just come from the sensations he was eliciting. His hand skimmed her side, barely touching the side of her breast, as she laid her hands on his hard chest.

León worked his hand to the long split at the side of her dress and thrust the fabric aside to run his fingers over her bare thigh. Bebe shivered, the whimper real this time when he touched the tips of his fingers to her pussy.

prayed for Orchis to be restored, but instead, the gods transformed him into the flower we know today as the orchid."

"Wow. That's kind of a harsh punishment for a dalliance with a priestess. Unless his attention was unwanted, then it serves him right."

León couldn't take his eyes off this woman as she spoke, her voice husky and seductive with a slight accent he couldn't quite place but guessed might be from Pakistan. He found himself fascinated by her. He wanted to know more, like how and why she got into this line of work. Nobody grew up wanting to be a mercenary or assassin, and certainly not one as beautiful and intelligent as the woman in his arms.

Without conscious thought, he found himself bending toward her, his nose tickled by the soft strands of her hair. Her scent once again surrounded him as she moved, angling her head towards him, so their faces were a breath apart.

"You need to kiss me and make it believable."

Like being doused with cold water, the erotic pull he was feeling broke, and he remembered this was a game, a show for everyone else and not the start of a romantic liaison.

But, by God, he'd put on a show that would make her head spin.

Stroking his hand up her spine, he pushed his fingers through the thick strands of her hair before gently fisting the hair at her scalp. A hiss of breath had him looking into her eyes to see surprise and arousal competing for dominance. Angling her head slightly, he tightened the arm wrapped around her waist and pulled her closer.

His head bent and he took her mouth, slanting his lips over hers until she opened for him. A whimper slid up her throat as his tongue danced along her lips before flicking inside to taste her. In all his years and the many first kisses he'd had, León had never felt this way. Compelled, drugged, lost in sensation as desire pummelled his body and his dick strained against his pants. Bebe leaned in, her hands feathering the back of his neck and it was like she had a line directly to his cock. It was intense and terrifying just how affected he was by her.

Pulling away, he saw the same look of shock on her face before she covered it. Her eyes, though, were like a mirror of the desire raging inside him. The fact he wasn't the only one affected was somehow comforting. "That good enough for you?"

Bebe licked her bottom lip, and hell, it took everything in him not to drag her from the room and finish what they started. But this was fake, and he'd do well to remember it.

Bebe turned to leave the dance floor, casting a flirtatious look over her shoulder. "It'll do."

Two

Stepping through the door of Prince León's apartment, Bebe wanted nothing more than to kick off her heels and take a few minutes to get herself together. Following the man who'd kissed her so thoroughly on the dance floor and then preceded to enchant her with his wit and conversation, all the while playing up to the people around them and cementing the fact they were suddenly infatuated, had taken a toll on her equilibrium.

León threw his keys in a turquoise ceramic bowl by the door, his other hand moving to the grey tie around his neck to loosen the knot. In her line of work, Bebe had met countless handsome men, yet none had made her skin tingle and her pulse pound the way this man did. He was taller than she thought, over six feet two inches, she'd guess. His build was muscular, which she put down to his years in the military and his subsequent love of rock climbing, or as he'd gone on to explain, he preferred free climbing.

With most men, she'd have put his admission down to posturing or showing off, but León didn't strike her as the type to need his ego stroked. He was confident and seemed to dominate the room as they moved around it, but never the conversation. He was a true alpha male, full of charisma and sex appeal. Which was why she could feel the daggers from almost every woman they'd passed tonight.

"Thank God, we can…"

Bebe grabbed his arm, spinning him to face her and putting a finger to her lips. Dragging him slightly, she pulled him toward the bathroom, while making moaning sounds as if they were kissing.

León caught on quick and slammed the bathroom door behind them, turning to turn on the shower. When the sound of flowing water filled the room, he turned to her, hands on his hips as he put distance between them. His eyes dipped to her breasts, and she knew he'd enjoyed their kiss as much as she had, and that was bad. This was a job, and she needed a clear head. She'd never, not once allowed a target or contact to become anything more and she couldn't start now with the most important job of her life at stake.

"You think my apartment is bugged?"

Bebe dug around in her bag for the scanner she always carried. "I don't know but until I clear it, I don't want to assume it isn't."

"What the hell is that?"

Bebe grinned as she waved the small dildo shaped scanner in the air. Shaped like a magic bullet, she knew anyone searching her bag would never give it a second look because of its shape, and that spoke to her warped sense of humour.

"Get your mind out of the gutter, Leo, this is a scanner. Although…."

She gave him a wicked grin and he rolled his eyes and took it from her hand.

"Hey, you don't know how to use it."

León quirked a dark eyebrow at her, his expression devilish, and Bebe fought the shiver as he leaned in closer. "I can assure you I do."

Bebe let her smart mouth get the better of her as she flicked her hair over her shoulder. "Need the help, Leo?"

His deep, gruff chuckle worked its way over her skin, leaving goosebumps in its wake.

"A real man learns every way to please his woman and then some. A real man isn't afraid of toys."

things aren't mutually exclusive. You take the bed and I'll take the couch."

Bebe shrugged, not wanting to give away how much his words affected her. "Fine. Let's go deal with this bug in the bedroom because I'm exhausted."

León walked behind her as she stepped into the bedroom.

A moan erupted from her mouth, and she watched his face go from cool and composed to the muscle in his cheek twitching as each loud, over-exaggerated moan and whimper slipped from her lips.

"Yes, Leo. Oh God, yes. Just there."

Bebe faked her breathing becoming rapid as she held the eyes of the man opposite her, her idea suddenly backfiring as the room became drenched in the heady feel of desire. Stuck in her own web, she had no choice but to continue as breathy sounds came out of her mouth.

León let his eyes wander over her body and her nipples beaded in response. Her womb tightened and her pussy ached as she imagined what it would feel like to have this man inside her for real instead of the performance she was putting on. His fists clenched at his sides. She could see the hard ridge of his cock in the dress pants he wore as she continued like this was just for him and not a ploy to knock the lamp over and have it removed.

"Fuck me, Leo, harder."

His eyes darkened and he stepped forward as she moved closer to the bed and the expensive lamp she was about to destroy.

"Harder. Oh, God, I'm going to come."

"Not until I say so."

Bebe felt her breath hitch as he spoke, his deep, rugged voice made her thighs clench. His hand snapped out to cinch her waist as her heart beat so hard she thought she might just come from the sensations he was eliciting. His hand skimmed her side, barely touching the side of her breast, as she laid her hands on his hard chest.

León worked his hand to the long split at the side of her dress and thrust the fabric aside to run his fingers over her bare thigh. Bebe shivered, the whimper real this time when he touched the tips of his fingers to her pussy.

Bebe fought the gulp at the visual of this man between her thighs using the bullet on her as his wickedly seductive eyes wandered over her body.

Before she could respond, León left the bathroom with her trailing after him as he scanned the room. His face lost its confident smirk when the scanner alerted him to a device in the lamp beside the bed. He glanced at her, and she shook her head, indicating he should leave it for now. His countenance darkened further as he found five more bugs planted throughout the apartment.

Beckoning him back to the bathroom, Bebe closed the door behind them.

"Fucking bastards bugged my personal space."

"Which says it's someone with full access to this room. But let's put a pin in that for now. We need to leave the bugs in situ. If we take them out, it will tip them off that we know or suspect something."

León's demeanour grew cold, his teeth gritting, accentuating the strong jawline, and giving her a glimpse of the soldier beneath the bespoke suit. "I'll leave the others, but I won't tolerate one in my bedroom."

Bebe nibbled on her bottom lip as she thought it over. "Okay. We can find a way to get rid of that one, but it means this has to be believable, even behind closed doors, unless we're in the bedroom or bathroom."

"So, we have to share a bed?"

Bebe cocked her head. "I can take the couch in your room."

"Absolutely not. My mother would turn in her grave if I made a lady sleep on the couch. You take the bed. I'll take the couch."

"Hate to break it to you, but I'm not exactly a lady. I kill people for a living."

León looked her over as if trying to see if what she was telling him was the truth. She knew her appearance made it difficult for people to believe she was as dangerous as she was, and that always played to her advantage. This time though, she found it irritated her. She needed this man to see her, to see who she really was.

"You may be a killer, but you're still a lady in my book. The two

Her head thrown back, she moaned as he stroked her through the lace before shoving the fabric aside and thrusting two fingers inside her.

"You're fucking drenched for me."

"Leo!"

Bebe didn't know at this point if it was a plea to continue or a warning of the foolishness of what she was about to let him do.

With his palm against her clit, he fucked her with his hand, and she moved against him, riding his hand with an abandon she couldn't ever remember having before. Feelings spiralled and she gripped his biceps, her head thrown back, her body searching for the release she knew would be phenomenal.

"That's it, Bebe, ride my cock."

At his words, her head came up and she looked into his eyes, which were dark and dangerous. Heat and desire flooded her pussy as she felt her body build towards that delicious feeling known as 'the little death'.

"Now you can come."

She tipped over the edge and came hard, her body pulsing and contracting in more pleasure than she'd ever known.

Leo knocked the lamp from the table with his hand and it crashed to the floor as she cried out, her knees buckling as he held her to him for support. Withdrawing his hand, he leaned in close to lick the taste of her from his fingers and she shuddered.

Bending close to her ear, he whispered, "Don't toy with me, Bebe. I'm not the man for that."

With those words, he backed into the bathroom, leaving her legs weak and Bebe wondering what the hell had just happened.

Three

LEÓN ROLLED OVER, HIS BACK CRACKING FROM A NIGHT SPENT ON THE couch in his own bedroom. He groaned as his mind flashed to last night and everything that had happened. When he'd come out of the bathroom last night, after a very cold shower, Bebe had been asleep. He'd felt like a creeper as he'd watched her for a moment but he'd wanted to see if she was awake so he could apologise, but she was either out or a damn good actress.

She hadn't been acting when he touched her though, nobody was that good. Rolling to his feet, he speared his fingers through his hair as he noticed the empty, perfectly made bed. He hadn't heard her get up, which was unusual. After years in the army, he hadn't thought anyone could get the jump on him, but she had. He didn't know if that was a testament to her skills or if he'd let his own get rusty.

After a quick shower and change into jeans and a pale blue shirt, León headed for the main living room. He still needed to apologise but for now, at least, it would have to wait. They had a show to put on.

The smell of coffee hit him as he entered the main living area. Bebe was sitting on his balcony in a short, black silk robe, her feet up on the balcony, her long and shapely legs on display. The vision made him pause as she looked out over the vista of fields in the distance to the left, the ocean to the right. It was still early, the air just starting to warm the sand-coloured stone of the streets of his land as if bestowing a gift.

It was hard to see the woman he knew her to be as he watched her. A killer, a dangerous deadly accomplice in this game they were playing to try and weed out a traitor. All thoughts of lust left his body at the thought of someone close to him being the culprit. When his butler had come to remove the lamp last night, a man he'd trusted fully, he found himself looking at him differently.

Bebe leaned back, looking over her shoulder at him, a smile touching her lips. "Are you going to come out and talk to me or do you have voyeuristic tendencies I need to know about?"

He hated that he didn't know if it was genuine or not. Forcing a relaxed smile, he moved toward her, resting his hands on her shoulders, and leaning down to drop a kiss on her upturned mouth. It was meant to be light, but the second his mouth found hers, it was like a fire was lit in his blood.

His tongue explored her mouth, and he felt like he'd never get enough of her taste. Bebe sighed, her hand finding his neck, and he knew she could feel how wild his pulse was as he struggled for control.

Pulling back, he searched her eyes for the answer and found only the same desire reflected back at him. "I'm sorry for last night." His voice was barely a rasp as he spoke low against her neck, so nobody else would hear his words.

"It's okay, I was partly to blame."

At her words, he felt lighter. Not that his soul would ever be clean again after the things he'd seen and done in the army. Yet Bebe made him feel hope. After less than twelve hours, he felt she understood him more than anyone else. Perhaps because they were the same in many ways.

León took the seat opposite her as Bebe dropped her feet to the floor, crossing her legs. She was totally make-up free and looked fresh-faced and more beautiful than she had a right to at this early hour. It was barely seven and she was up and ready to take on the day. He liked the quietness of early mornings until the small sounds that the world was waking up greeted him. The peace allowed him to mentally ready himself for the day ahead.

Pouring coffee from the carafe that was delivered every morning by his butler Hans, he watched her as he took a sip. "Did you sleep okay?"

Bebe nodded, her head tilted as she watched him, her gaze confident and bold. He felt like every secret he had was being uncovered, pried from his mind without a single word from her.

"Pretty well actually. Your bed is the bomb."

León felt his lips curve. "The bomb?"

"Yeah, you know, awesome, amazing. The bomb."

León lifted his chin. "Ah, I see."

"So, what's the plan today?"

He knew her words were directed at the plan for her to get to know people and plant her own bugs and cameras. "I have to meet my father at eleven for a short meeting with his advisors on foreign affairs and then I'll give you a tour of the property. After lunch, I thought we could go visit the orchid farms."

"That sounds lovely. Shall I wait for you here?"

"No, I'll let security know you're free to walk around the gardens."

Bebe finished her coffee and stood, stretching her arms over her head and sighing. He watched her long, lithe legs and the sweet curve of her ass as she walked away and wondered if he'd survive this mission without succumbing to her magnetism.

"You know, you could come and help me pick out something to wear instead of just ogling me."

León jumped to his feet, eager to play the role of a besotted boyfriend if his reward was that he got to look at her without censure. Wrapping an arm around her waist, he pulled her close, bending his head to her neck and inhaling the sweet seductive scent of her, his mind remembering the honey taste of her on his fingers last night. "Need some help getting dressed?"

Bebe chuckled, a deep intoxicating sound, but her expression told him she knew this was for show so the person listening believed their cover.

As they closed the door to the bedroom, sealing the outside world away, she stepped from his embrace and turned toward him. Arms crossed over her waist, the sun from the open blinds slanting across her body, she looked innocent. Yet her eyes told of a worldliness he ached to understand.

"We need to make sure this cover is solid. That means we need to act like we're falling in love with lots of touching, flirting, and kissing. Is that going to be a problem after last night?"

León shook his head as he widened his stance, his arms crossed over his chest now as he faced Bebe. "No, of course not. I know I was out of line last night and I shouldn't have touched you. It was a mistake, but it won't happen again.... unless you want it to?"

"Listen, Leo, it's not that I didn't enjoy it, or that I'm not attracted to you because obviously that's a lie and I don't make a habit of lying to myself, but this is a job. There's too much at stake for me to get scrambled up in emotional entanglements."

He rubbed his chest where the words lodged and tried not to acknowledge the sting of them, but she was right. The stakes were too high for him to let himself get carried away and it wasn't what he wanted either.

"Then it's settled. Out there we put on a show but in here we work the case."

Bebe gave a short nod and began pulling clothes from the case he'd had delivered from her hotel last night. "I need to see the Tanzanite and get cameras in that room."

León sat on the couch where he'd folded away all evidence of his night there. "There are already cameras in the room. Why don't we just hack those?"

"Because I don't like the idea of anyone but my team being able to access them. We need to assume the person involved will cut the feed or loop it when they make their move."

"True. Okay. When I take you on the tour later, we can get them in place. We might just need some good acting skills to distract anyone who's watching."

"No problem. I can pretend to like you, Leo."

Her smirk made his cock twitch, and he was glad he was sitting so she didn't notice.

"I need to change and then I'm going to check out the lay of the land outside while you do whatever you need to do with the King."

"It's a boring council meeting as far as I know. Hopefully, we can wrap it up quickly."

"I'll see you back here then."

León felt his phone buzz and withdrew it, frowning at the message from Roberto, his father's private secretary. "The meeting had been moved up to nine. I should probably change too."

Moving to the wardrobe, he peeled his shirt over his head, his back to Bebe and threw it on the bed as he reached for his navy suit and a pale blue shirt with a silver tie.

"You have a fair bit of ink for a prince."

León looked behind him to where Bebe was watching him, her clothes clutched in her arms. "You know a lot of princes?"

She shrugged and her eyes caught his, confident and unwavering, enchanting. "A few." She waved her hand at his body. "None of them look like that."

León tried not to be pleased by the unintentional compliment. "I guess not many have served their country in Special Ops either."

"Yeah, you're something of an enigma."

With that, she closed the bathroom door, and he was left wondering even more about the complex woman.

At five to nine he stepped into his father's office and found the King already at his desk. The room was on the opposite side of the palace to the living spaces he and his father kept and allowed a certain amount of privacy and division. Not that the King was ever not working; he was a good monarch. The King was also a good man, but a good man didn't always make a good husband. León still had a somewhat strained relationship with him because of his multiple affairs over the years, which had ended in his mother's early death over twenty years ago. The coroner had said it was a heart attack, but León was convinced she'd died of a broken heart.

"Father, you're working early this morning. Shouldn't you be taking it easier as the doctor suggested?"

The King looked at him over his glasses, a deep frown marring his features at the reminder of his high blood pressure and the warning from the family physician. "I'm fine. I like to be busy."

Sitting across from him, León crossed his ankle over his opposite knee and relaxed back in the chair.

His father pulled his reading glasses off his face and set them on the desk, resting his hands over his belly. León didn't look away as his father assessed him, as if looking for the future King León would be and not finding what he sought. "I hear you brought one of your conquests back to the palace last night."

León's jaw tensed at him calling Bebe a conquest and a feeling of annoyance streamed through his blood. "She's not a conquest." He paused wondering how far and how fast he should go with this and then realised time wasn't a luxury they had. "She's the one."

King Alfred's bushy eyebrow went up as if trying to make contact with his receding hairline. "The one?"

León dropped his foot to the floor as he leaned forward. "I know it sounds crazy and we hardly know each other, but it feels right. As if I've known her forever."

"It does sound crazy, but it was the same for your mother and me."

León held up his hand to stop whatever his father was going to say next. "I don't want to talk about mother."

The King sighed, and for the first time ever he looked every inch of his seventy years. It was startling and León was rattled by the sight of his father looking his age. His mortality had never been in question but now León faced the reality of what was going on. One day his father would no longer be around and despite everything, that filled him with incredible sadness.

"Either way, I'm pleased. I want to see you happy, and God knows you need an heir. Currently, if anything happens to you after I die, your dolt of a cousin becomes King and I've worked too hard and sacrificed too much to let an idiot like Alain sit on this throne."

"Wow, we're way off marriage, Father. We just met."

"But you said she was the one."

"Yes, but there's no need to rush things."

"I disagree. There's every need and I just outlined them. Bring her to dinner tonight. I want to meet her."

"Fine, but no booking the church just yet. I don't want to scare her off."

His father harrumphed as a knock sounded at the door. His father stood and he followed suit, facing the door. Five men walked inside, three of whom he recognised. His uncle Alwyn, Alain's father, Roberto, his father's private secretary, and Cyril Powel, their prime minister.

"Prime Minister." León shook the hand of the man who led their country in government.

"Your Highness. Good to see you."

"Likewise." León liked Cyril, he was a straight shooter and didn't suffer fools. As a military man, he'd served the country and shown great bravery.

Roberto nodded as he took the King's side and Alwyn positioned himself close to the King on the other side. A power move he knew to try and throw him off. Since he'd turned eighteen, his uncle had been making these little moves to try and press the fact he was more suited than Alfred to be King, and he certainly didn't think León had what it took. Since he'd returned from serving his country, the moves had become more obvious, and León wondered if he was threatened by him. He needn't be. Alwyn had no claim on the crown, and he knew it, so this was all unnecessary in his book.

"Prince León, this is Brody James. He's my new press secretary."

León looked at the man who he guessed was the same age as himself. He was fit and muscular with intelligent blue eyes. "Mr James, nice to meet you."

"You too, Your Highness."

His accent was American. South if he had to guess, with a lyrical and deep quality to it.

He turned to the other man who was standing a few feet from them all and stretched out his hand. "I don't think we've met."

"This is Albin Wojcik. He'll be working with me to help stabilise relations with our Eastern European friends."

León glanced at his uncle, who had the unofficial title of European Relations Ambassador because he liked to travel and party. He wasn't a good man and would make a horrible leader should that ever come to pass.

"Is that so." León swung his gaze back to Albin, who was watching them with a closed expression. His face gave nothing away and that in itself was telling as far as he was concerned. "Pleased to meet you, Mr Wojcik. I look forward to working with you more closely."

As the meeting got started and mundane press items were addressed, León found his mind wondering. Were these two new additions to the staff a mere coincidence or was this to do with the auction and the Tanzanite Tears? His gut told him it was but at this point, he had no evidence either man was involved, and he certainly didn't trust his uncle as far as he could throw him.

As they were wrapping up the meeting a call came through the landline in his father's office, which was unusual.

Roberto answered the call, his face paling and he glanced around the room in shock. "Yes, I understand. Protocol ten will need to be implemented immediately."

At the words, León's gut took a nosedive and he sat forward beside his father. Worry was etched on the face of every man there who knew the significance of protocol ten.

Roberto looked to the King before he dipped his head. "I'm very sorry to tell you but *The Grace* exploded about six hours ago. The coastguard just got word. It seems everyone on board was killed."

León jumped to his feet, his head spinning at the news his yacht had been destroyed and his cousin, oh dear God his cousin, was dead. He looked to his father, who was watching him as if needing him to lead at that moment. León didn't need it verbalised for him to act. They may not have been close, but he had always had his father's six. "Uncle Alwyn, my deepest sympathies."

His uncle, for all the hostility between them, looked thoroughly shaken by the news and accepted the hand he offered.

Roberto ushered everyone from the room, leaving the three family members to come to terms with the accident. Or was it more than that? After all, *The Grace* was his yacht.

Four

Her first sign something was wrong came from the sudden bustle about the gardens and grounds as she made her way back from the olive groves surrounding the palace. People dropped their heads and avoided eye contact as she walked past. Hushed voices and quickened steps caused an uneasy feeling to fill the pit of her stomach.

Her palms itched in sudden apprehension or maybe foreboding that something had happened, and it was bad.

Catching the eye of a housemaid as she rushed past, Bebe called to her. "Excuse me, is everything okay? Has something happened?"

That was when she noticed the girl had tears in her eyes. "It's not my place."

Bebe touched her arm. "Please?"

"The yacht. There was a fire. They're all dead."

"Who?" Bebe felt adrenalin kick in at the news and knew she'd been spot on. The shit was hitting the fan.

"All of them. His Highness Prince Alain and all his friends."

"Oh, my. I'm so sorry."

Shock at the turn of events had her mind spinning in a hundred different directions as scenarios played out. Bebe let the girl go and she rushed off as the household went into what was obviously a pre-arranged plan she assumed was protocol after an event such as this.

She thought of the man she'd watched with Leo last night and shook her head. He'd been a prime candidate for this auction. Then there was Atticus, another person of interest. More importantly was the knowledge that the yacht belonged to the prince, and he was known to use it often.

Was he the target and if so, was it because of this or was there more at play than she realised? Bebe shook her head. Either way, people had lost their lives and it was incredibly sad for all who loved them. At times like this it was hard not to feel guilty for the lives she'd taken in her line of work.

She hadn't grown up dreaming of becoming an assassin for want of a better job description. She'd wanted to be a doctor, for goodness's sake, to save lives, but life had other ideas for her. An image of her older sister came to mind along with the familiar ache in her chest at the loss of such a beautiful person. The ache, compounded by the guilt over not being able to help even though that was her sole purpose in life, almost choked her.

Shaking the depressing thoughts away, Bebe made her way to León's apartment to wait for him there. He'd no doubt be longer than expected and she didn't mind, she could do some work on her laptop. Anyone watching wouldn't be able to see what she was doing if she sat outside in the sunshine, and she could read through the background checks again.

Roz had sent detailed dossiers through to the encrypted laptop on every single person, even Leo. That way anyone, who by some miracle got past the encryption, wouldn't know he was in on this with them or that the leak was even remotely linked to the palace. Bebe had only given them a cursory glance before she'd been thrown into this melee, so now was as good a time as any to fix that.

As she sat down with a bottle of water and lifted the lid on the laptop, the door to the luxury apartment opened and León walked toward her. He looked handsome as hell, even with the frown and grief darkening his stormy green eyes.

Standing, she had the urge to offer him comfort. Even knowing she needed to keep some distance between them didn't stop that feeling. "I just heard. I'm so sorry, León."

With his hands on his hips, he looked like a man ready to go to war as he dipped his head. "Thank you."

His lips were tight as he spoke as if allowing more emotion to escape would be too much. She understood that grief had to be processed in a person's own time. He clearly wasn't ready yet and she instinctively knew he needed to fix this and find the culprit. She could help with that.

Sitting with her back to the wall of the balcony, she motioned for him to do the same. "Sit. Tell me about it and let's see if we can figure out if this is connected."

Her sweep of the balcony at six had shown it to be bug-free, giving them another space where they could talk as long as they were careful to be quiet and aware of their surroundings when they did.

León seemed to pause before he did the same, strategically making sure his back was to the opposite wall. She knew he was special forces and that his actions were as ingrained as hers were, but their paths couldn't be more different.

"I don't have long. My father was very shaken by the news, as was Uncle Alwyn. I'm not his biggest fan, but Alain was his only child."

"I can't imagine how hard this is. Nobody should bury their child. It's absolutely horrendous."

León was tense, she could feel it coming off him in waves and wished she could do more to help him. Her traitorous brain told her exactly what would relax him, but she shut it down. Sex would only help in the short term. Long term it was a horrible idea.

"Do we know what happened to the yacht?"

León looked toward the sea, which shimmered in the distance as if he could see the answers, but he shook his head. "No. As of right now, all I know is there was an explosion and everyone on board was killed."

"Perhaps I can do some digging while you do whatever you need to do here."

León frowned, his jaw tensing, and she could tell he didn't like the idea and was going to object, which would piss her off. Why did men always conclude that she'd be better off sheltered despite all the evidence to the contrary?

"Fine but be careful."

Surprised, Bebe tried not to show it, especially as very few people could shock her these days. "Badass, remember?"

Leo seemed to drag his eyes over her in a slow deliberate perusal, which had her tummy tightening. "Yeah, I remember or you'd be locked inside this room until it was safe."

Bebe sat up straighter, rolling her lips between her teeth. "I'm going to put that sexist comment down to grief and shock and not kick your ass, Leo, but don't do it again."

His lips twitched in a smirk and some of the darkness left his eyes as he leaned closer. "Why does the thought of getting hot and sweaty and sparring with you make me so damned turned on?"

Bebe swallowed, noting the desire in his eyes. "Because you were dropped on your head as a baby?"

Leo threw his head back and laughed before he leaned in close, cupped her cheek, and kissed her as if she was the only source of oxygen on the planet and he'd been starved of her.

A sigh broke free from her throat as she balanced a hand on his hard thigh for support. This man kissed like a damn god. All too easily she was swept up in the feeling and didn't notice the man standing in the shadows of the balcony door until he cleared his throat.

"Excuse me, sir, but the King wishes to speak to you."

Leo took his time pulling back, his green eyes heavy with lust as he pecked her lips once more before turning to his butler. "Thank you, Hans. Tell the King I'll be with him shortly."

Hans nodded, shooting a look of disapproval at Bebe before he turned on his heel and walked away.

"I don't think Hans likes me."

"Don't let it bother you. Hans doesn't like anyone."

Bebe tipped her head to the side. "Oh, I wasn't going to. It was more of an observation."

Leo leaned back as if he needed some distance between them and she sure as hell needed it. It had been way too easy for her to fall into the kiss and ignore her surroundings, imagining it was real. Their chemistry was off the charts, and she didn't like it one bit. A connection like that was a distraction and could get her killed if she didn't keep her head in the game.

"Talking of observations. We had two new appointments to the palace staff that I had no prior knowledge of, and that makes me nervous. Especially given what's happened."

"Oh?"

"Yes, Brody James who's the new press secretary, and Albin Wojcik. According to my uncle, he's here to help stabilise European relations."

"What happened to the old press secretary?"

"I don't know. I didn't get a chance to ask, but Mallory St James has been with us for years and was great at her job. Never took a sick day and she got on well with my father, which was a big help as he can be a stubborn so and so at times."

"I'll look into it. As soon as I have access to the security network or preferably my own feeds, I'll run facial recognition on them."

Leo stood and she followed suit. "Brody is American and, if I had to guess, he's CIA."

"What makes you say that?"

"Gut feeling and the way he was watching me as if he knew something. I should go find my father."

He turned to walk away, and Bebe touched his back to stop him. Lifting on tiptoes so she could speak into his ear as he bent lower, her lips feathered his stubbled jaw as his masculine scent enveloped her. "Leo, who approached you about working with me on this?"

Leo angled his body toward the balcony, the sun catching the natural highlights in his hair, making him look every inch the prince he was.

"A woman named Emily Reynolds. She works for MI6. We worked together a few times when I was in the military on special operations."

Bebe bit her lip in thought. "Yes, I know her. She's one of the good ones."

"She is and I trust her. The intel she gave us saved a lot of lives, including mine."

Dropping back to her normal height and taking his hand, she walked with him to the door, leaning into his body like a lover offering comfort, acting out her part for the cameras. This didn't feel like acting though. She genuinely wanted to comfort this man she'd known less than twenty-four hours.

At the door he turned and lifted his hand, brushing her hair from around her face. He was tall and she angled her head up to him as he looked down at her like a lover with other things on his mind.

Running his thumb over her bottom lip and sending sparks of desire shooting through her body, he frowned. "Will you be okay while I take care of some things?"

Bebe nodded, knowing he was asking for more than just the cameras and bugs. "Yes, I have a few errands to run in town."

Leo nodded and then dropped a sweet kiss on her mouth. It was innocent enough and yet packed with feeling. "Be careful."

"I will."

Leo gave a short nod, squeezed her hand, and left the room, the quiet click of the door closing behind him.

Leaning against the door, Bebe laid a hand over her heart which was beating wildly in her chest. How was she going to keep things professional when she had to pretend to be his new lover? With every touch, the lines were blurring wildly. For the first time in her life, she had no idea how to stop them.

Five

"Son, are you listening to me?"

Leo shook thoughts of Bebe out of his head as he focused on his father. "Sorry, what did you say?"

"I asked if you'd bring your young lady to dinner tonight."

Leo rubbed his chin, his head tilting to hide his expression from his knowing father. They may have had issues and an outstanding conflict between them, but his father still knew him better than most. "I'm not sure that's a good idea given what's happened."

"Nonsense, it's exactly what we need. This family has suffered an incredible loss today and perhaps some light would be good."

"I'm not sure Uncle Alwyn would agree."

"Just the three of us then?"

Leo narrowed his eyes at his father, who seemed to have aged since the news this morning. "What are you up to?"

"Nothing. Can't a father meet the woman who has his son so distracted?"

"I'm not distracted. I'm in shock from everything that happened today, including the two new appointments to the staff."

"Yes, well, I didn't have much choice about that. Mallory's son was injured in an accident and she needed to be with him."

Leo loosened his tie, hating those social dictates that made him wear one inside his own home when meeting his own father. "That's awful. Poor Mallory. And Brody James, where did we find him?"

"Mallory recommended him actually."

"Hmm."

"What does hmm, mean? Spit it out."

The King was sitting catty-corner to him in his favourite large, brown leather armchair in his private study. The view out over the gardens was one he knew his father loved. Many a time he'd find his mother in here reading as his father worked, and over the years it had become the place his father retreated to.

"Nothing, just with everything going on I'd prefer not to have anyone we don't know around the palace."

"Well, that may be the ideal, but this is the situation, so we need to deal with it. Our people are looking to us for comfort and we must show them hope and brightness. If it comes out that this was anything other than an accident, our subjects will be afraid, and I won't allow that for them."

His father was acting like they were under attack, making León wonder if his father knew more than he was saying. "Have you heard something?"

His father lit a cigar and Leo tried not to let his disapproval show that he was still smoking after a warning from the doctor about his health. The last thing his old man needed was a lecture, so he bit his tongue.

Smoke billowed out around him, the sweet smell so familiar and, in a way, comforting. A reminder of his childhood and the safe, protected feeling he'd had before it went to hell. "Just that the authorities believe it was a bomb."

"Who knows so far?"

"Just us two, Alwyn, the Police Commissioner, the Marina Manager, and the Prime Minister."

"So too many then."

"Hmm. Perhaps you know someone who can investigate this on the quiet for us. I know you have certain contacts from your time in the military."

Leo was cautious as he answered. "I do, but I'd prefer to do it myself for now."

"Absolutely not. You're needed here to bolster the people."

Leo leaned closer, swatting the smoke from his face as he did. "I'll be here and be seen by the people. I can investigate in plain sight."

"No, León. It's not lost on me that it was your yacht that exploded. I won't lose my only child."

"You think I was the target?"

His father's mouth fell open for a second before he regained his composure. "Don't you?"

Leo nodded slowly. "Yes, it looks that way."

"Is this to do with your military work or do you think it's a plot to destabilise the Crown?"

What Leo thought was that whoever was entering the illegal auction had somehow found out that he knew. But did that mean they knew about Bebe? If so, she was in danger too. His stomach twisted at the thought, and no matter how many times he tried to remember how deadly she was and how she could take care of herself, he was still uncomfortable with it.

He wasn't a sexist as she'd accused. He'd worked dangerous missions with Emily Reynolds and other female operators that had been more skilled than a lot of the men at his side. He had no issue with it at all but, somehow, she was different. "I don't think so, no. Let me look into it for a few days. If I can't figure it out, I have someone I can bring in to help."

"Fine but I'd still like to meet this woman."

"Bebe. Her name is Bebe Basu."

"Bebe, then. I'd like to meet her."

"Fine but not tonight. How about Saturday night?"

His father smiled and his eyes looked glassy as if he was lost in time, his eyes going to the chair where his wife had always sat. "Of course. I remember what it was like in those first few months and not wanting anybody to intrude on the bubble of perfection you had created together."

Leo didn't comment, not wanting to encourage his father too much. "When will the funeral be?"

The King seemed to snap out of his daydream and focused on his son, a look of grief and regret marring his features. "A week from today. Everything is handled, which is just as well as your uncle has taken this hard and retreated to his place in the country."

"Of course he has. Alain was his son and a good man. This should never have happened to him or those he was with."

Guilt was like a sore in his gut, painful and nagging. If only he hadn't been so preoccupied with his mission this would never have happened or maybe it would. Leo knew better than most that shit went sideways sometimes and innocent people died when they shouldn't.

A hand on his forearm made him look up at the man who'd been his biggest advocate and his closest adversary.

"Don't do that. Blaming yourself changes nothing. I, for one, am incredibly grateful that I'm not mourning my child today. Alain was a good man, but as much as it pains me to say it, he was troubled too. Remember that when you investigate what happened. It wasn't a secret that he often borrowed the yacht from you."

Leo sighed. "I'll keep an open mind." Standing he went to leave, a sudden sense of urgency to be with Bebe pulling at him. "Go speak with your brother. He needs you. I'll take care of this, Father. You can rely on me."

"I know that, son. You're my greatest gift and I only wish you knew that you could rely on me, too."

León left the study without answering because what could he say? He was a grown man still bitter over the loss of his mother and blaming the only person he could. More and more lately he wondered if he hadn't got it horribly wrong about his father. Exploring that meant admitting he'd been wrong all these years, and he'd wasted so many precious moments he could never get back.

The afternoon sun was high in the sky as he stepped from the palace into the large rose gardens and walked far enough away that any flapping ears wouldn't overhear his conversation.

He waited impatiently for Bebe to answer his call, cursing himself for not going with her. Even after a day he'd known stopping her would've ended badly.

"Hey, Leo. Can't really talk right now."

Her breath was choppy as if she was running and he began speed walking toward the car he used when he was in town. The red Ferrari may not be inconspicuous, but it was fast and fun to drive. His hand gripped the phone harder. "What's wrong?"

"Just some overzealous paparazzi that seem to have spotted me as the woman you were with last night. I need to get his camera before my picture is splashed everywhere and my career is down the toilet."

"Head to the bakery on Church Street and go inside. Tell them I sent you."

"Roger that."

Bebe hung up and León floored the accelerator on the car. He needed to get there and prevent their cover from blowing up before they had a chance to find out what the hell was going on.

Leo burst through the door of the bakery ten minutes later, leaving the car abandoned at the curb. His eyes scanned the space, looking for the shock of dark hair. For a second he couldn't find her, and fear raced up his spine. Then he spotted her talking with Soroosh, the owner and his old friend, and he let go of the breath he'd been holding.

It wasn't an act when he strode toward her and dragged her into his arms. He held her tightly, relief flooding him that she was okay. Her scent swirled around him, and he felt her stroke her palm down his spine, comforting him.

"I'm okay."

León pulled back to look at her and saw a tight smile on her face. "You sure?"

Her scowl should have warned him to proceed with caution, but he didn't care. He needed to know she was okay.

"Yes, perfectly."

His lips touched her forehead, and he felt the tension leave his body.

"Your Highness, we apprehended the man who was harassing your friend."

Leo tucked Bebe close to his side as he greeted Soroosh with a handshake. The man had saved his ass on a mission in the Middle East. When he'd needed a fresh start after losing a leg to an IED, Leo had encouraged him to pursue his dream of opening a bakery here in Soflye.

"Thank you, my friend."

Soroosh was a man of few words and merely tipped his head as he motioned toward the man at the back of the bakery being watched by two of his employees.

Leo walked towards the man who he knew to be a pap for a well-known gossip rag. "Give me your camera."

The man was around fifty, with long greasy grey hair he pushed off his face. It was amazing he was still alive if the way he was breathing was any indication. "You can't keep me here."

Leo leaned in, his arm not leaving Bebe. "Give. Me. Your. Camera." The steel in his voice must have convinced the man he was serious.

The man paled, but he still looked belligerent as he silently handed the camera over. Leo wasted no time deleting every picture of Bebe and a few of them together from last night, thanking God it was an old camera and didn't have an instant backup to the cloud linked to it. He handed it back to the man who glared at him as if he'd been wronged somehow.

"Leave this island and don't come back. You're not welcome here."

"I was only trying to earn a living."

"By chasing someone down the street and making her feel scared and cornered?"

The man whose name he couldn't be bothered to remember shrugged. "Freedom of speech. The public deserves to know what you lot get up to."

"My private life is just that. I give enough to my country and my people. When I'm ready to make anything public you can be sure it won't be with the likes of you or the rag you work for."

"Elitist."

"I'm not discussing this with you. Leave me and my friend alone or you'll regret it."

The weaselly little man seemed to stiffen at his words. "Are you threatening me?"

"No, I'm making you a promise. I hope you don't make me keep it." Leo turned to Soroosh. "Would you mind having someone escort him to the airport and ensure he gets on a flight?"

"My pleasure, Your Highness."

Walking to a corner table the furthest away from the scuffle now taking place, he pulled Bebe into his arms again.

"You're overreacting."

She spoke against his chest so only he could hear and the warmth of her breath across his chest made his dick hard. "No, people would expect me to act this way toward the woman I love."

He pulled back to look at her, those brown eyes wide and clear of any fear.

"You thought I couldn't handle it."

Leo shook his head. "No. I protect what's mine. For now, at least, you're mine to protect, Bebe."

Six

A DINNER OF COLD MEATS, CHEESES, AND SALADS WAS SERVED IN THEIR apartment that evening. Having an apartment inside the palace was certainly an advantage for this mission. It allowed her to keep close to the threat but gave her space to breathe too.

Bebe bit into a fig, the sweet taste exploding on her tongue as the man opposite her watched as he sipped his red wine. Her pulse fluttered as she held his eyes, not wanting to appear weak by dropping her gaze. This man made her want to prove herself in a way she hadn't needed to in a very long time.

"How's your uncle?"

They were on the balcony after spending the afternoon in the bedroom debriefing from his conversation with his father. That the King had no idea what was going on was a good thing but letting his only son investigate was a mistake. Although she was doing the same thing for different reasons.

León was an operator through and through, but he also carried himself in the way of a Prince and a proud one at that. A devastating combination for any woman, but Bebe wasn't any woman. Still, the attraction was impossible to deny, her body betraying her every time they were close. He made her feel like a woman, not the deadly assassin she truly was.

Bebe had been angry with him for rushing to her rescue in the town, so used to handling every little thing herself without a man riding in to save the day. She didn't need that or want it. Though her traitorous heart had skipped a little at seeing him stride through the door like an avenging hero as if he was going to destroy anyone who hurt her.

The thought that he didn't think she was good enough to outwit a pap photographer had stung until he'd pointed out how it would be expected for him to act as he had. She'd felt foolish over her reaction and a tiny bit sad that she wasn't the woman who could evoke such devotion in this man.

It was a throwback to another time when she'd been made to feel like she hadn't done enough, wasn't enough, and had failed. Sipping from her glass of rioja, she let the fruity flavours wash away the memories from a time long ago when she was someone different.

Placing the glass on the table in front of her, she leaned back, waiting for León to answer.

He sighed, resting his arms on the table as he leaned in toward her. "He's broken, as you can imagine. Alain was his only child. My father was spending the afternoon helping him with the details of the funeral, but I should imagine he's lost as to know what to do. He may not be my favourite person, but he loved his son. I have no doubt about that."

"Losing a child destroys people."

Leo balanced the rim of his glass on his lip without taking a sip, before putting the glass aside. "Personal experience?"

Bebe considered lying, her past and her family were never something she wished to talk about, but she found herself wanting to share with this man. Something about him made her want him to know her. "Some. My older sister died, and it tore our family apart."

"I'm sorry. That must have been difficult."

Bebe gave a dip of her head. "It was. Nina was a beautiful soul and the light of everyone's life. When she died it was like the world went dark."

"How did she die, if you don't mind me asking?"

Bebe shook her head, taking a sip of her wine to fortify herself. "She had Leukaemia. Battled it most of her life."

"Loss is never easy. It's the part of life we all run from because we know the pain is too much to bear."

"You lost people when you served?"

León rolled his lips between his teeth and sat back as if the question made him fidgety and uneasy. "More than I'd like to admit. Good men and women who were just doing their jobs and making the world a safer place. Taken from the world and lost to those they loved."

"I don't believe they're lost to us."

Leo angled his head. "No?"

"No. How can anyone who made such an impact on our lives be lost? They're there in every action we take in some small way. Each interaction is affected by the people we've loved and lost"

"Hmm, I guess I never thought about it like that."

"That's survivor's guilt. You came home and they didn't. It's bound to leave deep psychological scars and I'm sure you saw things no person should ever have to see."

"How are you so wise? Experience with survivor's guilt?"

"Oh, you have no idea."

"Tell me."

Bebe wanted to, she wanted him to know her, but the words stuck in her throat. "Not tonight."

"I understand."

The air was thick with awkwardness. Normally she'd let it go, not really caring, but the need to fill the silence was heavy. "Tell me about Soroosh. He seems quite the character."

After the journalist had been escorted from the building to the closest airport, Soroosh had served them Churros and hot chocolate to dip them in. It had been clear to see the easy camaraderie between the two men.

"Oh, he *is* a character and one of the best men I've ever served alongside. My squadron was training him and his men to take over when our division was pulled from Iraq. Soroosh is one of those men who has a story for every eventuality and each one is more elaborate than the last. He was always upbeat, keeping things light but he was a damn fine soldier and loyal to the bone."

"I can see that about him."

Leo dipped his head, a sadness about him as he spoke again. "One day we were on patrol, and he got caught by an IED. We flew him out of there and it was touch and go if he'd make it. He obviously did, but lost his right leg below the knee. He'd always talked about owning a bakery, said it was food that made the soul happy. So, I asked him to come here and he accepted. Now he's living a life he loves with a woman he adores, and their first baby is due in the autumn."

"He got his happy ending."

"I guess he did."

"Partly thanks to you."

Leo shook his head as she'd known he would. "No, he's behind his own success."

"True but you played your part. You're a good man, Leo."

Leo placed his glass on the table and stood, moving toward her. Taking her hand, he pulled her to her feet and wrapped his arms around her waist. Her hands landed on his chest and slid up around his neck to the soft hair at the back of his neck. Pressing every inch of her body to his, Bebe felt her nipples peak, the ache in her abdomen moving toward her pussy.

"You're dangerous. You make me forget what's real."

Her heart seemed to beat double time at his words which so mirrored how she was feeling. Dipping his head, he kissed her slowly, drugging her until she didn't know which way was up, taking his time to taste her as he walked her back inside the apartment.

The backs of her knees hit the couch and she would've gone down if Leo hadn't turned, making her land on top of him.

A laugh escaped her as he broke the kiss and sat up with her somehow astride him, her skirt riding up her thighs. The thick ridge between her legs had her wanting to rock into him to ease the ache he'd created.

"Wanna make out before I give you the tour?"

Her body was screaming yes at his question and the sexy little smirk he'd given her, but her brain was yelling a warning that this was dangerous territory.

As he nipped at her bottom lip, dragging his teeth slowly across her lip, the decision was made. Her body rocked involuntarily against his hard cock.

He dug his fingers through her hair, holding her a willing hostage. "Naughty girl."

His voice was a growl as he held her still, eyes such a deep dark green flared with desire, making her feel like the only woman on the planet.

"And what do naughty girls get?"

Bebe had never been one to fall into her role to this degree, but she admitted, if only to herself, that this wasn't a role she was playing. She wanted this man more than she'd ever wanted another.

"Jesus, Bebe. What are you doing to me?"

"The same thing you're doing to me."

Her admission pushed him over the edge, and he slanted his mouth over hers, holding her still as his fingers tightened along her scalp, making pleasure zing through her body. A whimper fell from her lips as they duelled for control. Hands explored wildly as if they couldn't get enough of each other fast enough.

The barking of a dog pierced her lust-induced delirium and Bebe pulled back, leaning her head against León's forehead as she tried to catch her breath and get her bearings.

Turning, she angled her face into his neck and spoke. "Perhaps we should calm this down before we put on a show we hadn't intended."

She stroked his face when he bit back a curse, his body practically humming with the same energy invading her own. Leo gripped her hips and gently lifted her until she was sitting beside him.

He didn't push her away though, instead, he pulled her to his side and kissed her cheek. "I lose my head around you."

She could tell by his tone that the idea wasn't one he liked but she admired his honesty and gave him the same respect. "I know the feeling."

He cocked his head toward her and smirked before he stood and offered his hand. "How about that tour?"

Bebe smiled and nodded. "That sounds wonderful. I just need to freshen up and give my hair less of a just-fucked look."

Leo growled as he drew her closer and dropped a kiss on her lips before gently pushing her away. "Go before I change my mind."

Bebe laughed and walked toward the bedroom, putting a little extra sway in her hips. As she looked over her shoulder, she saw him watching and winked. "Back in a sec."

Once inside the bathroom, she splashed her face with cold water before fixing her mussed hair. Meeting her eyes in the mirror she found a woman who looked the same but different from the one who'd arrived the day before. A feeling that everything was changing crept over her, and it had a lot to do with the man in the room next door.

Smoothing her blouse, she grabbed the tiny bugs and cameras from the secure compartment of her luggage and slipped her gun into her thigh holster. She had a garrot in the underwire of her bra and hoped she wouldn't need either of those things tonight but being prepared was second nature to her now.

'Trust no one except her team' was a mantra she lived by, yet she instinctively trusted Prince León Cataleya, and that in itself was unsettling and dangerous. It was time to get this mission kicked into the next gear and uncover who was entering the auction and, more importantly, the details of when and where.

Roz and the girls who didn't work missions anymore were handling the 'what', and she knew they'd have intel soon.

Her mind turned to her friends who were working this same case in different countries, and she wondered how they were getting on with the men they were undercover with. She hoped they were safe, her heart clenching at the thought of anything happening to them and not being able to help them.

She knew her desire to save the world was because of her guilt for letting her sister down but that didn't make the urge any less potent, no matter how hard she tried.

Seven

HER HAND FELT SMALL IN HIS MUCH LARGER ONE AS THEY WALKED down the wide staircase of the palace that was his home. His eyes darted all around looking for danger, which he knew was a very real threat and that saddened him beyond belief. The home where he'd grown from a boy to a man, where he'd mourned his mother and followed his father around like a shadow, was now marred with danger and uncertainty.

Everything felt off as if things were shifting beneath him and he couldn't stop the tide no matter how hard he tried. Glancing at the woman who looked radiant and fearless beside him, he knew it had something to do with her. She'd only been in his life for twenty-four hours and she'd upended his control like nobody ever had.

His nickname in the military was Granite because he never got flustered or lost control. He was always the solid, stable force everyone could rely on. Now, when he needed it more than ever, it was slipping away from him.

"So, tell me about these people. Who's this?"

León tilted his head to the portrait of his ancestor and began to explain.

They'd followed a similar routine as they wandered around the palace, hand in hand. Bebe would stop to ask questions, and with more discretion than he'd ever seen, plant a bug or a camera, often using the ruse of a kiss or an embrace to hide what she was doing. Not that he minded having his hands or mouth on her in any way at all.

Bebe was highly efficient and skilled from what he'd seen of her. She was also a beautiful distraction. The thought that she was as deadly as she was captivating made the pulse pound in his neck and other, more inconvenient, places. Confident women were his weakness, but this particular woman could be his downfall if he wasn't very careful.

Sliding his arms around her as he stood at her back, he pulled her close and loved the way she leaned into him, giving him her weight and trusting him to have her back. Her scent was stronger as if she'd sprayed perfume before they left the room, and it teased his senses.

"That's my great grandfather. I never met him, but I'm told by my father that he was a kind man who ruled this country with a fair hand and a lot of love. His wife, my great grandmother, was the true strength behind him though. She was his most loyal advisor and would attend every meeting of his council with him. Which as you know, wasn't the norm in those days."

Bebe angled her head until she was facing him, her lashes long and sultry surrounding those smoky eyes as she blinked up at him. "Sounds like they were truly in love."

"I think they were, and my grandparents were the same way."

"And your parents?"

A familiar tightness formed in his chest. He fought the urge to rub it away and reveal too much about himself. He faked a smile and bent his head to touch his lips to her exposed neck, the feel of her an instant distraction to the raging bitterness and grief he felt when he thought of his parents.

Her hand cupped his neck, fingers toying with the ends of his hair. "You don't have to tell me."

Leo lifted his head and caught the open honesty on her face.

"We all have things we'd rather not talk about, Leo."

He saw it then, the pain she kept hidden and he wanted to know what it was that put the sadness in her eyes. What made a woman like her, who could've been and done anything she wanted, do this job? Who'd shaped her and broken her heart? And why did he feel the resultant need to defend her and make sure nobody ever hurt her again?

"My parents were happy for a long time. Then my father cheated on my mother and broke her heart. I don't think she ever recovered from it and she died of a heart attack a few years later."

"I'm so sorry, Leo. That must have been hard for you."

Leo shrugged it off as he'd always done. "That's life, right? People hurt you if you let them."

Bebe turned in his arms and placed her hands on his chest. Looking down he saw her lips part slightly, her tongue flicking out to touch them. Leo felt the hair on his nape rise as his heart pounded under her hand and knew that she could feel it. His fingers itched to explore every inch of this woman. To forget the reason she was there and allow the desire between them to overtake all his senses.

"Not everyone hurts you, Leo."

"Don't they?" He wasn't even sure why he was asking, or maybe he was.

"No, some people enrich your life and show you nothing but love and friendship. Take Soroosh for instance. Your friendship is formed on trust and mutual respect, and I don't think you believe for one second that he'd betray you."

Leo blinked and pulled away slightly, letting her hands fall to her side as he stepped away. "That's different and you know it." Taking her hand, he walked them toward the Jewel room where the last of the bugs would be placed.

Her hand flexed in his and he turned his head to see her watching him. "It is and it isn't, and life is lonely if you keep people locked away due to fear they'll hurt you."

"I'm not afraid. I just have no intention of turning into my mother and allowing another person to break me like that."

He could feel his control slipping, his mouth going dry as he moved more quickly toward the final destination of the tour. He needed some space so he could regroup. Bebe was challenging his entire thought process and he didn't like the cracks that were beginning to show in his façade.

Her silence said a thousand words and crackled like electricity between them, making him regret his harsh words. Slowing his walk, he squeezed her hand in a silent apology and she rubbed his forearm in response. The smile she gave him suddenly made everything okay as her forgiveness washed over him.

If he were the falling in love type this woman would be the one. He could feel that in his bones, but he wasn't and that would never change. The scars were just too deep for him to change now. He would, of course, marry one day and produce an heir, but it would have nothing to do with love.

Throwing off the thoughts that now seemed so distasteful to him, he headed down the corridor toward the Jewel room, where every gem, crown, necklace, ring, and bauble the crown owned was situated. Two guards stood at the entrance night and day.

Leo nodded to them as he approached. "Gentlemen."

He recognised the two nightshift guards and wondered if either of these men were in on what was happening or if they were unwitting accomplices.

"Your Highness."

Both men dipped their heads in deference to his title and León placed his hand on the door and pushed through. The double oak doors opened with a whispered click, and he faced the security doors that were thick steel.

"Wow, this is impressive." Bebe clung to him, looking around in wonder and he knew it was for the cameras following their every move. It was amazing how he could already tell the difference between a fake smile and a real one. She'd probably hate that he could see through some of her act, and he had no doubt others would never know.

"I guess so. I don't really think about it a lot."

Leo keyed in the eight-digit code and placed his palm against the scanner waiting for it to turn green. It clicked, and the air-locked room was unsealed.

Taking Bebe's hand in his, he stepped over the threshold and let the door close, locking them inside. The room was circular with glass cases all around the sides in a large semi-circle. The middle of the room held two wide, oak cases with glass tops that stood around desk height, where more priceless jewels lay. Directly behind that, on a raised dais, was the Tanzanite Tears gem.

Bebe let his hand go as she stepped toward the gem, entranced as every person who'd ever seen it was.

Watching her intently and wanting to see her reaction, he took a step closer. As she rounded the dais, her gaze moved to him, and he could see the glossy sheen of wonder in her eyes was in no way pretend. Having grown up with this gemstone, he loved seeing it through the eyes of another.

"It's magnificent."

Leo pushed his hands into the pockets of his trousers to stop himself from reaching out and touching the entrancing creature who hypnotized him. Moving forward, he looked at the huge, rare stone in the deepest indigo. It had been shaped and polished, but left mostly in its original state, not broken down and turned into multiple pieces, and it still held that raw beauty he loved.

"It was mined in Manyara, Tanzania, by a local miner. It weighs just under ten kilos and is the largest of its kind. Queen Lydia II gave it to my family as a gift of peace between our nations."

"It's stunning; so natural in its beauty with its angles and shapes. Knowing the earth carved these facets over millions of years is mind-blowing."

Leo dragged his eyes from her to the gemstone and agreed its history was part of its beauty. "Tanzanite was formed over five and a half million years ago. It was here before dinosaurs and will be here long after we're dust, and there's comfort in that kind of permanence."

Her body straightened and she moved toward him slowly, her hands loose by her sides, her hips moving with a gentle sway. Leo removed his hands from his pockets and caught her hips as she got close enough, pulling her the last few inches so their bodies were touching.

Her hands smoothed over his biceps, and he flexed, making her look up in surprise, a smile on her face. He loved that he could elicit so many responses from her.

"You talking about history is sexy."

Leo tried to hide his grin as he looked down, seeing the curve of her breast at the edge of her shirt, the pale lilac lace teasing him. "Oh yeah? Want to hear about the sex and debauchery of Roman times?"

Bebe let out a deep husky laugh that made his dick harden in his trousers. His fingers gripped her harder, bringing her close so she could feel what she did to him. His tongue flicked the lobe of her ear and he bit down on the soft flesh, making her breath hitch unsteadily in her chest, those perfect tits pressing against him and making him crave the feel of her hands on him.

Kissing his way over her jaw, he sucked on her pulse, light enough to not leave a mark, but enough so the taste of her skin exploded on his tongue making him need more.

Her hands fisted in his hair as she turned into him, her mouth finding his. Bebe didn't kiss like she was holding back. She gave him everything, opening for him, her tongue skimming over his, igniting a fire inside. Nothing was a simmer between them. It was all-out explosive, and he loved it.

Desire flooded his brain, and his body tingled from head to toe with the need to lay this woman down and explore her body. His hands skimmed up her sides, his thumb rubbing over the tight, erect nipple, forcing a growl from his throat and whimper from her.

She arched into him, and he rocked his hips against the heat of her core, his cock almost punching a hole in his pants to get to her.

Bebe dragged herself away, her breathing hard, her eyes almost black with arousal and placed a hand on his chest. "Maybe we should finish the tour so we can take this somewhere more private?"

Leo tried to rein in his yearning, his breaths harsh as he focused on anything but the woman in front of him and how close he'd come to stripping her down and fucking her against the case holding the Tanzanite Tears stone. "Good idea."

He moved alongside her as he walked her around the cases,

showing her the different jewels and explaining some of the history to her. He saw her plant the bugs and the cameras so discreetly that nobody would find them unless they went looking, and there was no reason to think they would or that the person involved had any idea they were onto him or her. Although the niggle at the back of his neck made him wonder again about Brody James and Albin Wojcik.

"What about this one?" Bebe pointed to the crown with emeralds and diamonds fashioned in a Greek style, gifted to them by the King of Greece.

"That was worn by my mother on her wedding day to my father."

Leo unlocked the case and lifted the crown, which was heavy. The five emeralds were almost ninety-five carats combined and the hundreds of diamonds that made up the rest of the design were close to the same.

He placed it gingerly on Bebe's head, the crown sitting perfectly on her thick, dark hair. Stepping back, he looked at her and his stomach flipped in his body. An image of Bebe as his Queen flashed before him, her grace and beauty unparalleled and he knew in his gut she'd be a wonderful Queen. A true partner to any King ruling a nation, an inspired advocate of everything he held dear.

"You'd make a wonderful Queen." His voice shook slightly with the words, and he hoped like hell she didn't notice.

Bebe laughed. "God, no. I'm not exactly royal material. I can't even run my own life sometimes, let alone a country."

"I highly doubt that."

"It's true. I'm in the prime of my life, single, childless, and working my ass off."

Leo cocked his head. "Not what you saw for yourself as a teenager?"

Bebe lifted the crown and looked at it for a second before passing it back to him. "No, I saw a husband, kids, a family, and a job I loved."

"What happened?"

Bebe's lips pinched, and he could see the pain and bitterness she was trying desperately to bury. "I failed at the one thing I was supposed to do in this life—save my sister. So, you see, I'm as far from a Queen as you'll get."

With that she walked past him, her arm brushing his chest and waited at the door. Leo stayed quiet as he put the crown away and tried to process her words. She was hiding as much grief as he was but for different reasons. She blamed herself and he blamed his father.

Eight

Like a coward, Bebe had escaped to the bathroom once they returned to Leo's rooms. The kiss and the conversation had all been too much and she could feel her barriers falling. As she let the warm water fall over her skin, she tried to push thoughts of her parents, and all the hurtful things they'd said to her after her sister had died, away.

How it was her fault. How she'd failed her family and what a waste it had been to give her life. Leo seeing her as a Queen was a joke, and perhaps he'd meant it that way. She wasn't sure, but it had hit a nerve she hadn't expected. She cared way more than she should about how he saw her and that was scary.

Over the years and her time with Zenobi, she'd come to terms with her past as much as she could and vowed never to let it affect her present. What happened in the past shouldn't matter, and neither should the future. It was the moment she lived in that made the seconds count.

She'd been in the moment with Leo when he'd kissed her, throwing away every thought but him. He was such a complex man. A Prince, a soldier, but she saw only him, the whole person, each facet of him melding like the jewel she was here to protect.

That was what she needed to focus on, her job and finding out who was involved. Right now, she had very little to go on. Stepping out of the large shower cubicle onto the cool tile, she wrapped her thick hair in a towel and tied the robe tight around her body. The length of the robe was clearly built for a man, coming to the bottom of her calves, leaving only her feet and ankles exposed. She wriggled her foot, watching the flower tattoo she'd had done to remember her sister move as if the wind was blowing the flower around. Orchids had always been her sister's favourite, and maybe it was fate that had brought her here to the place with the largest orchid farm in the world.

Stepping back into the bedroom, she saw Leo making up the couch with sheets and paused. He stilled as if sensing her, his muscles freezing in place before he went back to what he was doing. "You can take the bed if you prefer."

Leo straightened but kept his back to her. "It's fine."

He went to move past her into the bathroom and she stopped him with her hand on his arm. "I'm sorry I snapped at you."

Leo angled his head to her, his face closed, and she thought she detected hurt beneath his eyes, which was crazy. Nonetheless, she wanted to fix this, to get the easy partnership they'd acquired so quickly back in place. "There's no denying the chemistry between us, Leo. But to take it further, no matter how much we want that, would be foolish."

"I agree."

Bebe blinked, her mouth falling open as she felt him turn into her body, and begin walking, forcing her to move or get ploughed over. "You agree?"

Her throat felt dry as her knees hit the back of the couch, his body pressed to her, and she wondered if he could feel the beat of her heart reverberating through her chest.

"An absolute disaster and yet we both know it's going to happen. This," he motioned between them, "is too hot to be extinguished."

He leaned in so his lips were almost touching hers and she struggled to draw oxygen past the thick blanket of need filling the air.

"We'll get burned." Her warning was just as much for herself as for him.

"I don't give a fuck if the world burns down around us, Bebe, but this is going to happen."

With that he stepped away and walked to the bathroom, slamming the door behind him.

Bebe drew in a shaky breath and moved to the vanity. She began to brush through her long hair as she processed the words Leo had spoken to her. The repetitive action calmed her frayed nerves. He hadn't sounded any happier about it than she felt but he'd seemed to accept whatever was between them easier than she did.

Lifting the towel, she dried her hair, rubbing the strands together before brushing it once more. She should dry it, or it would be a wild mess by morning, but she also wanted to be in the safety of her bed by the time Leo came out of the bathroom.

Stopping, she listened, moving so her ear was pressed to the door of the bathroom. She could hear the water running but also something else. A groan, her name spoken on a low growl that had her clenching her thighs together, her clit pulsing at the sound of him getting off to thoughts of her. It would be so easy to open that door and join him, to step into that shower and feel the hard, wet ridges of his body against her own. To let the lust consume them, but it would also complicate an already complex situation.

Instead, she shut out the light, put on panties, threw on an old t-shirt that belonged to her friend Waggs and had gotten mixed up with her laundry, and climbed into bed. The cool satin sheets were heaven on her fevered skin. She lay back, moving her damp hair to the side and knowing she'd regret not drying it properly in the morning.

As the shower kept running, Bebe slid her hand down her body, the slight touch making goosebumps break out on her skin. Pushing her panties aside she rolled her fingers over her aching clit, a moan escaping her as she imagined it was Leo. His hands on her, his big body over her, inside her.

Pleasure seared her skin and she lost herself in the feel of ecstasy that rippled over her flesh. A flood of light hitting the room had her hand stilling as Leo walked back in, a pair of grey sweats slung low on his hips. His physique was impressive, muscular and lean. The ripples in his back as he moved to the couch made her mouth water with the need to taste him. To see what he looked like when he lost control, gave up the fight, and just let the beast inside him free.

A man like him, who'd seen the hell of war, seen friends die and lived to come home, would hold themselves in check, but a King in waiting? He'd have an even tighter leash on his emotions.

Bebe dared to imagine how beautiful he'd be when he let that control go. To be on the end of his kind of intensity would feel like the world was at your fingertips. Even after only a short time together she knew he could love. That he could be everything to someone. A husband, a father, and a King, and he'd do it to the best of his ability because anything else would be a failure to him.

She wanted to feel that, to know that kind of love but was she enough? Could she ever be enough for anyone, let alone a man like him? A woman who'd killed, seduced, fought, and lost the biggest battle she'd ever faced.

It was why she lay there, looking at the ceiling, long after he'd slipped beneath the sheets of his couch.

"You should get some sleep."

His deep voice in the silent darkness made her jump and she rolled to her side to see him watching her. "I'm trying."

"Close your eyes, Bebe."

His command had her doing as he asked, the tone of his voice deeper, lower, and more intense than she could hope to ignore.

Bebe sighed. "Fine, they're closed. Happy now?"

His chuckle had her turning to her back, the sound soaking over her skin and the frustrated ache of her interrupted 'me time' earlier, making her tense.

"Not even close."

More silence but this time it was punctuated with the sounds of their breathing, heavy with unspoken secrets.

"I'm sorry I pushed you earlier. I didn't mean to upset you."

Bebe hated that he thought it was his fault, and the need to give him something to explain her behaviour had her unexpectedly opening up to him. Bebe drew in a shaky breath. "I was a saviour baby. My parents had me specifically to save my sister. When she died anyway, they blamed me. I'd had one purpose. To save her and I failed. She died and they were left with a child they never really wanted."

"That's horrendous."

The darkness made it easier for her to elaborate. "Nina was their world. The sun rose and fell with her. Don't get me wrong, while she was alive they were never hurtful or abusive. I was just there. My father was a revered cardiac surgeon in Pakistan, and he felt my failure was a slight on him as a doctor. They never had the time or the energy to give me more than the basics, even before she died. My life was a round of hospital appointments, blood tests, procedures, all geared toward saving her life and I didn't mind. I loved my sister so much."

Her throat clogged and she felt like she was choking, the grief and guilt she tried to keep buried rising to the surface. "When Nina died, I was just finishing school. I'd thrown everything into my grades, trying to be the best so my parents would love me. The day she died was the worst of my life. Nina loved me for me, not for what I was meant to do or not do. The truth is, I think she was tired of fighting and she hated how I was made to feel. Not that I told her or let on, but Nina was astute, and she saw me as a person, a real human being and she loved me. She told me she was ready to go."

Tears clogged her throat and she flinched as the bed dipped and Leo slipped in beside her, hauling her body close and holding her safe from the memories that shredded her every time she allowed them out.

Settling back against his chest, his breath feathered her hair and she held onto the arms holding her. One at her waist, the other across her chest and she felt as if nothing could hurt her now.

"My parents shouted and screamed at first. Telling me how I was useless, that I had killed Nina. How they wished it had been me and that I was their biggest regret, and I could handle that. I knew it already and I blamed myself. I should have done more, eaten healthier, not snuck that extra cake or portion of chips. After the initial loss though, they just shut down and ignored me as if I didn't exist. They were so lost in their own pain they'd go days, sometimes even weeks, without speaking to me."

His lips on her hair only made her tears fall harder. She didn't deserve his sympathy. She was a killer and her first victim had been her sister. "I don't know why I'm crying."

"Because you suffered something nobody should ever have to go through. You were a child. You deserved love for merely existing. Instead, you were made to feel like a spare part."

"I killed her. I should have saved her. It was my job."

"And that's why it's so important to you that you never fail another job, isn't it?"

His insight tore a sob from her chest, and she wondered if it was the hormones left over from her last failed IVF. Bebe had never discussed her sister with anyone. Not even her friends knew. Only Roz knew the truth and that was because it was essential, and part of the agreement they all had with her was that they'd always be truthful with her.

When Roz found her blind drunk on the anniversary of Nina's death not long after she'd recruited her to Zenobi, it had all come out. The ugly truth about her failure. Roz had forced her into therapy and the conscious part of her knew she was an innocent child, but the other part hated herself for what she hadn't done. "Yes. I can't fail another person."

"You didn't fail your sister. Your parents failed you. They should be whipped for ever making you feel like it was your fault."

His words made her cry harder, and she couldn't seem to stop. Leo just held her tighter, this man she hardly knew giving her comfort. In some ways she felt closer to him than she had anyone in a long time.

"Do you ever see your parents now?"

Bebe shook her head. "Not since the day I left. They still live in Pakistan in the house I grew up in. They set up a foundation in Nina's name and every year I donate to it, anonymously."

She could feel the anger on her behalf radiating off him, but he said nothing except, "Sleep, Bebe, I won't leave you."

As her sobs ebbed and the grief left her body, she felt sleep pulling her under and was relieved not to be alone.

Nine

Leo lifted his head to see the woman who'd exposed her heart to him sleeping soundly. Slowly, he eased out of the bed where he'd spent the night cuddled up to her, his body perfectly moulded around her. Pulling on a t-shirt, he took one last glance at the sleeping beauty as the dawn eased over the hills in the distance. She looked like an angel; her lips slightly parted, long lashes feathered over her cheeks. Her glorious hair spread over the pillow, a hand beside her face.

Her walls were down, as they'd been last night, but he knew she'd resurrect them this morning and go back to the operator she was. Last night had been a blip, a hiccup, and even only having known her for a short time, he knew she'd hate that she'd shown him her weakness.

Quietly he closed the bedroom door and went to the door of his apartment where he'd asked Hans to leave his coffee and food. Lifting the silver tray, he took it to the balcony where he could watch the sunrise and drink his morning brew. The peace at this time of day soothed his soul and had him thinking about last night and the revelations.

Bebe's confession and the pain in her voice had slain him. Getting into her bed may have been a mistake but he couldn't sit by while she broke her heart. His relationship with his father was strained, mostly by him, but he never doubted his father's love for him. To know you'd been born to save a sibling was one thing but to have your parents treat you how she'd been, was criminal.

His hand tightened on the mug he was drinking from as anger spread through him in a slow burn. Everything he knew about this woman who was turning him inside out made more sense now. Her job, her need to stay professional, she was trying to fix a wrong she'd never committed.

Movement at the door to the balcony had him looking up to see Bebe standing there watching him. He could see uncertainty and wariness in her eyes, her hands were by her sides, her long legs teasing him beneath the t-shirt she wore. "Coffee?"

"Please."

She moved to sit opposite him as he poured the coffee from the carafe, adding milk and sugar as was her preference.

Leo gestured to the man's shirt she wore, with a grey AW on the chest of the black shirt. "Nice t-shirt."

Bebe looked down and pulled at the shirt. "A friend gave it to me. We work together a lot and live in the same building. My machine broke so he let me use his. He must have left this in the washer because it ended up with my stuff and I claimed it."

"You seem close."

"We are. Waggs is a good friend."

Jealousy twisted inside him, and he hated this Waggs guy that lived and worked with Bebe so often. Not that it should matter to him. After this was over, he'd probably never see her again. That had him rubbing a hand over his chest as a heavy feeling settled on him.

Leo nodded because she was waiting for a response, and he didn't trust himself to speak.

"His wife and son are the loveliest, too."

Bebe sipped her coffee, hiding her face behind the mug and he coughed into his fist to hide his embarrassment at being so obvious with his green-eyed monster. He was never this guy. At least, he never had been, and he shouldn't be now. There was nothing between them except a red-hot attraction.

"We should head to the Marina today. I want to speak to the investigators. See if they know any more and check out the remains of the boat myself."

Bebe nibbled on a dry pastry, the flakes falling to her chest, and he tried not to let his eyes follow suit. "That's a good idea."

"Whoever planted the bomb must have gotten on board somehow, and as there's no footage we need to do this the old-fashioned way."

"That's another thing I don't like. Whoever this is either hacked the cameras or is skilled enough to know to stay out of sight of them."

"I think it's fair to say we're dealing with a highly trained individual."

Bebe shook her head. "I don't think it's an individual. I think this is a small team of at least three."

Leo sat forward, discarding his coffee now as he waited for her to continue. Watching this woman's brain work was seductive. He definitely shouldn't be thinking about sex right now, but she seemed to bring out that side of him, no matter how hard he tried to ignore it. "What makes you say that?"

"Too many variables. You need someone inside the palace who's high enough up not to get questioned, but the background checks show nobody other than you with the kind of skills needed to pull this off."

"Well, we know it's not me, so who?"

Bebe pursed her lips. "Originally, I'd have said Alain or Alwyn. But obviously, Alain is out. I don't see Alwyn killing Alain. His son meant the world to him from what you say."

Leo felt disloyal even thinking it, but it had crossed his mind briefly before he dismissed it. "Alwyn could still be involved, and his partner killed Alain to keep Alwyn in line."

"Possible, but to what end? Alwyn is hardly the master criminal. He may be ambitious for the crown, but I can't see him wanting anything from the auction."

"No, but it could be a quid pro quo situation. The partner helps him get the crown and he helps them get the stone he needs for the auction."

"So that leaves Wojcik and Brody James. They're the new faces here."

Leo didn't want to consider his own blood was involved but he couldn't rule it out. "So, if that's true, my father is in danger. The only way the crown goes to Alwyn is if my father and I are out of the picture."

"Exactly, but if we take your father out of the picture and put him in protective custody, we let the traitor know we know something and they could go underground."

"We should bring my father in on everything." It wouldn't have been his first plan, but things were changing.

Bebe shook her head. "No, we stick with the plan. Whoever it is won't make a move on you or the King straight away. If three members of the Royal family die, it brings too much outside focus to the Kingdom and an investigation would take place."

Leo considered this and slowly nodded; she was right.

"Of course, we could be off, and Alwyn isn't involved. It could be someone blackmailing the King."

"What? No!" Leo stood fast, knocking the chair backwards as he paced the space, his hands tugging at his hair to try and ground his temper.

"Hear me out. If someone found out something about your father, such as his affair or something else, then he'd want it kept a secret. If he thinks the person only wants the stone, would he sacrifice it to save you from embarrassment?"

Leo stopped, his heart pounding hard in his chest. He knew what she was saying could be true and he hated it. His father loved him and had never made it a secret that he'd always try and protect him. Leo always put it down to guilt, but he saw now that was harsh. "So, as of this second, we don't know who or when or where, just what."

"Well, we don't know that either until I can speak with my contact. I have a call scheduled for tonight."

"Right. Let's go to the Marina and see what we can find."

Bebe stood and sashayed back inside, and he knew the act was back on. The balcony had been cleared of bugs and she was checking twice a day for new plants, and her camera hadn't caught anybody coming and going inside his apartment except for the cleaners, and they'd only done their jobs.

Leo followed her, his eyes on her ass, a grin on his face but it was forced as he thought of the risks and connotations if his family were involved in this.

~

Leo settled his aviators in place as he got out of the car. He'd driven his more sedate Audi Q7 to the Marina, not wanting as much fuss as the Ferrari would cause. He moved to the passenger's door and opened it for Bebe, offering his hand as she exited. She looked sensational in white Capri pants and a yellow shirt tied at the waist. Wedged espadrilles on her feet gave her height and made her ass look amazing.

Taking her hand, he walked toward the dock where his yacht had been moored in the Royal slip. "I asked Hector, the Marina Manager, to meet us."

"We should have someone look into him, too."

Leo checked his black diver's watch and dipped his head. "Agreed."

Hector was waiting at the office when they arrived and he greeted first Leo and then Bebe, offering his condolences for Alain and his friends.

He and Bebe had agreed he'd take the lead. After all, she was there as his girlfriend, not an operator. "Thank you, Hector."

"Please sit, sit."

Leo waited for Bebe to sit in one of the office chairs before sitting beside her and taking her hand in his again. They needed to sell his complete adoration of her to anyone that could be involved. Her smile was genuine as she glanced at him.

"Would you like some water, tea, coffee?"

"No, thank you."

Hector took a seat behind his desk, bracing his hands together, elbows on the table.

"Tell us what you have so far, Hector."

It was no secret he'd been in the army, and he was familiar to his people, having made it his mission to be seen in the towns and villages. He eschewed a guard, knowing he was more deadly than any man on his security team and would likely spot a threat before they did. He kept them in place though, so the palace had extra cover. They were currently patrolling the grounds, ensuring none of the journalists surrounding the palace got close to the King. His involvement wouldn't be unusual to anyone, they'd expect him to get involved.

"The bomb was professionally made and placed inside the engine room. It was set on a timer. Most likely so that the boat would be out to sea by the time it went off."

This was the same information the police had given them. "Has the marina had any new faces of late? Any staff members, short mooring leases, that kind of thing?"

"We have a few summer hires to help with tourists day mooring their boats with us but all of them have been background checked and none are allowed near the Royal mooring."

"Any issues with clients in the last few months?"

Hector shook his head, his face getting redder as he did. "No, nothing like that. I run a clean operation. My staff are happy, and every rule is adhered to completely. I take my job seriously, Your Highness."

"I know, Hector. We're just trying to make sense of it all."

"I understand."

"Were you or any of the staff here when my cousin and his friends arrived?"

"Yes, Patty, one of our older crew members, was here. She said she saw them get on board the yacht."

Leo looked to Bebe who gave nothing away about what she was thinking. "Is Patty here? I'd like to speak with her."

"Yes. Yes, of course. I'll get her for you."

Hector stood and made his way across the marina to one of the floating docks that was beside a yacht he knew belonged to a Hollywood movie star.

"Why didn't the police mention this?"

Bebe shrugged but didn't respond, only glanced around as if not trusting this place wasn't bugged either. She was right to be cautious and he swore inwardly at his loss of focus. Too many possibilities were making it hard for him to piece things together in his mind.

Hector and Patty walked back toward the office, and he recognised the woman from his visits to the marina previously. She was nearing forty if he had to guess and was a competent sailor with a real love of the sea.

She had, in fact, filled in for one of his crew at a party he'd thrown for Alain last year. Did that put her on the suspect list? He figured it did and the list was getting out of control now.

Patty stood just inside the door, shoulders back, hands behind her back in a military position.

"At ease." He saw her relax and knew he'd been right in that she was ex-military. "What branch?" Although he thought he already knew the answer.

"Royal Navy, sir. Marine Engineers."

"May I ask why you retired?"

"Medical discharge, sir. I sustained a head injury during a routine exercise, and they deemed me unfit for duty."

Leo flattened his lips. "I'm sorry to hear that."

"Thank you, sir."

"I understand you saw my cousin and his friends the night they died."

Her back was ramrod straight and her chin lifted, not making eye contact with a superior. He'd guess she'd been a good sailor, competent and disciplined.

"I did, sir. I was making some routine repairs when they arrived. I saw him and four men board the yacht."

Leo frowned she made no mention of Chelsea. "Just him and four men? No women went on board?"

"Not that I saw, sir."

"And could you have missed anything?"

He saw Patty frown as if trying to remember. "I don't believe so, no. I was on the floating dock beside them from the time they arrived to when they set off, but it was dark so I can't be one hundred percent sure."

"Could anyone have arrived beforehand?"

"Yes, sir, I suppose that's possible."

Leo felt Bebe squeeze his hand as if she was trying to tell him something.

"Sweetheart, didn't you say that you were with Alain before we met that night?"

"Yes, darling, I did."

He glanced at Patty to see she was watching Bebe before she looked quickly away. Her furtive look at his woman could just be curiosity. He attracted attention everywhere he went after all. "Patty, what time did my cousin arrive?"

"Nine thirty."

Leo tried not to show his reaction but his blood chilled. If she was right then it couldn't have been his cousin and friends on that boat, because Alain was with him at the time, and he'd seen Atticus and Chelsea after that.

"Are you sure of the time?"

"Yes, sir. I remember looking at my watch because I had a text come through with an early weather warning for windy conditions."

"Thank you, Patty. That will be all."

Patty nodded once and turned on her heel and left.

"Is there a problem, Your Highness?"

Hector must have picked up on his emotions during the last few minutes because he seemed worried, cautious.

"No, Hector. We've taken up enough of your time, but if you hear anything please let the palace know."

"I will, Your Highness."

Leo walked quickly back to the car, Bebe silent at his side, neither one risking a word to the other about what they'd just found out. He opened her car door for her and closed it before heading around to the driver's side, his head on a swivel as every time he turned around the threat was coming from a different direction.

He watched Bebe take something out of her bag and flip a switch, placing it in the centre console.

"We can talk. That's a frequency blocker, in case they planted anything on the car while we were away."

"You think they would?" Jaw clenched in anger, his thoughts turned to his father again and the possible danger he could be in.

"No. But let's not take a chance."

He angled his body toward hers, the tinted windows keeping them hidden from prying eyes. "So, if my cousin was with me when he allegedly got on that yacht, whose bodies are in the morgue and where the hell are Alain, Atticus, and Chelsea?"

"Who identified the bodies?"

Leo shook his head. "I'm not sure."

"We need to find that out, and fast."

Ten

Bebe held Leo's hand as they crossed the large reception hall of the main Palace to get to his apartment. Her mind was spinning a million different scenarios as she tried to figure out the most likely. Seeing the distress and confusion on the face of the man beside her had made her belly clench with sympathy for him.

He was acting like this was a mission to him, but she knew it had to be hard when the threat was so close to home. Everything he knew was being challenged, people he cared about had the finger of betrayal pointed at them.

"León."

She felt León stiffen and then work a smile onto his face as he turned with her to face his father. "Your Majesty."

King Alfred was tall like his son, his hair grey and receding but he looked fit, with just a small paunch around his middle. Handsome, with a regal, straight-backed bearing, he walked toward them, his eyes taking her in and assessing her. Bebe kept her face neutral, years of practice at hiding her true thoughts and feelings from the world, giving her a much-needed edge.

"Son."

"Father, this is Bebe Basu, the lady I was telling you about."

Bebe let go of León's hand, remembering that he was a prince for the first time since they'd met. She dropped a curtsey and bowed her head in respect as the King waited for her to rise.

"It's a pleasure to meet you, Miss Basu."

"The honour is all mine, Your Majesty."

"Are you on your way in or out?"

The King angled toward his son, asking him the question, giving Bebe a moment to study the dynamic between the two men. Affection was as clear as day on the King's face as he waited for his son to answer.

"We've come from the Marina."

"Ah, wonderful. You can have lunch with me in my private quarters."

Bebe saw Leo clench his back teeth, his jaw going rigid and knew he was about to try and wriggle out of it. This was a good opportunity for her to get a read on the King though and, God willing, clear his name. She hated that there was now doubt in Leo's mind about his father's innocence. She'd considered keeping quiet, but secrets led to people dying in her experience and she had no intention of letting Leo die.

"That would be lovely, León."

She squeezed his arm, where he'd looped it, taking her fingers and wrapping them around his forearm in a gesture that made his feelings for her clear. A spear of regret shot through her as she wished for just a moment that it was real. That he did indeed crave her touch in such a natural and intuitive way. Leo smiled, his eyes warming, tiny lines around his eyes crinkling and it felt like this was real, like they were the only two people in the room.

"It seems, my darling, that I can't deny you anything."

She knew it was a ruse, a lie, but when he looked at her like he was and called her darling, it was all too easy to forget that this was fake and that she wasn't his anything. The thought made her ridiculously sad, regret like a knot in her chest.

"Then that's settled. I'll see you at one in my quarters."

She turned her eyes to King Alfred as he pivoted on his heel, his three-piece suit immaculate and walked away, his shoulders straight, head high.

"I can't believe you got us into that. You do realise he'll have the wedding planned by the time we get to dessert, don't you?"

Bebe smirked as she leaned into his arm, resting her head for a second, a smile teasing her mouth. "There's dessert?"

Leo shook his head, a bemused grin on his face as he opened his apartment door, holding a hand for her to precede him. "You do realise that you're completely crazy, don't you?"

He hooked his hands around her waist drawing her close, so she had to look up at him to reply. "Crazy for you."

"Yeah?"

"Yep." She let her mouth pop on the 'p' and hated the giddy feeling that was making her body ache for him. If this were real, she'd throw herself head long into this feeling, but it wasn't, and she wished so hard that she was a woman worthy of him.

"I've never met anyone like you. Beautiful, sexy, clever, confident with a heart as big as those gorgeous eyes."

"Did you just say I have bug eyes?" Bebe twitched her nose trying not to laugh, because her emotions were shot, and it could easily turn to tears.

"What? No. Stop twisting my words, you minx."

"Now, I'm a minx. Prince León, I may call off our imaginary wedding if you keep insulting me."

Leo placed a hand over his heart and feigned heartbreak. "Please, I beg you, don't do that. You know my heart only beats for you."

Bebe rolled her eyes. "Whatever."

She went to pull away, but he snatched her arm, dragging her back and bending his head to capture her lips.

Her breath left her lungs at his hot kiss, the earthy male scent of Leo mixed with the aftershave he wore making her dizzy. His hand gripped the back of her neck as he guided her head to the side so he could deepen the kiss. Bebe wrapped her arms around his neck, moulding her body closer, feeling the hardness of his cock against her belly. His teeth tugged at her bottom lip, and he growled as her nails bit into his neck.

"I need you."

"Your father," she reminded him as he palmed her ass, grinding his cock against her clit, making her gasp.

"Fuck my father."

Bebe pulled her head away so she could get some normal brain function working, his hands and mouth a distraction to her mental ability to think. "We can't just ignore the King's invitation."

"He's my father, and I'm due a rebellious phase."

Bebe laughed and his hands tightened on her ass, which she loved. His touch was becoming addictive. "We can't have him thinking I'm a bad influence. He might not plan our wedding."

"Argh, fine." Leo stepped back and put some space between them as he placed his hands on his hips and looked at the floor. "Go. Change or whatever you need to do before I forget myself and ravish you on the carpet."

Bebe was clever enough to know when to beat a hasty retreat and spun on her heel heading for the bathroom. She took her time freshening her make-up and smoothing her hair. She wanted to make a good impression on the King, so he'd believe this story they were weaving. At least that was what she told herself as she slipped into a cream crepe midi dress with a wide belt and tiny pearl buttons which did up to a peter pan collar. Slipping her feet into pale green suede shoes, she checked the blade that was embedded in the heel and secured the belt so she could easily access the garrot that ran through the middle of the stiff fabric.

She'd like to have her gun and throwing stars, but she could hardly arrive for lunch with the King with a gun on her person. Satisfied she was ready to do this, she exited the bathroom and found Leo relaxed on the bed in a grey suit and white shirt, a pale green tie around his neck in a complex knot.

He rose to his feet, coming toward her and taking her hands so he could spin her gently. "Breath taking."

Bebe felt an unfamiliar blush stain her cheeks and smiled, dipping her head, before her eyes moved over him. "Not so bad yourself, Leo."

He dipped his head in thanks and she felt the attraction between them sizzle hotter than a four-alarm fire.

"We should talk about what we discovered at the Marina." Bebe needed to get this back on track before she lost herself to lust.

Leo pursed his lips, his brow dropping in concern. "Yes, I'll try and keep lunch short so we can come back here and talk about things."

With her hand in his, her other holding the flat envelope purse with her phone and lip gloss, she followed Leo out of the relative safety of the apartment and down the elegant staircase. Her eyes moved around in what anyone watching would assume was wonder but was actually her checking the camera positions.

She knew someone back at Zenobi would be watching the feed and keeping an eye on the gem. She'd get an alarm through her phone if the room was breached. First chance she got Bebe needed to speak to Roz about the two new hires in the palace.

It could easily be one of them was the person she was looking for, but it was just as likely it was someone who'd been in the palace a long time and been bought off or tempted in some way.

Humans, she was all too aware, were fickle creatures and if you knew the right button to push, easily manipulated. The other thing she had to consider was whether this person knew the full details of the plan regarding the auctions and the other gems.

She stopped beside Leo as he reached the King's quarters and waited for them to be announced. When the door opened, she got a glimpse into the understated luxury of the King's apartment within the palace.

Where León's apartment was modern with modest luxurious touches, the King's was classic. With a lot of antiques and wood, deep leather couches, priceless paintings and artworks from a time gone by.

The butler showed them into the dining room where the King was waiting. He turned with a smile, a crystal glass of amber liquid in one hand. "Ah, León, Bebe. I hope you're hungry. I've had the chef prepare all of your favourite dishes, Leo."

"It smells delicious, Your Majesty."

A genuine smile spread across Alfred's face. "A woman who enjoys her food. A true find, my boy."

"Shall we?" Leo asked a touch of impatience in his voice.

Bebe frowned at the sharp tone, as the King's face fell for just a second before he rallied. "Yes, of course."

He sat at the head of the table with Leo to his left and her beside Leo. The table was set as if for a banquet, with polished silver cutlery, the finest of china and crystal wine glasses. Delicious aromas were coming from the covered dishes that were being carried out as if there were ten people dining and not just the three of them.

"Father, it seems you may have gone overboard."

King Alfred regarded his son and Bebe wished the breach between the men could be eased. "It's a long time since we dined together. I wanted to make the most of it."

Regret and sadness clouded his words and she felt Leo tense beside her. Without thought, her hand reached for his and squeezed gently in support. He turned her way and she smiled, giving him a small nod of encouragement. Encouraging what she wasn't sure, but she wanted him to know she was there for him.

His eyes held hers for a moment in time and something passed between them that she couldn't explain. Not lust or love, but a silent conversation between two people who knew pain and understood the complexities of family.

Breaking his gaze away he kept her hand in his as he turned to his father, who was watching them, intently. "You're right, Father, and for that I'm sorry. I'll do better in the future."

A sheen of tears came over the King's eyes before he glanced away, clearing his throat. "Please dig in. I hope you don't mind but I've asked the staff to leave us for this meal so we can just be a family for a change."

Leo lifted a plate of roast beef and offered her some, Bebe shook her head. "I don't eat beef or pork." Being a somewhat lapsed Hindu was a source of guilt for her and she had certainly not followed the spiritual teachings of her childhood into her work life, but not eating beef or pork had stuck with her. As had, some of the other things like her belief that samsara the continuous cycle of life, death, and reincarnation and karma were at work in the universe.

"Is that a religious belief or just a personal choice?" Leo passed the basket of bread, and she tipped her head in thanks.

"I was raised Hindu by my parents, but I don't consider myself one religion or faith. I feel more spiritual than religious."

"I have visited Pakistan and thought it was a Muslim country?"

"It is predominantly, but my family were among a very small percentage of people who were Hindu."

The king nodded, taking a bite of his bread. "I found Pakistan to be brimming with life and colour and, as you say, spiritualism. A beautiful country." The King smiled kindly.

Bebe smiled in return. "It is very beautiful."

"Do you go back often?"

Bebe bit her lip memories of the country of her birth and formative years distant and the beauty plagued by memories of rejection but seeing it from an outsider's perspective, she could see the beauty for what it was.

"Not as often as I would like."

"Perhaps you and Leo could visit in the future."

Bebe rolled her lips to hide the smile at the obvious matchmaking. "Maybe we could."

Feeling Leo's eyes on her, she glanced his way and saw him smiling at her with warmth before he turned it toward his father.

Bebe felt a warm sensation in her belly. This rift was healable, unlike the one with her family. This man loved his son, no matter his mistakes, and where there was love, there was hope.

Eleven

Leo braced his arm on the back of Bebe's chair as laughter rippled through him.

"I tell you he was barely two and he'd climbed that tree like he was part monkey. His mother, God rest her soul, almost had a conniption."

The mention of his mother almost had him shutting down until he glanced across at Bebe and something in her expression begged him to give his father a chance. He let the grin on his face stand as his father finished the story of his wild youth.

This lunch, despite his reservations, had been a good idea for both him and his father. He'd listened intently as Bebe had chatted with the King, slipping in questions that seemed innocuous but were meant to give her answers as to whether the King was in on the scheme to attend the criminal auction.

He'd known his father would never be involved. No matter their differences he had utter faith in that regard. He was a good man, just a terrible husband.

"Leo, this lady is a true delight. When can I expect to see an engagement ring on her finger? You'd be a fool to let her get away and I know for a fact you aren't a fool."

He'd joked with Bebe about this happening but hadn't truly believed his father would fall under her spell as easily as he'd done. His fingers brushed the back of her neck under her mane of silky hair. She was utterly enchanting, clever, strong, so beautiful it hurt to look at her for too long, and she cared perhaps more than she realised. Even after everything she'd been through, she wanted him and his father to heal.

If this were any other time, if she hadn't been here to find a traitor in his home, if this were real, he'd very likely be considering exactly what his father was suggesting. No matter what she thought, Bebe would make a fine Queen and wonderful life partner.

Her head angled to him, and she blushed at his father's words. A reaction he wouldn't have expected from her, but this was the second time he'd seen that delightful shade of pink tinge on her copper skin. Was it that she was as affected by him as he was her or was it something else?

"You're correct, Father. I'm not a fool. Bebe is someone I hadn't expected in my life, and you can bet I'll do everything in my power to convince her I'm worthy of her."

"You're worthy, Leo. You're so much more than the man you show the world."

His father clapped his hands, delight clear on his face. "I couldn't agree more, Bebe, and how wonderful that you see it too."

"You've done a wonderful job raising him into the man he is today."

"No, that was his mother. She's the reason he's the man you see today."

Leo blinked as if waking from a deep sleep. The reality was his father was responsible. He'd raised him, being more hands-on than many in his position. His mother, even before her death, had been absent. She'd been loving but so often she'd been tired or sick, and it had been his father who'd taken him riding or shooting.

"No, Bebe is right. I loved mother, but you're the person who moulded me into who I am today." His chest felt tight as he spoke, the memories he'd hidden flourishing now.

"Thank you for that, my son, but you have your mother's gentle heart."

"Maybe but I have your sense of family and loyalty."

A memory of his mother apologising for something lingered just out of reach, and a conversation he couldn't seem to access.

A knock on the door had him snapping out of the past and concentrating on the present. A gentle grip on his arm had him looking toward the woman who was throwing his world into turmoil in more ways than one. Upending everything he thought he knew and letting the world he knew settle into a new and more beautiful landscape.

"I'm very sorry, Your Majesty, but Chelsea Vos is here and insists on speaking with Prince León."

León's gaze cut to Bebe who schooled her features much more quickly than he did.

The chair scraped back as the King stood his eyes on Leo. "Son?"

Leo shrugged as he threw his napkin on the table and stood. "You know as much as I do, Father." How was Chelsea there when she was meant to be dead?

"Please show Ms Vos to the Library and I'll be with her shortly."

Turning to his father, he saw the shock and confusion on the older man's face and wished he could explain at least some of this to him. After today the thought of lying to him and keeping him in the dark left a bitter taste in his mouth. "Stay here, Father, and I'll be back shortly."

The King sat and took a sip of his brandy before waving his hand at Leo. "Take Bebe with you. Chelsea might need the support of another woman."

"Good idea."

He'd been going to take her anyway but now he didn't have to think of an excuse to do so. His gaze cut to Bebe as they walked across the hallway toward the library, a silent communication moving between them. He hated that he couldn't speak about this, but they had no idea if the rest of the palace was bugged and had to err on the side of caution.

Pushing on the double doors, his eyes swept the room and found Chelsea sitting by the window that overlooked the gardens. She startled and then stood, flying towards him so he had to let go of Bebe and catch her as she fell into his arms.

"Oh, León, thank God."

Her voice was full of tears, and he felt a second of sympathy before he gently pulled her away and led her toward the couch. Chelsea eyed Bebe who sat beside him as he took the couch opposite her. He offered her a tissue, and she gave a wan smile as she took one, dabbing at her eyes. She was a beautiful woman in many ways and could get almost any man she set her hat to but not him, not now.

"I have to say I'm surprised to see you. I take it you're aware of what happened on Saturday night?"

Chelsea cast a worried look toward Bebe. Some of her fear seemed to recede at what she saw as another woman on her turf. He'd been very clear with Chelsea that he was her friend and no more, yet she'd taken it upon herself to run off any woman who spent time with him. He'd selfishly let that happen because it suited him to have someone else do his dirty work, but he recognised now how reprehensible that was.

Reaching for Bebe, he made it clear who he was with. "You can speak in front of Bebe. We don't have any secrets."

Her liquid eyes moved over their hands before coming back to his face. "I woke up in my bed this morning with no clue where I was or what had happened. I put on the television and saw what happened and panicked."

"Didn't you go with Atticus to the boat?"

Chelsea shook her head. "Neither of us went. He and Alain had an argument, so we went home and got drunk at my place."

Leo knew that most likely had involved a hell of a lot of coke and champagne. "Where is Atticus now?"

Chelsea sniffed and reached for his hand, gripping it tight. "I don't know. I woke up and he was gone, and I can't reach him. What's happening, León? They're saying this is murder on the news. I'm scared. I could've been on that yacht and died."

Her crying began again, and Bebe rose and went to the bar to pour her a drink. She handed the brandy to Chelsea who took it with a shaking hand.

"I don't know, but I promise we'll find out."

Big eyes came to him, and she swallowed. "Can I stay with you?"

In normal times he might have said yes, but now things were different. He had Bebe and he didn't want Chelsea there. But he owed her safety if she'd been pulled into this because of someone in his inner circle.

"No, but I'll have guards assigned to you at home. The palace isn't the place for you right now."

Chelsea pouted, her puffy lips doing nothing for him but turning him off. "But she's here, and you hardly know her."

He took Bebe's hand in his but kept his eyes on Chelsea. "Bebe is my girlfriend and the woman I wish to share my life with."

"But you only just met."

Leo could see the rage building in his former lover and knew this could turn into a hissy fit. "When you know, you know."

"How do you know she didn't plant the bomb?"

Leo stood, his temper and patience going in opposite directions. "Chelsea, I'm willing to offer my resources to keep you safe out of respect for our history and friendship but don't test me. Bebe is important to me and if you make such outrageous accusations again, I won't be someone you wish to know."

Knowing when she was beat, at least for now, Chelsea backed down. "I'm sorry, León. I'm just frightened, and I feel so alone."

Well used to this kind of behaviour he nodded. "I understand and trust me. I'll look into everything and find out what's happening. I'll have two of my men drive you home and stay with you."

Chelsea stood. "Thank you."

Going up on tiptoes she kissed his cheek, and it took everything in him not to wipe the evidence of her kiss away. "No problem. Wait here and someone will come and get you."

Leo held his hand out for Bebe to go ahead of him. She did but then stopped at the door. "Try not to worry, Chelsea. Leo will get to the bottom of this, I promise."

Opening the door, he watched as Chelsea nodded, knowing she really wanted to snarl at Bebe. Chelsea was the epitome of a social climber, cunning, smart, and aware of her own body and what it could get her. What she didn't understand was that he'd only allowed her to climb as far as he'd wanted and now her time was done. Out of respect for her family though, and the past fun they'd shared, he'd keep his word and make sure she stayed safe.

He hurried to his apartment and put in a call to his head of security, who were all hand-picked by him and instructed them to stay with Chelsea at her flat. If she left the apartment or had any visitors, he wanted to know.

Bebe had headed straight for the bedroom, and he found her sitting on his couch when he entered, shutting the door behind him.

"Well, that was unexpected."

He sank down beside her, the exhaustion of the last few days catching up with him. He laid a hand on her thigh as he rested his head against the back of the couch. "The last three days have been unexpected." Lifting his head, he looked at her and saw the pinched worry between her brows. "What is it?"

"Too many variables. I don't like it."

"No, me either."

"Leo, can I ask who identified Alain?"

He sat up and angled his body toward her. "My uncle, but I'm told that his body was very badly burned. What are you getting at?"

"And the others? Who identified Chelsea and Atticus as being on board?"

"Dental records."

"And yet we know for certain that Chelsea is alive and possibly Atticus too. Unless he joined the yacht later on before the explosion."

"So, someone set it up to look like they all died."

"Yes, but then why leave Chelsea alive? It makes no sense."

León stood, pacing to the window. "Unless she was meant to die too. She's well used to cocaine and champagne. It shouldn't have knocked her out for so long. Maybe she was drugged, and they thought she'd overdose."

"But why not make sure, and why leave her body in her home? Surely the police checked her house as part of the investigation."

"Yes, they should have. None of this makes sense."

"Can I be honest with you, Leo?"

He spun, his hands on his hips. "Yes of course."

Bebe walked toward him her body graceful and fluid, distracting him from the nightmare his life was becoming. "My first thought was that Alain was involved, but when he was killed that kind of fell on its arse. Then I considered your uncle and if I'm honest, I still do. Now Chelsea and Atticus are involved but I don't know how. I'm certain your father isn't involved, and he was never really a suspect."

Leo didn't want to believe his family were involved but he was aware enough to realise he was too close to make that call. "What about Brody and Albin?"

Bebe nodded and lifted her hair off her neck and tied it into a knot on her head as she walked around the room. She was a pacer like him, the movement allowing her mind time to think.

"I still believe there's something there but whether they're the ones going to auction, I don't know. I need to speak with my boss and have some background checks done."

"Are you saying you don't believe Alain is dead?"

Despite everything Bebe was suggesting he still hoped that was the case. That he was an alive traitor sat better on his soul than the thought of him being an innocent dead man.

"Maybe."

"Is it wrong that I want him to be alive?"

His hand shook as he placed it on the window ledge and looked out at the view before him. His eyes didn't see any of it as he travelled over his memories and the times he and his cousin had played as kids in this palace.

A warm body crushed to his back as her arms came around and crossed over his chest. Leo lifted his free hand and placed it over her hand on his chest. He needed this closeness, this woman to stabilise him. She'd become his safety net in a sea wild with sharks and storms.

"No, Leo, of course not. No matter what happens, you and Alain have a past filled with laughter and fun. It's natural you don't want him to be dead. He's your family."

"And if he and my uncle have betrayed us?"

"Then you'll always have the memories and those are pure."

His mind turned that over as he thought of his father and the strides they'd made today. It had just been lunch, but it felt like so much more. Like a truce had been called or maybe not a truce, a cease-fire on his part. His father hadn't started the rift between them, that had been all him. This woman who'd flown into his life to end a traitor was fixing things she wasn't even aware of.

"My father really likes you. He'll be crushed when he finds out this is all fake."

He turned in her arms and caught the sadness on her face at his words before she could hide it.

Lifting her eyes, she held his gaze, her brown eyes reflecting his own uncertainty. "Is it all fake, Leo?"

He closed his eyes as her breath hitched and he wanted to say no, to tell her that for him this was as real as any relationship he'd ever had. That she'd brought something out in him that he'd never expected to feel.

His hands travelled over her waist and cupped her ass as he lifted her, encouraging her to wrap her legs around his hips. He backed her against the wall and felt her breath shudder from her body as she ran her hand over his cheek.

Dipping his head, he feathered her lips with his own. "No, Bebe, it's not all fake."

He wanted to tell her none of it was fake, but he knew an admission like that would do neither of them any good. So, he kissed her, telling her with his body what he couldn't put into words.

Her tongue flicked at the seam of his lips, and he opened for her, their tongues duelling for dominance. He ground his cock against the warmth of her pussy, and she groaned into his mouth. Her hands reached for his belt as her heels dug into his ass and his cock ached to be inside her.

"I want to fuck you against this wall."

"Yes."

He licked at her lips, his teeth nipping her bottom lip as her hand tunnelled into his boxers, her small hand gripping his length. Bebe stroked him from root to tip and he thought for a second he'd cum in his pants like a thirteen-year-old boy. Leo gritted his teeth as he pulled away to look at her, the dazed lust the sexiest thing he'd ever seen.

He pulled her hand away from his aching dick and kissed her palm as he held her arms up against the wall. His body was the only thing holding her up as he explored her with his free hand and mouth.

The tiny buttons on the dress popped as he tore at the fabric like a man possessed. He needed to touch warm, soft skin. Bebe tugged at his tie and the buttons of his shirt until she was running her hands over his chest, her nails biting against his skin making him shudder in pleasure.

Pushing aside the edges of her dress, he exposed the cream lace bra that barely concealed her gorgeous tits. His thumb stroked over the pebbled nipple, and he watched her eyes close in pleasure as she bit her bottom lip.

"Fucking hell, that's sexy."

A flirty smile creased her lips. "You gonna fuck me or not?"

The challenge in her tone brought out his dominant side. She may be a deadly assassin who took no prisoners, but in here, he was in charge. "That mouth's going to get you in trouble."

"Promises, promises."

The sexual tension in the room was so palpable he could almost touch it, it was so thick, and he realised they both needed this. This moment in time where there was nothing but pleasure.

Gliding his hands over her hips he caressed the bare skin of her ass, his fingers digging into the soft flesh and making her moan, her head falling back. Stroking a finger over her hip, he gripped the lace underwear and tore it from her flesh.

"Take my cock out of my pants, but no other touching."

He saw her pout, but she did as he said, even that slight touch delicious torture on his heated flesh.

"Good girl. Now show me those beautiful tits."

His eyes drooped with desire as she pushed the bra down and ran her palms over her tits before cupping them for him. A whimper whispered from her throat at the contact.

Leo bent his head and took a nipple between his teeth, flicking the tender nub with his tongue. Bebe arched into him giving herself over to the feelings he was creating. He continued his ministrations until she was begging him to make her come.

"Oh, God. Please."

"Please what?"

Her dark eyes came to his. "Make me come."

Dropping her legs to the floor he knelt in front of her, hitching the fabric out of the way before kissing his way up her thigh. He hooked her knee over his shoulder and wasted no more time. Lashing her clit with his tongue, using his fingers on her hot, wet heat, he slid inside her tight body, stroking her pussy as he nipped and sucked at her clit until her hand gripped his hair and pulled, making his scalp burn with absolute bliss.

"Oh, God. Oh fuck, yes."

Her walls clenched around his fingers and her body stiffened as she came hard, squeezing him as she let her climax overtake her body with total, spectacular abandon. He lifted his head and she looked down at him, an unmistakable connection he couldn't get away from between them.

"Do you have a condom?"

Leo reached for the drawer beside his bed and pulled a string of condoms out, quickly ripping one from the strip and rolling it down his length as she watched with desire-laden eyes.

He stood, lifting her into his arms and kissing her like she was the air he needed to survive this storm. Bebe held him close, her arms and legs wrapped around him as he positioned his cock at her entrance.

"You sure?"

"Yes."

Leo thrust inside her to the hilt and heard the hiss of breath in his ear at the intrusion. "You good?"

"Never better."

A smirk tipped his lips at her response. His body took over and he was doing what he'd promised, fucking her against the wall. It sounded base and without emotion, but it was anything but those things. He could feel her heart beating against his chest, her lush breasts pushed against him. Her eyes watched him as he leaned back slightly to get a good look at the beauty of them together.

Pushing his thumb into her mouth, he watched her close her eyes as she sucked it, the sight and feel of her warm mouth making him want to watch her on her knees with that mouth around his cock.

Pulling his hand free he drew it down her body, leaving a wet trail until he got to her clit, and he circled the tight swollen bundle of nerves and felt her body ripple around his dick. Her orgasm climbed as her breasts heaved with each breath and he tried to hold on to his own climax.

She looked at him in almost panic as her pleasure rose. "Leo."

"I'm right here, Bebe. Let go, I've got you."

He felt her pulse around him, squeezing him tight as she cried out her release, triggering his. Electric pulses of pleasure erupted as he spilled his seed inside her, the feeling almost taking his breath and making his legs sag as he leaned one hand against the wall to brace them both.

Silence in the room was only magnified by their harsh breathing as they both sought to understand what had just transpired because he knew for a fact that was more than just fucking. That was everything.

Twelve

Bebe had been grateful for the reprieve when Leo had been called away shortly after they'd had sex to speak with his father. She needed a few minutes to get her equilibrium settled after that. She was no stranger to sex, and certainly not a virgin but that had been different to anything she'd ever encountered.

She'd had good sex and that was so far up the ladder from good, Bebe now feared he may have ruined it for her for life.

Now, changed into jeans and a pale pink tee with her favourite converse on her feet, she felt more settled. Picking up the vibrator wand, she checked for bugs in the bedroom again and when she found none, put in a call to Roz.

"Hey, you."

"Hey, Pax. Did I call you by accident?"

"No, I answered Roz's phone because she's dealing with something else for a second."

"Shall I call back?"

"No, she won't be a second. How are things going?"

"More questions than answers right now."

"Anything I can help with?"

"Maybe. What do you know about Chelsea Vos?"

Pax's superpower was her ability to find out any information on anyone. She never went into the field but was the person who handled all the logistics. If they needed a place to stay, she found it, information, Pax found it, guns, weapons, exfil, Pax handled it all. Bebe had cried at her wedding when she married Calvin Blake, one of the men from Eidolon.

"I know her parents are diplomats and that she's a spoiled social climber who posts everything she does on Instagram and TikTok. Why? Is she a suspect?"

"Well, we thought she was dead, but she just turned up here most definitely alive."

"Oh, wow. That's suspicious. What does the prince think?"

"Leo has offered her his guard, but I don't think he trusts her either. The problem is there are so many variables right now."

"Leo?"

Bebe felt the blush on her cheeks and thanked God this wasn't a video call, Pax would spot her guilt a mile away. "It's what he told me to call him."

"Mmmhmm."

"I sent Roz some pictures of the two new hires at the palace. Did she manage to find out anything about them?"

"Yeah, hang on. Here she is. Stay safe, Bebe. Love you, lady."

"Love you too, Pax."

"Bebe, how are you?"

"Fine, I'm safe but I have so much information and I need to narrow it down. Do you have anything for me?"

"Yes, and you aren't going to like it."

Bebe groaned. "Wouldn't be a Zenobi mission without a little FUBAR thrown in for entertainment."

"True story. So, Brody James is CIA. Looks like they didn't trust us after all and sent in one of their own to try and figure it out first. That's the good news."

"Great."

"Yeah, Albin Wojcik is actually Albin Symanski."

"You've got to be kidding me."

"Nope. We don't think he's there for you but if he finds out you're there, he won't waste the opportunity to kill you. He's still furious you killed his brother."

"It's not my fault his brother was an evil, child-murdering bastard."

"No, but he's the same in that he's a contract killer. If the money is right, it doesn't matter to him who dies, man, woman, or child."

"You want me to deal with him?"

"Not unless you have to. The mission is the priority here."

"Okay. So here's my news."

Bebe went on to tell Roz about the new developments and theories she and Leo had come up with.

"That's a lot to unpick but let me get the girls on it this end and see if we can get you any information that will help. So far, there are no reports of anyone going near the gem so there's that."

"Yeah, but that doesn't help us. We almost need them to make a move so we can wrap this up."

"I did find out the date for the auction is set for a week from Friday coming, so we don't have a lot of time."

"How did we find that out?"

"Lili managed to find out the date of her auction and as it's the second one with four weeks between each, we now know yours is in a month."

"How are they all?"

"Good, wading through information and false truths the same as you."

"That's good." Bebe nodded to herself. "Here is the thing, you said the first auction triggers the next and so on, but if we stop the auction from going ahead won't we ruin the mission for the other girls?"

"I thought about that, and my thoughts are we stop it if we can. But if the others need the time, we let it go ahead and switch out the gems."

"But won't The Collector know who they're dealing with? We need to leave them in play. It's too risky to swap the gems. It will expose the lie and we could lose The Collector." Bebe looked up as she heard the door to the apartment open. "Hang on a sec, I have company."

Bebe stood with the phone to her ear and walked to the door to see

Leo striding toward her looking handsome and sexy in jeans with a white shirt rolled up his muscular, tan forearms.

Stepping back, she pointed to the phone, and he nodded before closing them both in the bedroom.

"It's fine. It's just Leo."

His brows rose and a playful smile flitted on his lips at her words.

"So back to what I was saying, can't we leave them in? It would be a huge risk to take them out."

"No, we can't and I'm working on a plan for that, so leave it with me."

"You're the boss."

"Now you sound like my daughters."

Bebe grinned because she loved the girls Roz and her husband Kanan had saved from a child trafficking asshole Roz had killed personally.

"Give them all hugs and kisses from me. Tell them I'll try and bring them something nice back from my trip."

"Don't you dare, they have enough. Spoiled little wenches."

"Oh, toffee. You adore them."

Roz sighed. "Fine, but nothing too expensive like last time or I'm cutting your pay."

"Ouch."

"Be safe, my Bebe."

She heard the softness in her friend's voice.

"I will, boss."

"Check in tomorrow and I'll have more information for you."

"Will do."

Bebe hung up and looked at her phone. She didn't know what would've become of her if it hadn't been for Roz and her girls. They were her family and she loved them fiercely.

"Just Leo?"

Bebe turned her gaze to the man sitting quietly beside her on the couch. "Just Leo."

"You know, in some circles, the rumour is I'm a Crown Prince."

She loved that he could make her smile. "Oh yeah? Who are these poor, delusional people?"

"Hey!" He grabbed her around the waist and hauled her across his lap as his fingers dug into her ribs, making her squeal with laughter.

"No. God, no. Please."

"What?" He cupped his ear as if he couldn't hear her.

"Please, Prince León."

Leo stopped and ran his hand down her back. "Nah, I like being just Leo to you."

Bebe snuggled closer, allowing her natural softness to show instead of hiding from the world like she so often had to. She trusted this man, which might make her a fool, but she did. He made her feel safe. She didn't need it, but it was nice to have it.

"How's your father?"

His hands twisted in her hair as he twirled the strands around his fingers. "Confused, shocked, worried. He's concerned it might be a threat from another government trying to destabilise our nation. I wish I could tell him the truth."

"I do too. He's a good man and he adores you."

"He is and I'd forgotten that for a while. Thank you for helping me remember."

"I didn't do anything."

"You did. You forced me to spend time with him today and reminded me of the man he is."

"Maybe we should read him in on this. I'm just worried the more he knows the more at risk he'll be."

"I know, me too."

"Let's sleep on that one. He won't do anything without your knowledge will he?"

"No. He's grooming me to take over, so we make all these decisions together."

"And your uncle?"

"He's at his home in the country until the funeral."

"Well, that's good at least." Her body was becoming languid from him playing with her hair, a weakness of hers, but she needed to tell him about her call with Roz and what she'd learned. "So, I have an update."

"Yeah, what is it?"

"Brody James is CIA. Seems they weren't sure I could get the job done so sent one of their own in too."

"And Wojcik?"

"Ah, well, that's complicated. He's a contract killer who just so happens to hate my guts."

Leo pulled back and looked down at her. "And why is that?"

"I might have assassinated his brother for being a child-murdering bastard."

Leo lifted his hand and waited until she tapped it with hers in a high-five.

"Is it wrong that I find that a huge turn on?"

Bebe giggled. "What? Me killing a man?"

"No, you killing a piece of scum."

She shrugged. "Maybe."

"Hey, not the answer I was looking for."

Bebe straddled his lap, placing her hands on his chest. "Well, Prince León, if you want a yes woman, I'm not the one for you."

His face lost its humour as he looked at her intently. "But what if you are?"

Her heart was beating wildly in her chest at his words. This was crazy, she was on the biggest mission of her life and all she wanted to do was fall into this fairy tale feeling with this man.

"It's not real."

Her voice was a whisper as she struggled to get the words out and believe them. She had to stay focused. "But what if it is?"

Bebe stood, putting distance between them. "It's adrenalin and hormones. We're playing a role and maybe things will get confused, it happens but if you let yourself believe in it, things will end in tears and heartbreak, Leo."

He stood and grabbed her hips, pulling her closer as if he couldn't stand the space between them after what they'd shared.

"Are you saying you didn't feel it?"

Bebe shook her head. "No, I felt it but I'm saying it isn't real. It won't last."

"Then be in the moment with me. Let's see what happens?"

Bebe was tempted. God she wanted that. "We have a job to do."

"Yes, let's go all in and do this together and when it's done if we decide it wasn't real, we walk away."

"I've seen this movie, Leo, one of us will catch feelings and the other won't. Then there are broken hearts and promises, and I can't deal with that in my life right now. I have a plan."

"Then we promise to not catch feels. We have fun and walk away."

Bebe had no clue if she'd be able to keep up her end of the bargain but she wanted the extra time with him so she'd try. If it went wrong, she'd go home to her friends and have the memory of it to last her a lifetime. "You're a stubborn sod, aren't you?"

A grin stretched across his face, making him look younger and more carefree.

"I'm a Prince. I like to get my own way."

"Well then fine, Prince Leo. But when I break your heart, no locking me in a tower."

He waggled his eyebrows. "Now, there's an idea."

"Yeah? Well, it will have to wait. I need to figure a few things out. Can we get away from the palace for a bit so I can breathe?"

"Sure, I know just the place."

"Do I need to change?"

"No, you're perfect as you are."

"Charmer."

Leo laid a hand over his chest. "It's true."

"Fine let's go."

Thirteen

Leo wasn't sure where his desperation for Bebe to agree to keep their affair going came from, but he suspected it had something to do with the best sex of his life. He certainly wasn't a boy scout and had definitely enjoyed more than his fair share of female company over the years but there was something unique about Bebe that called to him on a primal level that he couldn't seem to walk away from. Not yet anyway.

"The Orchid Farm, I was dying to see this place. My sister's favourite flower was orchids."

He parked the car and turned in his seat to Bebe, to see her toying with the end of the plait she'd threaded her hair into. He fingered the soft strands as he smiled at her look of happiness. "I noticed the tattoo on your ankle."

"I got it after I left Pakistan and our home so she'd always be close to me."

"And the wolf on your ribs?"

Bebe placed a hand over her left rib and grinned. "All the Zenobi girls have one. It represents the pack mentality and how we're all one family and look out for each other."

"You always seem to show such joy in things. You never hide your enjoyment or try and temper it, do you?"

Bebe shook her head. "No, joy is a rare commodity. I've learned to relish it when I feel it."

"Well, you'll enjoy the Orchid Farm and as a bonus, it offers us complete privacy to try and figure this out."

"Yeah, and boy, do we need it."

Leo got out and walked around the front to open her car door, but Bebe was already out of the vehicle. She turned to reach in and grab her bag, which he now knew contained her wild array of weaponry. He'd never known such an assortment and would probably never look at a simple lipstick again without wondering if it could kill him.

Hooking an arm through his, she allowed him to lead them toward the rare variety section of the farm. It was vast and he knew only a few people would be there at this time of the day. He listened to her ooh and aah at the stunning blooms and relished the simple joy of being with her in the late afternoon, wishing her cover story was real and she was just here to check out the blooms for her perfume company.

Entering the field from the east, he kept his head on a swivel, making sure there was nobody around him before he led her further into a field filled with an array of rare orchids.

"This place is pure heaven. The scent alone is astonishing."

"Did you know we're the only growers in the world to offer these types of blooms for perfumes? Most orchid-based fragrances are manufactured."

"I didn't know that."

"Well, now you do."

They strolled for a little longer, Bebe as aware of her surroundings as he was. The sea was to the south of them and the lush green of the hills to the north offered protection from the wind the island was prone to. It was also the perfect vantage point for a sniper and the thought had him feeling exposed in a way he didn't like and steered her towards the opposite end of the field. "We need to go on the offensive with our approach. I originally thought it was best to be discreet and not openly challenge any suspects. But with there being so many now, we need to narrow things down."

"I agree. Where do you want to start?"

Bebe looked at him, but her sunglasses were hiding her expressive eyes so he couldn't read her. "You're happy to let me lead?"

"You're the expert."

"Thank you. It's nice to have that recognised. I've worked with a lot of people who only see a woman and think she's weak or stupid, or worse, only good for one thing."

"Oh, you're definitely good at that, but your worth is multifaceted and beautiful, and I'd be a fool to ignore that."

The way she dropped her head as if shy, made his body tingle all over with unknown feelings. "Well, given that, I think we need to speak to Brody James and see what he knows. It stands to reason that if he's here, he probably has information that wasn't shared with us. We thought we knew everything, but I think more is at play here than we realised."

"That's a good idea."

"We should also get a feel for Emily and see if the same is happening with her. Have you had any contact with her since I arrived?"

"No, but I wasn't expecting any to be honest."

The hairs on his neck rose a split second before a bullet pinged past his head. Before he could react, Bebe threw herself on top of him, knocking them both to the earthy ground of the field.

Time slowed as he listened, letting his senses concentrate on everything around him as he pulled his weapon from the holster beneath his jacket. He grabbed Bebe, angry for a split second she'd been the one to put herself in danger to save him before he saw the gun in her hand and remembered who she was. He still didn't like the idea of her risking her life for him, though, and would be expressing that later.

"We need to move. Is there a second exit from this place?"

"Yes, but it's toward the mountains where the shot came from. We'd need to run toward the shooter."

"Fuck."

Another bullet hit the ground where they were now crouched with nothing but flowers to hide them from the sniper.

Bebe glanced around them, barely flinching as another bullet hit close by. "Okay, new plan. I want you to move back the way we came. I'm going to cover you and head towards the mountain. Stay down and see if you can come around behind them."

"No fucking way. You're like a sitting duck." It wasn't in his nature to let someone run into danger while he ran from it, and especially not this woman.

"Yes, way. This is my job and I know what I'm doing. Now go or stay here and argue and we both die."

Before he could answer, she was already up and running, firing towards the mountain and drawing heat from whoever was shooting at them. With no choice, Leo cursed and took off in the direction they'd come from, keeping low and doing everything he could not make too many big movements.

As he arrived at the gate they'd entered through, he didn't hear any more shots being fired and chanced a look toward the mountain to see if he could identify the shooter. His eyes scanned the space, taking in every familiar tree and bush of the vista he knew so well before he backtracked, running his gaze over the space. There, on the second ridge, between two olive trees, was something that didn't belong.

He cursed not having a long gun, he could've taken them out from here with a rifle but it was what it was. Dropping low again, he scanned the area looking for Bebe. In her pale pink top he should have been able to spot her easily, but she was a ghost. There was no sign of her on the mountain or in the field of flowers.

With no time to dwell on the twisted feeling in his gut at the thought of her down from a bullet, he focused on what he could do, and that was take out the shooter. Skirting the gate, he rushed down the side of the field, keeping as close to the ground as possible. He made it to the edge of the mountain where the ground beneath his booted feet was coarse gravel, and began to edge up the path, keeping his eyes on the area where the shooter had been.

More shots rang out towards the field but there was no return fire and he prayed it was because she'd made it past the mountain ridge. He should have stayed or followed her, gone at this together, but his operator's brain knew this had been the best plan.

As he neared the tree line where he spotted the sniper, he used the olive trees to shield him from view. Heart pumping hard from the adrenalin, he glanced to the left and saw a shadow moving and recognised Bebe as she came up behind the man lying flat on the ground.

Watching Bebe was like a lesson in how to operate. Her movements were lithe and fluid, like a panther on the hunt for a kill. She didn't fumble or hesitate. She was confident and sure as she bent and held her gun to the man on the ground.

"Hands out to the side where I can see them."

Leo walked toward them, his eyes scanning the landscape for any other threats.

Bebe glanced up at him and he noticed blood coming from a wound on her arm. He motioned at the cut which looked like a deep scratch and tried to resist the temptation to take her in his arms and check her all over for any other wounds. "You, okay?"

Bebe glanced down and shrugged. "Meh, I've had worse cuts shaving my legs."

Leo grinned and rolled his eyes before concentrating on the man on the ground, relief like the removal of a thorn in his side.

He bent and pulled the weapon away from the man's reach. "Turn over slowly and don't give me an excuse to end you."

The man who was dressed head to toe in black turned and Leo took a staggering step back at the sight.

"Hey, cousin."

"Alain?"

"Alive and kicking."

Alain moved to sit up and Bebe raised her weapon. "Slowly."

His cousin turned to her, seemingly understanding who the real threat was as Leo tried to get his shock and confusion under control.

"I just wanted to talk, and this was the only way I could think to get you to come to me."

"Are you fucking with me? You didn't think to just call and say, *Hey, Leo, guess what. I didn't die in a fiery inferno*?"

Leo paced away, knowing without a doubt that Bebe had his six as he wrangled his emotions into place.

"Listen, I know you have a lot of questions but I don't have a lot of time."

"Start talking then." Bebe cocked her hip as if getting bored, but he could see the controlled tension she was hiding.

Alain sighed and he tried to find any signs of the lazy, spoilt rich kid he'd grown up with. He realised he'd greatly misjudged his cousin because this man was anything but those things. He just didn't know what he was.

"About a year ago I got arrested for drunk driving after I hit a girl with my Porsche and almost killed her."

"Jesus, Alain."

Alain held up a hand, dropping his head. "I know, I know. I get it. I was lucky she pulled through but in exchange for escaping jail, I was asked to go undercover at the palace and just give this person what at the time seemed inconsequential information that could most likely be found on the internet. So, I agreed."

Leo cast a look at Bebe and saw the same look of disgust on her face as he was probably wearing. He went to take a step forward and pound his cousin in the face, but she gave a slight shake of her head, which had him stilling.

"Listen, Leo, I know what you must be thinking, and you're right. I'm a fuck up, but I didn't betray this family like you think I did."

"Explain it to me then, because from where I'm standing it looks like you did."

"About six months after I started, the man began to ask for more detailed information about you and the King and the details around the gems in the vault room. I told him I wanted out and wasn't going to help any longer. Then five days ago I was summoned to my father's place in the country. Albin Wojcik was there and he was eating lunch with my father."

"Wojcik is the man who helped you?"

"No, the man who helped me initially was American. But I never met him, just spoke to him over the phone. It seems Wojcik works for him and has been sent in to keep me on track. I thought at first that he'd threatened my father, but boy, was I wrong."

Leo could feel the tension building like a bomb was about to drop, and it would be worse than the knowledge his cousin was alive.

"Father is working with Wojcik and asked me to find a way to get access to *The Grace*."

"Why?"

Both men looked at Bebe. "They wanted me to fake my death and steal the Tanzanite Tears for them."

"That makes no sense. You'd have more chance of stealing it if you were alive. Nobody would question you going inside the room."

"Look, can you point the gun away?"

Bebe looked to him at Alain's question and he nodded. She dropped the gun to her side but stayed vigilant, she obviously didn't trust Alain any more than he did right now.

"All I know is that I headed to the yacht with Atticus and Chelsea and was to meet a few others at the marina. I was planning on ditching Atticus and Chelsea. I've made mistakes, but I had no intention of getting my friends involved. But I didn't have to because Atticus got his ass out of joint and accused me of flirting with Chelsea, which I wasn't, and they stormed off. I didn't argue because I was relieved. Then Wojcik arrived at the marina and said there was a change of plan, and I was to go with him. I thought they were going to call it off but when I got to my father's house, I heard the yacht had exploded. My father was going to identify my body along with Atticus and Chelsea."

"Atticus and Chelsea are alive too."

Leo could see this piece of news had surprised his cousin.

"That doesn't make sense. Why would my father let them live but identify the bodies?"

"Because he isn't pulling the strings, and whoever is wants him to go down for it."

Leo glanced at Bebe at her comment, her clear brown eyes on him. "Go on."

"Whoever is behind this is setting your father up. He thinks he's getting something from this obviously, but by you faking your death and your father identifying the bodies of people who are alive, he looks guilty. And by faking your death and stealing the gem, it all comes back to you. Whoever Wojcik is working for will most likely have you both killed when he gets what he needs."

"Fuck." Alain pushed his fingers through his hair and turned his back to them before rounding on them with a gun aimed at Leo. "Drop your weapons."

Leo let his gun fall to the ground and watched Bebe do the same.

"Alain, what are you doing?"

"You have to help me."

"And you think pointing a gun at me and shooting me will get you that?"

"I don't want to hurt you, Leo. You're like a brother to me but I'm desperate."

Before he could get out another word, Bebe dove forward and had disarmed Alain and had his gun pointed at him before he could figure out what had happened.

"You ever pull a stunt like that again, I won't just point this gun at you, I'll ram it so far down your throat your prostate will flinch."

Alain dropped to his knees and started to cry. His pathetic sounds would've had sympathy edging into his emotions in the past, but he'd used up all his good favour from their shared history when he'd pointed a gun at him for the second time. "So, what's the plan now, Alain? Where does Wojcik or your father think you are?"

"I snuck away and followed you here."

Bebe dropped to the ground just as a bullet peeled past her ear. "You fuckin dumb ass, you didn't sneak anywhere. They followed you here."

Leo ducked, grabbing his gun as Alain snivelled like a punk. "You really fucked us, Alain. Now our cover is blown and you probably just got your father killed."

"I'm sorry, Leo."

"Shut up and let me think." Bebe snapped at Alain, and he went silent.

Leo stayed quiet, letting her form a plan as he tried to figure out, how he'd keep his father safe.

"Did Wojcik have any other men with him?"

"Yes, two that have been staying with me and my father."

Bebe turned to him. "Call your father's secretary and have him request an urgent meeting with Wojcik and Alwyn regarding the funeral arrangements. Tell him it's time-sensitive."

"Okay." Leo put in the call and made the request, ignoring the confusion in the man's voice as he gave the orders.

"Good. Now, if that's Wojcik, he'll leave. He has no choice if he wants to maintain his cover. If it's someone else, we deal with them."

Leo dove for the sniper rifle, flattening his belly to the ground and knowing he was safe while Bebe had his back. Looking down the scope, he watched as two men in all black tried to get through the orchids. "I have eyes on two men."

"Take the shot."

"Roger that."

Leo executed the two shots quickly and efficiently, watching as each man fell. Not his best work but both were clean shots. "Targets down."

"Good. Now we need to get back to the palace and ensure our cover isn't blown." As Leo stood Bebe turned to Alain. "Does Wojcik suspect Leo is on to him?"

"No, but he knows you're not here for Leo. He says you're an assassin and a crazy bitch."

Leo ground his back teeth. Hearing anyone refer to her that way made him want to kill the person, even his own cousin. Yet Bebe seemed unaffected by the insult. That made him angrier that she thought it was okay or was so used to it that it ran off her back.

"Wojcik is an idiot." She moved close and laid a hand on his bicep, making his skin heat from her touch as his heart rate skidded up from just that small contact. "We need to call Emily and have her handle

Alain. We can't send him back in, he'll blow our cover. He's way too unstable."

"I can hear you, you know."

Bebe glared at him, and he seemed to pale. "Then I suggest you don't give me a reason to show you if Wojcik is right about me and shut the hell up."

Leo smirked but nodded. "I'll call her."

"No need. We'll handle Alain from here."

He and Bebe turned guns raised as Brody James stepped out from behind a tree, his hands raised to show he was unarmed, or at least not pointing a gun their way.

"Can this day get any worse?"

"Alain!" He and Bebe both yelled as the man tempted fate with his stupid comment because everyone knew when you uttered those words shit always got worse.

Fourteen

"You should get back to the palace and meet with Wojcik. If he isn't suspicious of you right now, we need to keep it that way."

Leo looked down at his feet and huffed out a sigh. Bebe knew he didn't want to leave her to deal with this, but she had a job to do and any feelings between them came second.

"I've got this, León."

His eyes moved slowly over her body, taking her in to make sure what she said was true and she fought the shiver.

"Okay, if you're sure. I'll see you back at the palace later."

He hesitated just a second and she could tell he wanted to say more but stopped himself in front of Alain and Brody. A tight smile was all she got as he turned and made his way back down the mountain, his gait agile and smooth.

"So, what about me?"

Bebe closed her eyes, placing her hands on her hips to stop herself from reaching for Alain's throat and squeezing the life out of the stupid man. How in all that was holy could two brothers such as Alwyn and Alfred produce such different children? It was a question for another time because she had work to do.

Ignoring him, she angled toward Brody James who was glaring at Alain. "So, you can handle Alain?"

"We have a boat anchored a mile out to sea. We can hold him there until this is done."

"And give me one good reason why I should trust you?" She waved her hand in the air. "It's not like you've given me a single reason to. You were meant to stay out of this and let Zenobi handle things."

Brody smirked but he didn't back down or show her weakness, and she had to respect that to a degree. "And you think nobody else has eyes inside? It never occurred to you SIS has Emily Reynolds working this but from a different angle?"

"Fucking spooks. Can't trust any of them."

"Just doing my job."

Bebe cocked her head. "Is that a line they brainwash you with, so you don't question anything?"

"Whatever you need to believe, Bebe."

She hooked her thumb behind her at Alain. "So, you heard what this one had to say?"

"I did and it's a cluster fuck, but a workable one."

Bebe shook her head. "No way. You stay out of my way on this or I'll fucking shoot you."

"Not gonna happen and let's be honest, you need more bodies. I have the support and how are you going to explain those bodies down there unless I get rid of them? Your boss sent you on a suicide mission by letting you handle this alone."

"I'm not alone and I have support." She'd need Roz to send a clean-up crew and hoped one was close.

"Oh yes, Prince Charming going to save you if you get caught?"

Brody snorted and Bebe clenched her teeth to keep from reacting even though she wanted to. He was goading her to get a reaction and prove she wasn't up to the task. "I don't have time for this shit. Just stay out of my way."

"We should work together."

"Oh, because you're such a team player?"

"I can be when I need to. I'll handle Alain and get rid of the bodies if we agree to swap any important information."

"Fine, I'll let you handle him and swap info, but I can handle the bodies."

Bebe had no intention of trusting this spook. She didn't want to owe him too many favours and wanted to search the bodies herself. But he might prove helpful to her, so she agreed.

Brody walked to Alain and grabbed his upper arm. "Start moving."

"Unhand me this minute."

Brody turned to Alain and Bebe began picking up the weapons on the ground and figuring out a place to stash them.

Brody pointed her way and she glared daggers at both men and saw Alain take a step closer to Brody. "You prefer I leave you with her?"

She had to look away, so he didn't see the grin twitch on her lips.

"This is preposterous."

"Yeah, well, you play with the big boys, you get hurt sometimes."

Stashing the guns under a large bush that was easily identifiable, she followed Brody at a distance until he made it to the road and headed left toward the flowers. So much beauty and in the midst of two people who wanted her dead. It would scare a normal person, should scare them, but she was far from normal. Her entire adult life had been spent with one target or another on her head. Maybe even her whole life in some ways if she considered her parents' use for her.

Shaking it off, she moved to where the bodies had been and found only pools of blood. Looking up and around, she scanned the area for signs that they were alive or had gotten away and found only the tranquil silence of the island.

Her phone in her pocket dinged and she took it out, glad it hadn't got damaged and looked at a text from her landlord, Mitch.

MITCH: GOT YOUR BACK GIRL. WILL HIT YOU UP WITH IDENTITIES WHEN WE HAVE THEM.

Bebe grinned and looked around again for any sign of the Eidolon team, who were as much family to her now as Zenobi. They had a very different job, mainly to protect the British Royal family, and worked directly for the Queen as her personal team. For that reason, nobody knew exactly what they did, just that national security was a big part of it.

It stood to reason they'd be helping on this. But unlike the spooks, they were happy to trust her and let her take the lead because they had faith in her.

She didn't text back but knowing she had them there was a blessing as things got messier by the second. She hoped her sisters had that too, especially Mercy, who'd been through enough already.

Lifting her arm to sweep her hair back, she winced as she opened the cut on it again. A damned rock with a sharp jagged point had cut her when her foot slipped on the climb. Her converse trainers were awesome but climbing shoes they were not.

Heading back to the car park, she pondered what to do next when a car pulled up in front of her. She frowned until the window went down and she saw a smiling Soroosh.

"I understand you need a lift."

"Hey, Soroosh, that would be amazing. Thank you." Bebe hopped in the front passenger's side and clipped her belt. "Is there any way we can go somewhere I can clean up first? I don't want to head back to the palace like this."

Soroosh was nodding his head wildly. "Yes, ma'am. We can go to the bakery and clean you up. My wife has some clothes you can borrow, and I can feed you my newest creation, pistachio and white chocolate cannoli."

Bebe's tummy grumbled, and she realised she was starving. "Don't toy with me, Soroosh. That sounds like heaven on a plate."

"No toys, Miss Bebe, only heaven."

"Your wife is one lucky woman,"

"I tell her this every day."

Bebe smiled. She liked Soroosh. He was funny and sweet, but she didn't miss the way he kept glancing around as if on high alert. It was easy to see why he and Leo got on so well. They were the same and yet very different which, to her, showed a true friendship. If you could be opposites and still be friends, it meant the friendship was based on something deeper than a shared interest.

Soroosh led her inside the bakery through the back and was met by his wife, her neat baby bump adorable under a flowy, lilac summer dress.

"Thank you so much for this." Bebe had no desire to endanger this wonderful couple and wouldn't overstay her welcome.

"My name is Polina and I'm happy to meet you. Let's get that arm cleaned up while Soroosh sorts us some lunch."

Polina was petite but curvy, with long dark curly hair and startling blue eyes. She had the kindest manner about her, instantly putting Bebe at ease and she could see how well suited she and Soroosh were as they interacted.

"Here are some clothes. They might be a little shorter on you than me but you're welcome to use them."

"I just need a blouse or tee really. The jeans are fine."

"Take whatever you need. It will be a while before I get into them again with this one growing so fast."

Bebe glanced down and felt a tug at her heart, not jealousy but a little envy. The yearning for a child wasn't something she'd anticipated having had the start she'd had, but it was hard to ignore when it hit. She'd been trying to go it alone for two years but two cycles of IVF had failed. Not unusual from what she'd heard but time was ticking, and she wondered if she'd ever have a baby or if it was a pipe dream.

As she cleaned up her arm with the first aid kit Polina had given her, she wondered about Leo and what he'd think of her wanting a baby knowing who she was and the things she'd done. Would he think her selfish for wanting a child? Did he want them? It didn't matter, really. After this was over, she'd probably never see him again.

The thought stung more than the cut she'd covered with gauze. She'd known him less than a week and yet the impression he'd made felt life-changing. She was breaking every rule she had by getting involved with him and potentially putting the mission at risk. Yet the thought of going back to her life before him was hollow and empty. He'd shown her a passion and friendship she hadn't expected, and she didn't want to lose it, but how could she keep it?

The prince and the assassin sounded like a romance novel while her life was more like a suspense or action-adventure novel. Doing the buttons up on the pale green blouse with white flowers, she was glad to see it covered her wound. Running her fingers through her hair, she tied it up in a messy bun and washed her face, trying to get rid of the dirt and grime from the mountain.

Voices outside the bathroom door had her finishing up and heading out to find Leo talking with Soroosh and Polina. His eyes came directly to her, sweeping over her body in a sensual wave before holding her gaze. The intensity and emotion in that one look almost made her stagger back.

"Are you okay?"

Bebe got her feet moving and fell back into her role as his girlfriend with such ease it was terrifying how well they fit. His arms came around her and he drew her close as she wrapped her arms around him. "I am now."

Fifteen

Leo rolled onto his back, dragging Bebe's body on top of him. Her moans as he angled his hips up as she rode him made him harder than steel. "You look like a fucking goddess riding my cock."

Her hair was wild, her plump lips parted with lust, her eyes dark like a stormy night. Her tits bounced, the dark nipples teasing him. Holding her hips, he leaned up, pulling a tight bud into his mouth, and sucking as she ground against him, rolling her hips in a way that made him groan.

"I'm gonna come."

Her words were breathy and jagged as his hand speared her hair, holding her gaze on him as she splintered. Her walls tightened around his cock like a vice, pulling his own climax from him. He exploded as she cried his name, pleasure rocketing over them both. Leo sagged back against the headboard, holding her limp body to his chest and soaking in the feel of her, the scent of her, the very essence of the woman who was fast becoming the only thing he could think about.

"I'm gonna need more cardio if you want to keep this up."

Her words made him smile as he rolled her to her back and kissed her thoroughly. He loved how she gave herself to him with no worry as to how she looked and not a single ounce of concern or shyness. Her trust meant more to him than he could say, so he kept it to himself, and enjoyed the moment.

"I need to shower before I go to sleep."

It was barely eleven but after the last few days they'd had, he could see she needed sleep. Much as he'd like to spend the whole night making love to her, he would, he realised with surprise, be happy to just hold her while they slept. It was a new feeling for him and not one he was used to.

He watched her as she rose from the bed and ambled to the bathroom door, admiring every luscious curve as she walked away from him. Her head appeared back around the door frame, a teasing smile on her lips. "Give me five minutes to wash my hair and then you can come wash my back if you want."

Leo placed his arm behind his head as he looked up at her, his dick already stirring into action at her invitation.

"I'll give you three."

A light squeal from her made him chuckle as she disappeared around the door and seconds later, he heard the shower running. Leo felt his mind go back to two days ago on the mountain and all the revelations Alain had shared.

His cousin had always been a wild card, but he'd never considered he could be involved in this. But then, Alwyn was leading it or at least he thought he was. His uncle had always been a jealous bull of a man with his eyes on the Crown.

First thing tomorrow his father would be apprised of the situation in full and encouraged to go into protective custody. He and Bebe had agreed it was time with the potential threat being about him as much as the gemstone.

The fact they still didn't know the identity of the American behind it was annoying but they were further than they'd been, and it had only been five days. The funeral for Alain was meant to be in two days and he wasn't comfortable with the funeral going ahead and his people mourning a man who was in no way worthy and not even dead. If he could convince his father to leave the island under the pretence of ill health or a minor procedure, they could delay the funeral too.

Of course, that still left Atticus missing and that was a huge concern. Was he dead or involved in some way? It was all ifs, buts, and maybes at this point and now they had Brody James involved. That was a risk he didn't like, even if he'd dealt with Alain.

Bebe had told him that her friend's team had dealt with the two dead men shooting at them, or at least Alain. She'd spoken of them with warmth and love, and he knew these people meant something to her. Even going so far as to say she lived with two of them.

A burning sensation in his chest made him sit up and rub his hand over his heart. It was the same feeling he got every time she mentioned Waggs or Mitch or any of the other men she was friendly with. She obviously cared about them, but the mere sound of their names made him want to go toe to toe with them and warn them that Bebe was his now and didn't need them.

It was a childish and pathetic response and one he could hardly control, but he managed to for her. They'd made no promises to each other. In one way he was glad that she had people in her life who cared enough to have her back, but he recognised he wanted to be the one she turned to, now and always.

Rising from the bed, he headed for the bathroom, stopping when he saw the t-shirt she'd worn to bed the first few nights peeking out from under her pillow. He tore the fabric from under its hiding place and threw it into the hamper in the corner of the room. Moving to his drawers, he pulled out an old white cotton tee with his army unit on the front and replaced the one he'd discarded.

If she had to sleep in a tee, he was damn sure it wouldn't be one that belonged to another man. Over his dead body would it touch her naked skin ever again, no matter how innocent she insisted it was. Although his absolute preference was her butt naked and pressed tight against him all night.

A smile of satisfaction pressed over his lips as he walked into the bathroom full of steam. The outline of her body in the shower stall made him hard as he opened the door, the steam flooding out as he stepped in behind her. His hand went around her front, pressing into her belly and he pulled her wet body against his own.

Arching her neck so she could see him over her shoulder, she dropped her hands from her hair and stroked a palm down his thigh.

"That was longer than three minutes."

Leo kissed her neck, sucking lightly on the pulse point that beat faster at his touch. His fingers brushed over her pussy lips before sliding inside, swallowing the hiss of pleasure that fell from her lips with his kiss. He rolled his thumb over her clit as he finger fucked her into a shattering orgasm that made her knees give way.

"Sorry I kept you waiting."

"I forgive you. In fact, if that's how you say sorry, feel free to be as tardy as you wish."

Turning, Bebe placed her hand on his chest, tracing the lines of his ink over the muscle on his chest before she dropped to her knees. She grasped his hard, aching shaft as she looked up at him, wetting her lips with her tongue.

His hand swept into her hair, pulling back on her head lightly, making her look up as he growled in pleasure at her touch.

"Suck my cock, Bebe. I want to see you take my dick in that sweet mouth."

His words made her moan as she licked her tongue up the underside of his sensitive dick and engulfed him in her warm, wet heat.

His fingers tightened in her hair, his thighs burning with the tension not to lose control and fuck her throat like a wild man. The light sucking mixed with the harder bobbing of her head as she took him deeper into her throat almost made him lose his mind. Her hand moved to cup his balls, rolling them in her fingers as electric intensity zipped up his spine, warning him that he was going to come.

"I'm gonna come," he warned, his voice gritty and deep from the pleasure riding him hard.

Bebe didn't move away, she moaned around his dick, the vibration a sweet torture as she used the flat of her tongue to drive him insane. His back snapped straight, his knees locking as his climax hit him and he came down her throat. His free hand shot to the shower wall to keep him upright as she licked up every drop before releasing his spent cock with a pop.

Her smile was delicious and sultry and one of a woman satisfied with herself, and so she fucking should be. That had been the best head of his life, but he shouldn't be surprised. Everything with her seemed to be the best of his life and he wondered how he'd move on from a woman like her or even if he wanted to.

Dispelling the thought, he hooked his hands under her arms and helped her stand before turning her away and grabbing the sponge. They spent the next fifteen minutes washing and caressing every inch of each other's bodies until the water became lukewarm. He got out and wrapped her in a towel, before covering himself.

He liked this part as much as the sex. Taking care of someone was new to him. He'd never done it before and he found he enjoyed the intimacy of it. But again, he suspected it had more to do with the woman he was doing it with than anything else.

As she dried her hair in the vanity mirror, the towel drying her skin, he slipped into the bed they'd shared for the last few nights. His huge bed felt too big now when they ended up curled together in the middle by morning, their bodies entwined as if seeking each other out during the night.

"What?"

His eyes shot up from the arch of her shoulder to see her looking at him in the mirror, the dryer now silent and her hair a soft mass around her. "Just thinking how beautiful you are."

Bebe rose and walked toward him, her towel pooling at her feet and causing arousal to lick through his blood like a fire. She placed a knee on the bed as he peeled back the covers for her and crawled to him, her body lithe and sensual like a cat, a damn sexy one.

As she settled her naked form against his, she placed her head on his chest as he cradled her in against his side.

"You aren't too bad yourself. You know, for a prince and all."

"Yeah?"

"Yeah, you got a little something going on that does it for me."

Leo smiled and he realised he'd smiled more in the last five days than he had in the last two years. "Well, I'm glad I do it for you."

He settled them back against the pillows but turned when she shifted and pulled the t-shirt he'd placed under her pillow free.

Her brow arched as she held it out to him. "And what's this?"

Leo felt his face heat with unusual nerves. "I won't have my woman wearing another man's clothes. You want to wear a tee to bed, you wear mine."

Bebe pursed her lips and he waited for the explosion of her temper, but it never came.

"I can live with that."

He kissed her slow, taking her mouth as she surrendered to him. He released her mouth as he rolled her to her side and settled in against her back, his arm under her pillow, his free hand hooked over her waist.

"Sleep now, Bebe. We have a lot to get done tomorrow and I have every intention of waking you early so I can make love to you as the sun rises."

"Okay, Leo."

Her simple acceptance did something to him, making his heart leap in his chest and he wondered what the hell he'd gotten into because he knew for sure no matter what, he wasn't getting out of this without some substantial scars. He also knew it would be worth every one to spend it with her.

Sixteen

Studying the interaction between Leo and the King was fascinating to Bebe. The dynamic might be one of father and son, but it was easy to see that the King looked up to his son as much as Leo did him. A mutual respect between the two men, but still, an emotional distance was evident from León's side of things.

"This is all a little much to take in. I just...."

Alfred seemed to flounder, his words, the enormity of what Leo had revealed to his father landing like a boulder in the man's lap. Bebe moved to the antique table and poured Alfred a glass of his favoured brandy, handing it to him with a sympathetic smile. He raised his chin in thanks before taking a hefty swig, the pinkie ring he wore with the royal crest glinting as his hand shook ever so slightly.

"I know this is hard to accept, but Alwyn and Alain are involved up to their eyeballs. Alain admitted it to us."

King Alfred looked from his son to her, as if seeing her for the first time. "And you were sent into my home to find the perpetrator of this attempt to steal the gem and join this auction?"

"Yes, Your Majesty." Bebe stood facing the King who was sitting beside his son on the couch. She didn't out Brody James. She and Leo had decided to keep his involvement quiet for now at least.

"So, you two aren't in love?"

Bebe was taken aback by the question, and she glanced at Leo to get his reaction. The deer in the headlights look he wore probably mirrored her own. "We've only known each other a week, Your Majesty."

Alfred took another sip of the brandy and then lowered the glass. His eyes followed the movement as he looked to the ground at his feet, his shoulders heavy with dejection before he looked up and pinned her with a look she couldn't determine. "I only knew my wife three days before I realised, she was the love of my life."

Bebe didn't know what to say to that. She did have feelings for Leo but was it love? She didn't know and now wasn't the time to get into it, or so she thought.

Leo, on the other hand, seemed to have other ideas. He stood and paced to the window, the rigid stance uncompromising and alone. "Look how that turned out."

Tension racketed through the room at his words, decades-long pain and anguish building up until it could no longer be contained. "I should leave you two to talk."

Bebe went to move to the door and Leo turned, pinning her with a look. "No, stay. Please."

Torn between her desire to run from this awkward emotional family drama and stay and support Leo, she opted to stay.

"León, I've tried everything in my power to make amends for not seeing the signs of your mother's unhappiness, but I can't keep apologising."

"Maybe you should have tried staying faithful."

Bebe could hear the bitterness in Leo's voice and her heart broke for the little boy who'd lost his mother. She knew the pain of losing someone she loved so young, and it never went away. It became a part of you, a hardened, tough scar that bled when least expected.

"Son, I never, not once, cheated on your mother. She was, and will always be, the love of my life."

Leo spun, his jaw ticking with the anger he was trying to restrain.

"Lies. I overheard you talking about the affair and how sorry you were."

The King seemed to pale at León's words, his hand shaking as he drank the last of the brandy and set the glass aside. "I didn't know you overheard that."

"Well, I did."

Leo turned back to the window, and she couldn't stand the lonely, isolated grief she saw in him. Walking slowly toward him she stopped and placed a hand on his back. He flinched but gave her a small smile when he realised it was her.

"Perhaps you two should talk in private and get this all out. There are enough secrets in this home and you two need to be united."

His hand covered hers as she rubbed his shoulders. "Stay."

Bebe looked to the King who nodded. "Please, my dear, I feel it would be good for my son to have you here for this."

Gently she applied pressure on Leo's shoulder to turn around and come back to the couch. He followed but took the seat beside her instead of his father this time, and she felt sympathy for the King.

"Most don't know this, but when I met your mother she was here with Alwyn as his date. It was a party for your grandfather's birthday and Alwyn arrived with the most beautiful woman I had ever seen. Not just her outside beauty but inside too. She shone with a radiance I've never seen before." He looked up at Bebe and gave a tip of his lips, the pain of losing someone he'd clearly loved fresh on his face like it had happened yesterday. "At least not until you walked in with my son."

Bebe felt a blush heat her cheeks at the compliment he'd delivered and the spotlight it shone on hers and Leo's relationship, whatever that was.

"We locked eyes and from that moment I knew I'd marry her. She broke it off with Alwyn that night and he was fine with it, never looked back. He was always with a different woman and said he was happy for us. We married and then you came along, and life was perfect until it wasn't. I had only been King for a short time when your grandmother on your mother's side died. Your mother was devastated and became horribly depressed. She stopped coming to state functions and kept to her bed. Then one day I came home to surprise her and found her in bed with Alwyn. It seemed they'd been having an affair for a few months."

Bebe glanced at Leo who was ashen, his face grey with shock and realisation. Reaching for him, she curled her fingers around his and held tight as he leaned toward her seeking comfort, which she was happy to give him.

"Alwyn said it was my fault for ignoring her and putting the crown first. For her part, your mother was devastated, and I realised there were more people to blame than the two of them. Yes, they'd had the affair but only because I'd failed to see the signs of her loneliness. Your mother was devastated and wracked with guilt but we talked for many hours, and we wanted to fix things. Love was never an issue for us, communication was. We agreed to try again but out of the blue, three months later she had a heart attack and was gone forever."

King Alfred's voice wobbled, and she fought the desire to reach for him too and offer the comfort she knew he desperately needed.

Leo stood and moved to sit by his father, both men lost in grief and memories. "I blamed you."

"I know, son, and you were right to do so. I gave too much of myself to everyone else and not enough to those who mattered."

"No, you deserved her fidelity, no matter what. Mother could've told you how she felt but chose to seek comfort elsewhere. I remember her saying she was sorry to me over and over and never understood why. She felt guilty and so she should have."

"Perhaps but I never blamed her."

"You are too good a man. How can you stand Alwyn being in the palace? I'd hate him for his betrayal."

"I did for a long time, but I realised my son needed family and whatever he's done, he and Alain were family."

"You forgave him for me?"

"I'd do anything for you. You're my blood."

"I don't deserve you."

Alfred gripped his son's shoulder, tight. "Of course you do, my boy. You've grown into a man that would make any father proud. You'll make a wonderful King one day."

"In the meantime, we have to figure out how to stop this auction and find out who's behind it."

King Alfred looked at her and smiled. "Thank you, my dear. You've opened a lot of eyes since your arrival and healed some wounds too."

Embarrassed to have the eyes of these two powerful and broken men on her, Bebe blushed once more, dropping her gaze to her clasped hands. "I didn't do anything."

"You did more than you know."

"Well, then I'm glad. For my part, I agree with Leo that we should move you to a safe location. It will help us postpone the funeral and keep you safe."

Alfred stood and, for the first time since she'd arrived, she saw the will of steel behind the gentle man. "No. I won't run from this. I've allowed Alwyn enough freedoms in my life, and it's time I stood up to him."

Leo glanced at her, and she saw the worry for his father, written clear across his features.

Bebe stood, walking closer, anxious for the King's safety now that she knew what a kind and forgiving man he was, ratcheted tight in her chest. "Your Majesty, please."

Alfred took her hands in his as he looked up at her. "My dear, I know you mean well and wish to shelter me, but I'm the King, and a good leader never runs from a conflict. A true leader stays and fights."

"I'll fight, Father."

"No, we'll fight side by side as it should be. Now, tell me who you think this American is behind all this?"

"My best guess is Atticus. He's the only person unaccounted for and although he comes across as a playboy, I know for a fact he's very cunning. Bebe has her people running checks now."

Leo ran his eyes over her as he spoke, and she felt his gaze like a caress over her skin.

"I must speak to Alwyn."

"That's not a good idea. We need him to think we don't suspect him. It's bad enough that Bebe's cover is blown thanks to Wojcik."

The King raised his brows in surprise. "Wojcik knows about Bebe?"

"I might have killed his brother." Bebe had never hidden who she was, and she wasn't about to start now.

"Oh?"

She wasn't sure the King's brows could go any higher on his forehead, but she was wrong. "He was trafficking women and children for the sex and organ trade. I was tasked with bringing him to justice. He resisted, so I shot him."

She wasn't sure why she was being so provocative with her choice of words, except to say she was testing the King in some way to see if he could tolerate her past.

The room was utterly silent, as if waiting for the other shoe to drop, the tension in her shoulders making her neck ache. Would the King have her removed from the palace? Would he shun her choices as so many people would in his position?

"Then he has nobody to blame but himself."

That was all he said on the matter as a stunned Bebe looked to Leo to find him grinning at her.

As if she'd revealed no more than a disagreement, Alfred continued. "Alwyn doesn't have the faith in my son that I do, and in this instance, it plays into our favour. He'll believe my son is an ignorant pawn in this game. With Alain missing, he'll think you've taken him and become outraged. Wojcik will likely have his work cut out handling my brother. I'll call Alwyn and tell him the funeral must be postponed because of the police investigation. I'm the King after all, and my word is final. He won't like it but he'll have no choice."

Bebe didn't like the idea of Alfred in danger. He was older, more vulnerable than she and Leo were. "May I make a suggestion?"

Leo cocked his head slightly and the King nodded.

"I know you trust your guard, but in this instance, if you insist on staying here, I'd feel happier if I get my own people in to help guard you. Only two or three, not an army that would need explaining."

"I thought your team were all on similar assignments to this?" Leo folded his arms over his chest, and she swallowed as the muscles in his arms bulged, temporarily fogging her brain with lust.

Blinking she pulled herself from the memories of last night and the shower and then how he'd held her all night. "They are but we have others who don't go undercover anymore and still work for Zenobi."

"And they'd come?"

"Yes of course, and it will add one more layer of protection for you and peace of mind for Leo and myself while we try and get to the bottom of things."

"Won't this tip Wojcik and his boss off?"

Bebe smiled as she shook her head. "No, they won't realise the guards are guards."

Leo cottoned on and smiled wide. "Because they won't expect female guards."

Bebe rubbed her hands on her cream linen trousers and nodded. "Exactly, and to be clear, these women are as deadly as any man."

"Oh, my dear, I suspect more so. My wife, God rest her soul, had the temper of a lioness when she was in protector mode."

Leo dipped his head to his father and offered him a consolatory smile. "That's settled then. I'll make the call today."

"Good and I'll call Alwyn after that. Now, what else can I do to help?"

"Nothing, just stay safe."

"I have my guard for now and no plans to leave the palace."

Bebe and Leo left the King to mull over the news she knew must have been harder to hear than he let on.

Leo linked his fingers with hers before bringing them to his lips as they crossed the large hallway, her heels clicking on the marble floor. "Thank you."

Bebe blinked in surprise at his words. "What for? I haven't done anything yet except get us shot at."

"That's not on you and what you did was show me the truth about my father."

Lifting on tiptoes, she brushed her lips over his. "I just hope it helps."

Leo palmed her cheek, and it made her feel cherished in a way she never had before. She was the protector and it had always made men feel emasculated but not Leo. He was the real deal and she wanted so badly for this to last, no matter how unlikely it seemed right now.

Seventeen

Leo watched Bebe walk into the bedroom they shared and finally allowed his head to catch up with what his heart already knew. He was in love with her. It was the craziest thing but hearing his father speak about his mother, he'd felt the same connection to Bebe. His pulse raced when she was around, and his heart ached with worry when he hadn't laid eyes on her for a while. Every facet of her intrigued him and he wanted to sit and listen to every story she had just to hear her talk.

He found himself noticing things that he thought she might like and wanting to tell her, and more, he trusted her with his intimate pain. She was like the other half of him, his equal in everything but he didn't feel worthy of her. She was fierce in her devotion to her friends and loyal to the bone. To some, her moral compass might be seen as skewed but he knew it wasn't. Right and wrong were never black and white, they were murky and hard to decipher sometimes but Bebe always came out on the right side.

He was in love with a warrior, a woman who would die beside him, not standing behind him and asking him to face danger alone. He would. God, he'd do anything to keep her safe, but she'd never thank him for it. If he had any chance of convincing her to stay and be his, he had to let her be who she was born to be, a saviour.

"You okay?"

Leo stood and reached her in two short strides, his arms circling her waist and pulling her close. His eyes found hers and he watched her wet her bottom lip with her tongue, making his body go hard instantly. She was so beautiful, so perfect, and yet she carried her pain around like he did.

Her hands caressed his chest, her fingers flexing against his shirt, and he wished he had time to show her exactly how okay he was when she was around. "I am now. How was your call to your friends?" He wanted to say more but he had to be careful with ears in the room all the time.

"Great, they can't wait to meet you."

"We should set something up when the funeral is over."

He knew she was telling him they were coming, not that he expected any different. From what he could tell they were as loyal to her as she was to them.

Leo dipped his head and kissed her softly, letting his feelings deepen the kiss until he felt drugged by her. Lifting his head, he looked into her deep brown eyes and saw the same dreamy expression as he felt. "You're amazing, you know that? Since the moment we met, I've been swept away by you, mesmerised by you."

Her lips parted and he could feel her heart beating against his chest. She knew this was real too, that what he was saying was the truth and no longer an act for those listening. "I feel the same and it terrifies me."

Leo kissed her forehead, inhaling the scent of her like it was oxygen to his love-struck brain. "I know, but we'll figure it out. I won't let you down, Bebe."

"I know. I trust you."

He saw in her eyes that she did, and his heart soared with the hope that maybe this whirlwind nightmare could be the best thing to ever happen to him.

A knock on the door had them breaking apart.

Leo sighed and turned to the door but didn't release her from his hold. "Yes?"

His butler poked his head in the door. "Apologies, sir, but Miss Vos is insisting she speak with you."

Leo sighed again, his frustration with Chelsea outweighed only slightly by the fact she might have information that could help them wrap this up. "Tell Miss Vos I'll come and speak with her shortly."

"Yes, sir."

The door clicked closed and Leo dropped his head to Bebe's shoulder in a groan.

"You should go speak with her."

Lifting his head, he studied her and saw no sign of jealousy or irritation. "Come with me."

Bebe laughed. "She won't want me there."

"All the more reason to come. You can protect me from her."

Her body vibrated against this with laughter. "You don't need my protection."

"I do. She's like a praying mantis and I'm scared for my manhood."

"Perhaps you should have considered that before you slept with her."

"Ouch."

Bebe laughed again.

"Yes, I was stupid but you can't hold that against me. Can you?" He gave her his best impression of puppy dog eyes, trying to get her to agree. He didn't want her out of his sight and that might be stupid, but it was how he felt.

"Fine, I'll come."

Leo grinned and kissed her neck, letting his lips linger with the promise of more. "Thank you, I'll make it up to you later."

"Damn straight you will, mister."

God, he loved this feisty woman, but he wouldn't tell her, not yet. When this was over though, he'd lay it all on the line and hope she felt the same.

Fifteen minutes later he was parking outside Chelsea's home, which was less than a five-minute walk from the Marina and the luxury nightclubs the island had to offer. Her home was lavish and stood beside only two others on this road. The gates opened and he drew his car inside and parked at the entrance.

He got out and rounded the car to offer his hand to Bebe, who graciously took it. "We won't stay long."

The door opened and Chelsea greeted him in nothing but a silk dressing gown, her make-up an inch thick and her hair falling around her shoulders. He ground his back teeth at her obvious attempt at seduction and Bebe squeezed his hand in support.

Chelsea pouted, her lip curling in dislike. "What's she doing here?"

He turned, about to walk away but stopped when Bebe placed a hand on his. "Talk to her. I'll wait in the car."

He cupped her cheek, ignoring a fuming Chelsea beside him. "Are you sure?"

He didn't want to be there. His gut was telling him to leave, his army instincts itching with a warning. But these days every time they went out, he felt that way.

"Yes, she might be able to help, and I can wait in this awful car of yours for a few minutes."

His lips twitched at her description of his Lamborghini. "I won't be long."

He kissed her lightly and waited for her to get in the car before he followed Chelsea inside the house. The home, like the woman, was over the top with large, garish artwork, pictures of herself in every room, and lots of animal prints scattered around the house. Including a rug he knew was real fur.

Chelsea moved to the bar and poured herself a neat vodka, her choice of drink and held the bottle up. "Drink?"

"No, thank you."

"Oh, come on, Leo, don't be mad. I just wanted to talk to you. This whole thing has me shaken."

"Fine but only a soda water. I'm driving."

Chelsea smiled and poured the drink while he walked to the window of her living room and looked out over the perfectly maintained gardens. He wished it looked out over the drive so he could have eyes on Bebe but it didn't.

"Here."

Chelsea moved close and handed him the drink before she sashayed her way toward the couch. He watched her, wondering what he'd ever seen in her and realised it had been easy and convenient. That was the only reason he'd ever taken this woman to bed. He felt a modicum of sympathy for her but shot it down. He'd hear her out with decency and then get the hell out. He owed her that at least.

Moving, he sat opposite her as she crossed her legs, allowing the fabric of the gown to fall open and reveal her almost invisible underwear to his eyes. The gape in the middle told him she wasn't wearing a bra and instead of desire, he felt disgust sting his veins.

"Cover yourself up, Chelsea, or I'm out of here."

Chelsea huffed and straightened her clothes. "When did you become such a boy scout?"

"When I met the woman I love and grew some self-respect."

He sipped the water, wanting instead to leave.

"You love her?"

Tears threatened and he hated that he cared enough to soften his words. "I'm sorry, Chelsea. You don't choose who you love, and I love Bebe. We were never about that. It was fun between us but never serious."

Her liquid eyes came to him. "It was for me."

God, was it hot in there or was it him? He drank some more of the soda water to try and get rid of the overheated feeling and the discomfort this conversation gave him. "I'm sorry for that. I was always clear with you that we were never more."

"But you were kind to me."

"Of course, I was kind to you. I'm not an asshole."

Leo rubbed his finger over his collar to try and loosen it, the feeling of constriction almost overwhelming. Chelsea stood and walked closer to him, as she swayed in front of his eyes. The vision blurred as he tried to stand and found his legs were useless.

"What did you do?" The glass fell from his hands as he fought against whatever she'd drugged him with.

"I'm sorry, Leo, but I had no choice. You wouldn't listen to me, and Atticus needs her gone. If you'd only chosen me, there would've been no need for this nastiness."

Fear and rage overcame him as he fell to the ground, his body working against him as his slurred words fought their way to the surface. "If you hurt her, I'll kill you."

The last thing he heard was Chelsea laughing before the world went dark.

Eighteen

BEBE RAISED HER CHIN, LOOKING AROUND AT THE LAVISH DRIVEWAY that led to manicured gardens beyond. Chelsea Vos looked to have it all, but she had very little of any real worth. Her life was focused on the material things and what those around her could give her, and what she wanted was Leo.

Bebe knew that even if she hadn't met Leo, he never would've settled for Chelsea. Leo had a depth about him that the shallow woman would never understand. She'd certainly never meet his intellectual needs or become the strong gracious Queen Leo would need beside him one day

Opening the passenger door to let some air into the car, Bebe listened to the sounds around her. She could hear cars in the distance and the honking of a large boat as it came into the marina, but then there was utter silence. This island offered a slice of peace, and tranquillity despite the rich and famous islanders, even if it was all a smokescreen to the drama playing out behind closed doors.

Her gaze moved to the house, and she wondered how Leo was faring with Chelsea. She had no doubt the woman would pull out all the stops to seduce him, but Bebe wasn't worried. She didn't get to this age and go through the things she had to not understand her self-worth regarding men or anyone else for that matter.

If Leo wanted Chelsea, then that was his choice. If he wanted her, that was great, but she wouldn't spend her life worrying about a man cheating. If he betrayed her, he was gone and she'd move on, dragging her broken heart with her.

Leaning her head back on the cream leather headrest, she sighed. The truth was they hadn't made any promises and they'd certainly not discussed the future. Did she even want a future with Leo? How could she, an assassin, be what he needed in a partner as a future King? The Monarch of this beautiful land needed a woman who didn't have the baggage she did.

A movement off to the side just behind the house caught her attention and had her sitting up higher in her seat. Her eyes darted to the corner of the house as she slid the small but deadly handgun from her bag. Listening intently now, Bebe drowned out the sounds of cars and listened for the small clues that someone was coming that shouldn't be there.

Tilting her head, she toed off her heels knowing it would be easier to fight in bare feet than the four-inch heels she'd chosen to wear.

There!

The sound of a weapon being cocked. She should warn Leo but as four men advanced from the front side of the house, she realised she had no time. This was an ambush created to split her and Leo up. She had two choices, fight and she could probably take these four men, or surrender. It wasn't her nature to back down from a fight but there was more than just her at risk.

"Get out of the car and keep your hands raised."

The lead man, short and muscular spoke in an accent she didn't recognise at first. Then it came to her it was Proenian. The place where Mercy was infiltrating the palace as she spoke. What did this mean? Was Mercy in trouble? It couldn't be a coincidence that the man before her had that accent.

Her stomach turned to lead at the thought that the beautiful woman she knew could be in danger. Yes, she was as trained and dangerous as they, perhaps more so, but she had a vulnerability after everything she'd been through. Bebe couldn't fathom the thought of her enduring more.

Making a split-second decision, she raised her hands and dropped her gun to the floor, as she exited the car. "Who are you?"

The two men who'd sidled up behind her grabbed her roughly by the upper arms and hauled her forward to face the man in charge. "Who I am doesn't matter. All that matters is that you do as I say, or Prince León will die a horrible death."

Bebe leaned back, wanting as much space between her and this horrid man as she could get. An ache hit the back of her throat as she thought about Leo and his safety. That had to be her priority now. She could work on an escape plan afterwards when she got where they were taking her. If they wanted her dead, she'd be dead by now. This was her chance to learn more and gather information.

No, they needed something from her first and her acting compliant would give them cause to believe she wasn't as deadly as she might have been painted. "Okay just don't hurt him. I'll come with you." Bebe added an extra wobble to her voice to give the impression of fear when all she wanted to do was rip their throats out with her bare hands.

The leader angled his head to the house. "Hurt him? I expect our Prince is getting his cock sucked by the very talented Miss Vos about now."

Not an image she needed in her head, right then or at all. She knew they were taunting her, trying to break her spirit, and she wouldn't let them see how much the words impacted her.

Keeping silent as she was dragged to the back of the house and toward a blacked-out transit van, Bebe was surprised they didn't put a hood over her head, but then realised it was because they didn't expect her to leave alive.

A clue at least to their intentions if not their motive.

Her knees hit the hard metal of the van as she was shoved forward onto her belly. A body pressed into her back, the disgusting human grinding his hard cock against her ass as he pulled her arms behind her and zip-tied them so tight her skin pinched painfully. A hand curled over her ass in a caress that made her stomach roil with bile. She was going to slice this motherfucker up for touching her.

"Hey, Denis, we don't have time for fun. Let's go."

The man shoved her forward and her chin scraped against the floor as the door shut behind her and the van was thrown into darkness. Bebe blinked, trying to adjust her eyes as she listened to the two men argue outside.

"Don't use my name, dumbass."

"What do you care? She'll be dead in twenty-four hours anyway."

"Yeah, well, the man I work for is more careful and won't appreciate you being so careless."

"If the man you worked for was any good, we wouldn't be here helping you out, would we?"

That second voice was the man from Proenia. So, he'd been sent to help the man here get the job done. The bickering continued for a few moments as they got in the front seats before the vehicle started up and moved away.

Bebe tried to keep track of the turns as they drove, knowing it would be useful when she got away, and she would. She'd been in worse situations than this and walked away.

As she lay there waiting to see what would happen, her mind went over the conversation she'd heard between the two men.

If the man from Proenia was here to help, that meant whoever was after the gem was failing in some way and her guess was they were close to revealing the identity of the traitor. The success of the second auction depended on the first, so the second auction was Proenia and whoever was involved with that had sent people to ensure this one worked out.

They'd got it wrong about the auction invitees being isolated and not knowing about each other. They knew and were in contact. Bebe didn't know what that meant right now but it was food for thought for when she got out of there.

The vehicle stopped and she stilled, listening for signs of where they were. The sea. She could hear the ocean and smell the salt. Scrambling to her knees she waited as the men exited the vehicle and the door was thrust open. Blinking, she tried to look around, but the sun was bright as they grabbed her by her hair wrenching her neck back.

Bebe fought the desire to head butt the asshole and whimpered in pain because damn, hair pulling hurt like a bitch when it wasn't done in a sexual way.

"Now, bitch, you're going to walk toward the boat I tell you to and climb aboard without making a fuss or I'm going to make a call and have Prince León's throat slit. Do you understand?"

"Yes." God, she was going to make this bastard pay when she got free.

"Good."

Hauling her from the van he steadied her on her feet and threw a jacket over her shoulders to hide the fact her arms were bound. They were at the marina. She could see the manager's office not five hundred feet from her, but she didn't dare make a move yet. The tarmac beneath her naked feet was warm and rough as she walked between two of the men who'd taken her. The leader in front and a man behind her made it difficult to see much of anything.

Boarding the large yacht, which she couldn't see the name of, was tricky and she almost lost her balance a few times before her upper arm was grabbed painfully hard and she was wrenched inside the main cabin.

"Quit fucking around, bitch."

"Oh, I'm sorry for the inconvenience of nearly falling on my face because my hands are tied." Bebe bit her lip at her outburst with fear in her voice to give the impression she was terrified for her life.

"Oh, this one has more fight than I thought."

The steps down to the living quarters were steep but she managed to stay steady as she was shoved into a bedroom with a double bed, a beautiful teak wood dresser and wardrobes, and a desk and cream chair by a small round window.

Twisting fast, Bebe kept the men in front of her, not wanting a repeat of Denis's hands on her.

Denis grabbed his crotch and shook his vile body, his tongue stuck out. "How about some fun, now?"

"Not even if humanity depended on it."

Bebe saw his face change from cocky to angry as he pounced at her and pushed her to the bed, his long, greasy dark hair falling over her neck as he pinned her to the bed.

"You think you're too good for me, whore? You only fuck royalty?"

Bebe reared back and spat in his face. "I know I'm too good for you."

She then raised her knee and smiled as he cried out in pain and fell back, grabbing his balls.

"Bitch."

Bebe saw his hand coming but couldn't do a thing to stop the blow to her cheek. Pain smarted as her eyes watered and her nose stung with tears, her ears ringing from the blow to her face.

"Enough!" The loud cultured voice bellowed from behind Denis.

Bebe looked toward the sound and smiled inwardly. Now they were getting somewhere. "You look pretty good for a dead man, Atticus."

Nineteen

His mouth felt like cotton wool as Leo blinked to clear the fog from his brain. Something was very wrong, but he couldn't put his finger on what. He rolled and fell to the floor from the couch he'd been sleeping on. The air rushed from his lungs in a loud 'oof' as he came to his knees. Nausea roiled in his belly and his head was banging like Phil Collins was playing the drums in his brain.

Swallowing against the dry feeling in his throat, he looked around trying to remember what had happened. Slowly conscious thought came back to him, and he realised he recognised the room. This was Chelsea's house, but he couldn't remember why he'd come here. Standing, he pushed his uncoordinated body onto the couch and sat with his head between his legs for a minute as he fought to remember.

The swirls on the carpet kept moving so he looked up and out the window to the back, the dark night sky turning blue as the sun rose. How long had he been out? A flicker of memory had him grasping to take hold of it and clear the cotton from his head.

Bebe!

They'd come here for some reason, but where was she now?

Staggering upright, he found his legs a little steadier as he walked to the bathroom off the hallway, using the walls to hold his weight. Reaching the entranceway, he looked to the front door and then the bathroom. Water. He needed water to help him metabolise whatever was in his body. Reaching the bathroom, he turned on the cold tap and splashed his face with water, before cupping his hands and taking several large gulps. Resting his hands on the sink, he looked in the mirror. Seeing the bedraggled man in front of him made him frown as he tried to capture the memories chasing through his brain too quickly.

Where was Bebe? Was she with Chelsea somewhere in the house?

Taking a last drink of cool water, he felt his mind begin to clear, his body already feeling more in his control as he walked unaided to the front door. He pulled it open and saw his yellow Lamborghini with the passenger's door open. The sun began to crest over the horizon, and he shielded his eyes. Whatever drug he'd ingested made everything feel overly bright.

Urgency sprinted through his veins as he moved toward the car and saw Bebe's handgun on the floor. Dread filled his belly with lead as he looked for any evidence of what had gone down. Seeing her shoes in the footwell of the car, he reached out to pick up one of the nude sandals and turned it over in his hands as if it might give him the answers he sought.

A sound from the front of the house made him look up to see a smiling Chelsea headed his way.

"What are you doing up? You should be resting."

As she got close, she reached for his arm, an enchanting look he knew so well on her face, but he reared back. "Don't touch me."

Chelsea's smile faltered, and she stepped back, a look of uncertainty on her face. "León, why are you being like this?"

"Where is Bebe?"

Her bottom lip dropped, and she tried to scowl at him, but years of Botox stopped her expression from forming. "How should I know? Perhaps she got bored and went back home, where she belongs."

No, she wouldn't do that. They had a mission to finish, a job to do and she'd never leave him without saying goodbye.

As he glanced back at the shoe in his hand, he remembered Bebe putting them on to come here. Her sexy smirk coated her face and made him crave her like a drug addiction he never wanted to recover from. His mind flew to arriving here and Chelsea opening the door and being salty about Bebe's presence. Bebe saying she'd wait in the car, and the feeling he'd ignored that something was wrong.

Dropping his hand to his side he stepped forward and grasped Chelsea by the upper arm, seeing fear in their blue depths. "No, you're lying. What did you do, Chelsea?"

"León, stop. You're hurting me."

"Tell. Me. What. You. Did." He could barely restrain his desire to strangle this fickle bitch just to get the truth out of her.

"I had no choice."

Leo shook his arm as she tried to cling to him. "Tell me!" He roared his demand and thrust her away from him, not trusting himself to have his hands on her right now or he might do something he'd vowed to never do and strike a woman.

Chelsea hit the floor, her body collapsing on itself in dramatic fashion as she wept at his feet. "Please, Leo you have to understand."

"I don't have to do a single thing. Now tell me what happened to Bebe."

Bits and pieces of memory were returning now, and he remembered the water and how she'd drugged him. Any empathy he may have felt for this woman in the past evaporated.

"Atticus said if I could get you alone, he'd handle Bebe and take her away so she wouldn't be in our way. We can be together now she's gone."

His body felt numb at the revelation that Atticus was behind this. "Did Atticus tell you to come to me with the story about you being drugged?"

Chelsea looked up at him through big eyes filled with tears as she sat on the floor, legs outstretched in front of her. "Yes. He said he had a plan to make us rich and I'd end up on the throne with you as King if I did what he said."

Leo crouched to her as she spoke. "What did he say?"

"That we had to leave the marina and let Alain get on the boat. People would think we were dead and then I'd come to you and tell you I'd been drugged and he was missing. Prince Alwyn would get in trouble for lying about that, and when Atticus made Alain steal the gemstone, he'd get the blame."

"How would that help Atticus?"

Chelsea shrugged. "I don't know. Just that you'd turn to me, and we could be together but then she got in the way. Atticus offered to help me get rid of her."

"Where did he take her?"

"No clue."

Leo stood, he had all he was going to get from her. Time was moving on. By the looks of things, it had already been the best part of twelve hours. Looking at his watch he confirmed it had been twelve hours since he arrived at Chelsea's.

Picking up the sandal he'd dropped, he retrieved Bebe's gun knowing it was her favourite and stowed it in the glove compartment of his car before he gunned the engine and tore down the driveway, headed for the palace.

He hit dial on the console and his call connected to his private security. "It's Prince León. Please have Chelsea Vos picked up at her residence for treason and escorted to the private jail."

He ended the call quickly and wished he had more to go on, but he had very little. He knew a man who did though, and he was going to answer some questions or Leo was going to make his life a living misery.

Striding into the palace, León was a man on a mission. The early morning staff working to clean the palace sensed it, scattering like leaves on the breeze as he marched past them toward his father's rooms. A single knock before he entered, he stopped to see the very man he'd been about to summon already there with his father. Anger and rage built in him, making his fists clench as they itched to take a swing at his uncle.

His father looked up at him from his seat opposite his brother, a worried look on his face. "Leo, where have you been? I've been trying to contact you."

Leo didn't slow his pace, he prowled towards his uncle and stood in front of the man who'd caused a lot of the pain in his life and saw him for the weak man he was. "Where is she?"

"Son?"

Leo ignored his father's question and stared his uncle down as the man sat back, trying to seem unconcerned. The pulse in his neck gave him away, and Leo fought the urge to smile, although he felt no humour.

"Where is she? Don't make me repeat myself."

"Really, León, I have no idea what you're talking about. I've been sitting with your father as he was concerned after you never came home last night."

"Save it," Leo bit out, his temper boiling over as he leaned close.

His uncle seemed to sense the danger he was in now. Like a rat backed into a corner, he glanced at the door as if looking for a way out, but he had none here.

Leo reached down and hauled his uncle up by his lapels, ignoring the squeak of outrage. Moving close he saw his father stand from the corner of his eye but didn't remove his focus from Alwyn. "Stop. We know about Alain. We know you're working with Wojcik, and he's using Alain to obtain the gem for the American. Now you have five seconds to tell me where he took Bebe, or I'm going to beat the snot out of you."

Alwyn looked to the King, sweat dripping down his brow, as his eyes went wide. "Alfred, please."

The King stepped forward and for a horrible second, Leo worried he'd try and stop him. His father wasn't a violent man, he was known as a peacemaker, not a war-hungry animal.

Positioning himself beside Leo, he lifted his chin, as Alwyn swallowed. "I stand beside my son, Alwyn. What you're involved in is abhorrent to me. If you have any knowledge of where Bebe is I suggest you tell us because I'll have no hesitation in having you arrested for treason after my son has finished extracting information from you by force."

"You'd do that to your own brother?"

"My brother died the day he took my wife to his bed."

Alwyn must have seen the truth in his brother's eyes because he seemed to sag in León's hold. He closed his eyes and Leo waited for him to decide, even though he wanted to shake him and demand he hurry up.

Bebe was out there, God knew where, and she could be in trouble. The only thing keeping him from going full-on Hulk was the belief that she could handle herself, probably better than him.

"I don't know where she is."

Leo tightened his hold until his uncle's shirt was choking him, his fingers grabbing at Leo's hold.

Red-faced and fearful, he seemed to come to terms with the fact this was over. "I'm telling the truth."

Leo felt his father's hand on his shoulder and obeyed the silent command to release his uncle. Alwyn fell back onto the sofa; his hand moving along his collar to try and ease the tightness.

Leo stepped back once and folded his arms over his chest as his uncle looked up at them.

"I admit I did bring Wojcik here to help me get the throne. He wanted Alain to steal the Tanzanite for him, but it quickly got out of hand. He demanded Alain fake his death, and then I was to identify the body. Alain would then sneak back in and steal the gem."

"Why would you agree to that?"

Alwyn looked up at him and he didn't see the arrogant man from his childhood, but a jealous and bitter man who'd spent his life coveting what his brother had. "I'd have made a better King. Alfred is weak. He couldn't even keep his wife happy."

Leo put his arm out as Alfred stepped forward, ready to defend his honour and his wife. "Never speak her name again. You preyed on an emotionally fragile woman and betrayed your family. And for what? Power? Greed? You'd never be half the man or King my father is. You're pathetic."

Alwyn huffed his shoulders, sagging under the weight of the dawning realisation that he'd failed in his plan to overthrow the King, because it wasn't regret Leo saw on his face, of that he was certain. "Perhaps that's so, and now Alain is missing and Wojcik is threatening my life too."

Leo almost rolled his eyes as his uncle tried to gain sympathy for his predicament. "Alain is safe."

Alwyn looked up fast his blotchy face full of surprise, as his eyes widened in relief. "He is?"

"Yes, and he'll remain that way if you help me. Where is Wojcik now?"

"He had to go and help the American with something. I don't know what."

"What do you know of the American?"

"Not a lot. He's the one pulling the strings. He made sure Alain and I were perfectly placed to take the fall and keep himself in the clear. I thought I was in charge but evidently, I was wrong."

Leo angled his body toward his father. "Chelsea Vos demanded to see me and then drugged me. When I came to, Bebe was gone. Chelsea says Atticus is the American. That he set this whole thing up."

"No!"

Leo glanced at Alwyn who'd stood, regaining some of his bluster now the immediate threat was gone.

"Yes, he set Alain and you up and brought in Wojcik. We just don't know why yet."

"The auction?"

Leo pinned his uncle with a steely-eyed stare. "What do you know of an auction?"

"I heard Wojcik mention it a few times. It seems the gem is some sort of payment."

"Did he say where or when or what the auction was selling?" Leo knew the answer to when but wanted to see if his uncle knew anything different.

Alwyn was shaking his head as he leaned against the back of the sofa, rubbing his chin in thought. "Not what or when, but I did overhear him say it would be in Proenia."

"Proenia?" Leo frowned knowing that Bebe's friend was there currently working this case from a different angle.

"Yes, and I believe it's soon."

A moment later the door to the King's rooms burst open and two men and two women stood before him. Leo sighed in relief because he knew backup had arrived at the perfect time.

Twenty

After the first words she spoke to Atticus yesterday, he'd approached and jabbed her in the arm with a drug to knock her out. Bebe had been out much of the night, only waking as the sun came up and flooded the cabin with light as the seagulls above made a racket.

Now Atticus was back, standing before her looking fresh-faced and well-rested, while she felt like utter shit. Her wrists were thankfully numb because she knew when the blood began to flow freely again it would hurt like a bitch.

Bebe wiggled her fingers trying to get some feeling back into them as she faced Atticus. She needed as much information as she could get right now. "So, what now?"

"Now you tell me how much León knows."

"About?"

Atticus stepped forward, his perfectly pressed tailor-made suit making him look elegant and refined when he was nothing but a common criminal. His hand flew out like a whip and smashed into the side of her face where Denis had hit her yesterday, forcing her head back as pain exploded on her cheek. Her teeth cut into the side of her mouth, and she tasted the metallic flavour of blood, but she didn't cry out. She'd die before she let this bastard think he could frighten her.

Raising her head, she licked the blood from her lip and held his gaze. He was handsome until you looked closer and saw the mean tilt of his lips. She didn't blame Chelsea for falling for his charms or wanting Leo instead. She knew from his file that Atticus was charming but any illegal dealings he'd done had flown under the radar. Whatever his story was it was well hidden and buried under a pretence of affability and charisma.

"You're a feisty one, aren't you?" He turned his back, stepping away to show he wasn't afraid of her. "But then I'd expect nothing less from an assassin. Tell me, do you kill them while they lie satiated between your legs after fucking you?"

Bebe didn't try to hide her disgust, her lips curling as she spat blood on the floor near his polished loafer. "I'm going to slit your throat."

Atticus laughed. "Oh, silly girl, you'll do nothing of the sort."

He moved lightning fast and gripped her hair, wrenching her neck back. His furious face almost touching hers, his breath warm on her face, he waited for the fear that wouldn't come from her.

"You'll tell me what Leo knows and where Alain is, or I'll let Wojcik take his revenge for what you did to his brother."

Bebe was under no illusions that he'd do that anyway. "Wojcik doesn't scare me."

"We will see."

He let go of her and pushed her away, letting her fall back on her wrists which sent pins and needles of pain racing up her arms. "Tell me, what is it you want from this auction badly enough that you'll betray and kill your friends for it?"

Atticus, smiled, seemingly pleased she knew the details. "A program that will make me the most powerful man on earth. Every nation and leader will bow to me, fear me, and court me."

Bebe almost rolled her eyes at his performance. Why did men like him think power held the secret to happiness? "Oh, just you're a run-of-the-mill bad guy wanting power and money, yada, yada. So, you're over-compensating for a small dick then?"

"Watch your tongue."

"Why? You won't do anything to me. You need me to find Alain."

"So, you have him. I did wonder."

"Not me personally but someone I know has him safe."

Atticus waved his hand as if this made no difference to him either way. "It matters not. I have Alwyn under my control. He can get to the gem easily enough."

It was time to try a different tactic. "Who's The Collector?"

Atticus seemed to pale at her question, his eyes darting around the cabin as if the man himself would jump out at any given second. "I don't know what you're talking about."

"Of course you do. He's the one collecting the gems, but then you knew that didn't you? Did he tell you where the auction would be? Or doesn't he trust you enough?"

"I know."

Bebe shook her head. "Nah, you don't have a clue."

"Proenia."

Bebe would've pumped the air with triumph at Atticus's need to peacock and prove her wrong if her hands were free. "Proenia. So that's why they sent people to help you get control. They need this to work so they can get their auction approved by The Collector."

"Enough." Atticus sliced his hand through the air with finality. "Time for you to have a few moments with Mr Wojcik to remind you who's in charge here."

Wojcik appeared in the doorway behind Atticus, the slight rock of the boat reminding her of where they were. She'd felt the yacht moving so guessed they were a mile out to sea by the time she was knocked out, which meant they could be God knew where by now. If she got away, she could probably swim to shore but she'd rather not do it bleeding and attracting sharks.

"Albin, how's the family?" Bebe had never been one to face danger timidly and more than once it had gotten her into trouble. Usually, her attitude worked in her favour and threw the enemy off their game. Men were easy creatures to read and being bested by a woman, either verbally or physically, didn't sit well. She didn't have the physical strength to bust the ties, but she might be able to convince him to cut them off so he could prove what a big man he was.

"You whore. You're going to pay for every single second that my brother suffered."

Bebe shrugged. "I can't be held responsible for him having to grow up looking at your ugly face."

Wojcik produced a flick knife and rolled it in his fingers like some B-movie thug. Her heart rate remained calm as she assessed the situation. Atticus had left the room, but she knew there were at least the four men who'd grabbed her on board as well as Wojcik on the ship. "What's he paying you, Wojcik?"

The man paused at her question and cocked his head to the side. "Shut up."

He placed the knife on the side table out of her reach and removed his jacket, rolling his sleeves up his forearms, revealing an ugly burn scar on the right. She'd heard rumours that he'd killed his parents in a house fire for hurting his brother but that was unconfirmed. If she were normal, perhaps she'd feel guilt for killing his brother, but the images of the things he'd done to those women and children absolved any feelings of regret. It was a blessing to the world he was dead, and given the first chance, his brother would be joining him.

Kicking the chair from the dressing table closer he yanked Bebe by the arm and sat her on the chair, her arms still behind her, tying her ankles to the legs, with zip ties from his pocket. Of course he'd carry zip ties. Bad guy 101.

Satisfied, he stood and smirked at her, his slick, dark hair falling over his forehead before he pushed it back with both hands. "Now we have some fun."

Bending his knee, he punched her in the gut in a low jab that had the air leaving her lungs so fast she struggled to draw oxygen. Wojcik followed up with several right jabs to the ribs that made her grunt in pain before she could hide it.

"Ah, now we see if you're so big and scary or just a little girl playing games."

Coughing, Bebe took a second to get her breathing under control before she responded. "Anyone can beat a person who's bound, but I doubt very much you could beat me if I was free. You don't have what it takes, Wojcik. You're soft like your brother."

"Don't speak of him."

"Do you know he wept as he lay dying in a pool of his own piss and blood? He cried like a baby wanting his mama."

Rage coated his features, blood vessels on his cheeks so prominent she thought he might do the job for her and have a stroke.

He pounced and grabbed her chin in a tight hold. "I'm going to enjoy fucking your body while you die beneath me."

Bebe ejected that vile thought from her brain and smirked. "I thought we established you haven't got what it takes."

A below of rage left him as he bent and cut the ties on her ankles, before grabbing her elbow. He kicked the chair away as he spun her, so she was face down on the bed, before kneeling on the base of her spine, causing her ribs to scream in pain. The sound of his flick knife opening had her stilling as he ran the blade down the back of her neck. The sting of the blade nicking her skin almost made her flinch, but she resisted the impulse knowing she was getting what she wanted. He was responding exactly how she'd predicted he would.

"Not so brave now, are we?"

"Cut these ties and let's find out."

Wojcik ran the blade down her spine, cutting through the fabric of the blouse she wore, and she was glad the bra she'd chosen was silk and not lace. If she had to fight in it, she didn't want her body exposed to that hideous man's eyes. Spreading her feet wide to add balance, she got ready in case he did cut the ties on her wrists and she had her shot.

As he touched the blade to the plastic, a sound outside caught his attention.

"Wojcik, get here now."

Frustration made her grit her teeth and Wojcik swore in his native tongue.

Shoving her away, Wojcik grabbed his jacket and headed toward the sound of Atticus's voice, closing, and locking the door to the sumptuous bedroom. Flipping to her back, Bebe sat up, taking a deep breath to calm her breathing as pain from a rib she suspected might be cracked made her blink away tears. Flexing her arms, Bebe put some pressure on the ties and like she suspected they would, they gave. He may not have cut them, but he'd weakened them enough with the nick of the blade to give her enough strength to snap them.

As blood rushed into her wrists and hands, she winced in pain, rubbing, and flexing her fingers to get the blood moving. She'd already checked for obvious cameras and found none so she got up and began to look around the cabin for something of use.

She didn't need a weapon, but it was always nice to have one. Finding nothing of any note, not even a pair of nail scissors, Bebe sighed in frustration. As she neared the door, she did hear something interesting as she listened silently, her head pressed to the wood.

Wojcik was close as he spoke. "What do you need?"

"Get back to the palace and find out what's going on. I haven't heard from Chelsea, and she was meant to call me when she'd secured León."

"What do you want me to do when I find the prince?"

"Bring him to the marina. If they have Alain and Alwyn, we need leverage. He can get the gem for us."

"You think he'll do it?"

Atticus laughed but it was ugly and full of hate. "Oh, yes. We have the woman he thinks he loves."

"You don't think he knows she's a plant?"

"You heard the recording from the apartment. He's head over heels for her, poor schmuck. If we have her, he'll do as I ask."

"It won't be easy getting to the prince."

"Details, Albin, details. You figure it out. Kill the King if you need to get him to comply but my guess is he'll come when you say you have her."

"Alright, boss."

As footsteps came closer, she rushed back to the bed and assumed a foetal position with her hands behind her back. The steps kept moving but Bebe remained where she was, ready and waiting for when the next attack came. She'd be ready this time because there was no way she was going to let these animals use her against Leo or the King.

Twenty-One

"Who the hell are you?"

Leo raised his hand for his uncle to shut his maw, a look of irritation forming on the older man's face before he faced the newcomers again.

The palace security came rushing in and Leo again held up his hand to stop them. "It's fine, you can leave."

The guards looked warily at each other before doing as he bid.

"León?"

Ignoring his father's question, he stepped forward and offered his hand to the woman with short dark hair and a resting bitch face that said she'd fuck you up if she didn't like the look of you. She was very beautiful, with full lips and wide captivating green eyes. "Roz, I assume?"

The woman eyed him before taking his hand and giving it a firm shake. "You assume correctly." She turned and motioned to the man behind her who was keeping very close and watching him like a hawk. "This is my husband Kanan and these two are Alex and Evelyn."

Her husband was around his height with a short scruff of a beard, brown hair, and knowing eyes that said he'd seen and done things most people could never even imagine.

Leo moved his focus to the other two people. The man was tall and built with golden blond hair and looked like a film star. The woman beside him smiled and gave him a wave, her long dark hair and petite build making her look sweet and innocent like a girl next door when he suspected she was actually hell on wheels.

"It's a pleasure to meet you and I'd love to stand and make introductions, but Bebe is missing."

He saw Roz's jaw tighten as she stepped forward and went nose to nose with him while the other three merely watched. "I beg your fucking pardon. I send my girl here to help you and you let her get taken?"

Leo felt like a small boy being reprimanded and hung his head in shame, guilt at allowing this turn of events already a deep wound in his psyche. "You can't speak to him that way. He's a prince."

Leo closed his eyes and almost groaned at his uncle's words. Not a few minutes ago he'd been admitting his betrayal to the crown and now he was offended someone hadn't addressed him properly.

Roz looked his way and pinned him with her gaze before she strolled toward Alwyn like a panther stalking a mouse. Her husband watched on with what looked like pride and adoration on his face.

Her leather jacket and black skinny jeans led to biker boots, and if she was anything like Bebe she was loaded up to the eyeballs with weapons.

"And who do we have here?"

"I'm Prince Alwyn, third in line to the throne of Soflye."

"Hmm." Roz looked behind her at Kanan and then toward him. "Do you allow treasonous bastards on the throne here?"

"How dare you."

Her hand shot out and she grabbed Alwyn by the throat and squeezed. "Oh, I dare. Bebe is one of mine, and because of you she's in trouble, and I don't take that lightly. So here's what's going to happen. You're going to tell me what you know and leave nothing out or I'm going to cut off your tiny pathetic cock and feed it to you until you choke."

Leo and every man in the room winced at her threat. He had little doubt she'd indeed follow through on her threat.

"I already told Leo what I know."

Roz pushed Alwyn into a chair and reached into her pocket for a wickedly sharp looking blade. Evelyn pulled Leo to the window and his father looked to Alwyn before following them a little way off.

"Let her do her thing. She needs to get this out of her system. She's pissed she had to leave her kids at home and fly here so it's best she takes it out on him rather than us."

Leo palmed the back of his neck and sighed, the effects of the drugs still making him a little nauseous.

"I'm King Alfred. I'm sorry about this business."

Leo lifted his head to see his father introducing himself to the other three. "Sorry."

"It's fine, my boy. I haven't had this kind of excitement in years." His father frowned. "I just wish it didn't involve my family on the wrong side of things and that lovely girl of yours getting taken."

A scream of pain had them all looking to where Roz had Alwyn in a compromising position where if she slipped it would mean no more fun for Uncle Alwyn.

"You've got company."

Alex motioned for the window and Leo saw Albin Wojcik pulling up outside the palace gates.

Tensing Leo clenched his fists at the sight of the man. He wanted nothing more than to rip his face off with his bare hands. "I expect he wants Alwyn."

"Want us to go and offer him an escort off a cliff somewhere?" Alex asked, his hands in his pockets looking relaxed and calm, but Leo could read people, and these were all top-notch, tier-one operators.

Like recognised like.

Leo shook his head. "No, we need him. He might know where Bebe was taken."

Roz joined them at the window, wiping the blood from her knife on her jeans before tucking it away. God, this woman had kids and she was utterly terrifying.

"Your uncle doesn't know where she is, but he did say that you have a member of staff called Hans who'd planted the bugs in your rooms."

Leo glanced at his uncle who was sitting with his head between his knees as if he might pass out. Again he'd lied, keeping relevant information from them. Alwyn would never learn, and Leo would never trust him again.

"God damn it." He punched the wall by his head, feeling the sting of flesh hitting stone as he took out his frustration at the situation.

"One of yours?" Alex asked his hand on Evelyn's shoulder.

"My butler. I'll have someone pick him up and put him with Chelsea."

Wojcik was making his way on foot down the drive, laughing with the security teams as if he didn't have a care in the world.

Leo gave the newcomers an abridged version of the last fourteen hours. "So now you know as much as I do."

Roz glanced at his uncle who was too busy feeling sorry for himself to even listen. "More actually. We found out that Atticus is Alwyn's son. Alwyn never acknowledged him. When he found out he went to your uncle, and he turned him away. Seems Uncle Alwyn has been shaking it about all over the Kingdom."

Leo felt stunned by the news but had no time to react before Wojcik was shown into the room by Roberto, his father's private secretary.

He glanced at the people he didn't recognise and frowned. "Prince León, Mr Wojcik would like to speak with you."

"Bring him in, Roberto," the King beckoned with a nod and wave of his hand. All formality was seemingly out of the window right now.

"Yes, Your Majesty."

Albin Wojcik stepped into the room, looking confident and sure of himself, and stilled at the sight of the newcomers surrounding the King. His gaze swept to where Alwyn was now sitting quietly drinking a brandy, his hand shaking, sweat covering his brow.

Leo imagined it was quite the surprise for the hitman.

"Prince Leo, might I have a word?"

"Of course."

"In private, sir."

"Come, have a drink." Leo beckoned him closer and like a rat, he scurried forward, even as his senses must have screamed danger because he was cocky and thought he was still in control.

"This matter is rather pressing."

Leo poured himself a brandy and took a sip, placing himself in front of the King as the others moved toward the door blocking the exit. "I imagine it is since you kidnapped my girlfriend."

Wojcik glanced around the room, wary now as if he'd just realised he'd walked into a trap. He moved his arm to his hip and Leo had him on the ground before he could even finish the action. His face slammed against the antique rug, his arm pressed up his back until he squealed like a pig.

Leo kept his knee on Wojcik's spine as he patted him down removing two knives, and a handgun. "Where's Bebe?"

"I'll never tell you and if you kill me, she dies."

Leo leaned his knee into the man's back, forcing a groan from him before he moved back and pulled him to his knees, keeping his arm pinned behind him. Anger slid through his veins like ice, his fury almost more than he could contain. But he did because losing his cool wouldn't help the woman he loved.

It was crazy and fast but the reality of it was he could no more have stopped it than he could hold the tide from the shore. She was his everything. He'd get her back safely so she could decide if she wanted to take the chance on him and sit beside him as his Queen one day. "Wrong answer."

Evelyn stepped in front of Wojcik. Her man, Alex just behind her, not interfering but letting her know he was there. She angled her head as she watched the hitman before letting fly with an elbow strike to his face. Leo heard the crack as Wojcik's nose broke, the scream loud enough to bring the palace staff running.

Roberto opened the door, where he must have been standing listening, and gasped, his eyes flying to the King. "Your Majesty?"

"It's okay, Roberto. Just make sure the staff stay clear of this area, please. We need to take care of a few things and then I'll explain."

Roberto seemed to pause but nodded his acceptance of the situation.

Leo cast his eyes to Roz, who was looking bored. "Is Roberto cleared?"

"Oh yeah. That man is as loyal as a Golden Retriever."

Leo tightened his hold as Wojcik tried to get free of him and smiled inwardly when he pushed his arm a little too high up his back and he yelped like a puppy. "Stop moving. We know you work for Atticus, we know about Alain and Alwyn and the gem, and the auction. We know the venue, blah blah blah. So, you see, this is over. You might as well talk so at least when I kill you, I'll do it fast." Leo was growing tired of the delay, every second she was gone the stakes rose.

Wojcik sagged but remained silent.

"Do you have a room where we can perhaps try and persuade him without the staff hearing?" Roz asked, stepping up beside Evelyn.

"Yes, we have an old dungeon below the palace."

Roz laughed. "No shit? A real-life dungeon? Lead the way, Prince León."

"It's mainly used for storage now, but it will work for what I suspect you're thinking."

Roz shrugged, placing her hands in the pockets of her leather jacket and producing what looked like a set of knuckle dusters but instead of spikes, it had wickedly sharp hooks like something Wolverine would wear.

"What the hell are those?" Wojcik asked saving Leo the time.

Roz twisted her hand this way and that, admiring the device he was sure was antique. "What, these? These, my friend, are called Spanish Ticklers and you're going to become very well acquainted shortly."

Wojcik looked up and seemed to come to a sudden realisation. "You! You're her. The one they fear. You use antique torture devices on your victims."

Roz grinned. "I'm semi-retired but it's nice to know you've heard of me."

Wojcik looked like he was about to piss himself as Leo hauled him to his feet and marched him to the door.

Roz, Kanan, and Alex followed as he led them toward the dungeon. They went down two flights of stairs and into a tunnel that led from the kitchens, and past old boxes and files that hadn't seen the light of day in years until he came to the area with the steel grid cell door where prisoners of old would've been held until their execution.

He pushed Wojcik inside, letting him fall to his knees on the cold stone. "Last chance, asshole."

The man had seemingly got some of his courage back because he merely spat on the ground at Leo's feet.

Leo put his hands in his pockets as he turned to Roz. "Okay, have fun. I'll be with my father when you're ready."

He had no doubt, as he left the three people who'd dropped everything to come for Bebe, they'd get what they needed.

Leo almost shuddered at the thought of getting on the wrong side of Roz. The woman was terrifying, and he suspected each of her girls was as deadly as she was. Strangely, it only made him love Bebe more.

Twenty-Two

On his way back to his father who he'd left in the capable hands of Roberto and Evelyn, who he knew would defend the King to the very death, Leo put in a call to his personal security. "Is Miss Vos detained?"

"Yes, sir."

Leo's personal security team was headed by Lance Martin, a man he'd served with in the army and a great leader. Leo was sure he'd have made it all the way to the top if an IED hadn't taken his right arm. He was still an excellent soldier and Leo had jumped at the chance to give him a commission at the palace leading his personal team, which he'd thankfully taken up. His palace team were made up of men he'd selected personally and some he'd served with so he knew he could trust them to get the job done. He spent much of the time not using them, instead, he'd made them part of the palace security. Now he was glad he had because the Palace needed locking down.

"Good, please come to the palace and secure Hans and Prince Alwyn in the same way."

Leo heard his friend whistle through his teeth. "Wow, shit is hitting the fan big time."

"Yes, it is. I can't go into details except to say I need the palace locked down. Nobody in or out unless I give the order."

"And the four people in the dungeon?"

Leo smiled as he walked through the kitchen, the staff all looking away in fear as if they could sense the danger around him right now. "Mr Wojcik will be staying there as our guest, and the others are free to come and go. They're with me."

"I have no idea how they got in, sir."

"That's a conversation for another time. We clearly need to review our weak spots and eliminate them."

"Copy that, sir."

"I want the Palace guard on full alert. Nobody in or out unless myself or the King approves it."

"Roger that."

Leo hung up and went to his father who was sitting in his favourite armchair with Roberto standing guard between him and Alwyn. Evelyn nodded at his return and headed for the door, most likely to meet up with the others.

"Roberto, Prince Alwyn will shortly be taken into custody for treason. As are Miss Vos and Hans, my butler. Mr Wojcik is also being detained for further crimes. I'd appreciate it if you could keep a lid on this and make sure the staff don't discuss it. I've issued a lockdown of the Palace, and nobody gets in or out without mine or the King's direct authority."

"Yes, Prince León. I'll handle it." Roberto paused as if unsure if he should speak, the shock on his face showing he was struggling to understand and take it in but rallying to do as he was instructed.

"Speak, Roberto, now isn't the time to lose your spine."

Leo put his hands in his pockets as he watched his father step up to the plate, taking control of the situation for a few minutes while Leo got himself together.

"Is this about the bombing of *The Grace*?"

"Yes, in some ways. But at the moment I can't comment further except to say I want a complete press blackout. Lives are at stake here, and I'd value your ability to handle things as asked."

Roberto dipped his head. "Consider it done."

The man went to do as he was bid, but Leo stopped him. "Roberto, is Mr James on-site?"

"I'm not sure, sir. I'd need to check with the security team."

"Do that and have him sent to me immediately, please."

Leo didn't know where Brody James was, but he suspected he was off running his own investigation, but it was time to bring this together. They couldn't function in this splintered way.

"So, you're going to have me arrested?"

Leo glanced from his father to his uncle, who was looking ragged and pathetic even in his three-piece suit. Reality had finally caught up with him since Roz had her chat with him. She hadn't, as they'd thought, done any real damage just nicked his hand, the hand that had been covering his manhood. It had been a damn close though, having him believe that she'd done the worst imaginable to a man. Not that he considered his uncle a man. A real man would've acknowledged his son no matter the circumstances. He didn't have time or the energy to dwell on the fact Atticus was his blood relative right now. The man had chosen his path of revenge instead of coming to him or the King. Now they were, and always would be, enemies.

"You committed multiple crimes against the crown. Not to mention the calculated manipulation and blatant disregard for human life and familial loyalty."

Alwyn looked at his brother, ignoring Leo's words, hate burning in his eyes. "You took her from me."

Leo stepped back as his father faced his younger brother with a straight spine. "I didn't take her, we fell in love. If I'd thought she meant something to you, I would've backed away, but you told me she was nobody to you."

"She wasn't until she was."

"You mean she only got your attention when she picked me over you?"

"You have it all, Alfred. The Kingdom, the adoration, the power. What do I have? Nothing."

"You had a family who loved you, a son who looked up to you.

Money, a life of luxury, your health and security. You were blessed beyond your own comprehension, and you never appreciated it. Always wanting more and more until it poisoned you, made you toxic."

His father glanced at him, and Leo dipped his chin in support. Alfred laid a hand on his brother's shoulder and Leo knew this was hard for him. He wasn't a man to hold a grudge, that had been proven with the way his father forgave the affair. "Perhaps you can think about the life you could've truly had if greed and jealousy hadn't leeched the good from your soul. Maybe there's some good still inside you."

The door opened and Lance and three of his men walked towards Alwyn and took his arms, leading him from the room as he cursed and struggled. Blustering about his title and what he perceived as his right.

As the door closed, Leo sat beside his father who was slumped in the chair. He seemed to have aged a hundred years during that short conversation. "This isn't on you, Father."

Weary eyes met his and his father offered him a wan smile. "Perhaps, but I could've been a better brother."

Leo touched his father's arm. "No, you're a good man, a wonderful King, and a better father and brother than either Alwyn or I deserve." Guilt was crushing as he thought of all the times he'd shunned his father's company or conversation out of a misplaced sense of loyalty to his mother.

Alfred palmed his cheek a look of love on his face, reserved only for a child and parent. "You're the greatest gift of my life. I'm proud to call you son and one day I hope to call Bebe daughter. You love her. No matter how this started, it's real."

Leo looked away, emotion clogging his throat as he tried to fight it. He didn't show his emotions often, locking them away was safer, but he found himself wanting to share this. "I do love her. It's fast but the first time I saw her, I knew. Deep in my gut, I knew she was mine."

"Then we'll get her back and give you the chance to tell her that."

The quiet in the room was so at odds with what was happening in the palace dungeon below and the nightmare that Bebe could be facing right this very moment. It was like a normal day, with no urgency, just a father and son.

Leo stood, a sense that he needed to do something to fix this pressing on him. Helplessness wasn't an emotion he could tolerate. Action was his comfort zone, not politics and waiting around. This had always been the hardest part of any mission for him. Waiting for intelligence to be gathered before they could go out and operate.

He paced under the watchful eye of his father, waiting for news, looking out at the blue vista, the sun high in the morning sky.

He didn't wait long before the door opened, and Brody James walked inside.

Leo spun toward him and levelled him with a cold glare. "If you know anything, now is the time to tell me before you join Wojcik downstairs with Roz and her team."

Brody James looked to the King but didn't say anything about the breach in protocol. "I have someone at the marina who saw her being pushed onto a yacht late yesterday afternoon. We have a satellite tracking it right now."

Leo got up in Brody's face, his feet planted wide, his fist clenching with anger that the CIA officer had let this happen when he could've told someone sooner. Could've stopped it from happening. "You bastard. You let them take her as bait."

"We need The Collector."

Leo was seconds from punching James out when Roz stepped in behind Brody James, followed by Kanan, Alex, and Evelyn.

"They don't know who The Collector is. None of them have met him or have even spoken to him."

Brody placed his hands on his hips and squared up to Roz, making Kanan growl and move to block him. "How do you know he isn't lying?"

Roz put a hand on her husband's chest and smiled at him, and it completely transformed her into a different woman. "It's fine, K." Looking back to the CIA officer she glared at him, her eyes flinty. "Mr Wojcik barely had the capacity to say his own name, so he wasn't going to waste his breath lying to me. Neither he nor Atticus have met or spoken to The Collector. I do, however, have the details of the auction and the bid item they're going after."

"And?" Leo didn't give a fuck about any of that right now. There would be time later when he had Bebe back where she belonged beside him to go over the other details. "What about Bebe? Does he know where she's being held?"

Roz glanced at him. "She's a mile out to sea on a yacht called *The Triumph*."

Leo cocked his head to Brody James, accepting he'd told the truth. "We need to board that yacht. Right the fuck now."

"It will blow our cover."

The spook was pissing him off, now. "There's no we. You're not a part of this and are trespassing on foreign soil. So I suggest you shut the fuck up or you'll be joining Wojcik in the dungeon."

James leaned toward him, chest out as if he was ready to go to war and wouldn't back down. Leo stood his ground. He had more skin in the game than anyone else in this room.

"This is a matter of national security, not some romance novel you're playing out here, Prince."

James was asking for a punch in the face and Leo was happy to supply it. His fist shot out and caught the man in the jaw. Brody charged at him with a growl and took him to the ground, his back hitting the edge of the antique coffee table and smashing the fine wood with his weight.

Rolling, Leo held his hand to James' throat as he let fly with a punch to the nose. Twice more he laid into him before the bastard flipped him and got the advantage. Leo went to block a strike when James was hauled off him by Alex and Kanan.

"Enough!"

Kanan helped him from the ground as the two men heaved in a breath from the exertion. His lip was bleeding, and he wiped the blood with the back of his hand before locking eyes with the man who'd let Bebe be taken as bait and was still trying to use her for his own gain.

"You two, calm the hell down." Roz glanced at the King. "If I may?"

His father nodded and held out his hand for her to take the floor.

"This is what's going to happen. Alex and Evelyn will stay here and guard the King because we have no idea if The Collector has eyes here we don't know about. Leo, K, and I will take a boat as close as we can to the Triumph and board the yacht. James, you can come if you're prepared to follow orders. If not, you stay here."

"You can't trust him," Leo shot out, no sympathy for the man as he held a hanky to his bloody nose. If he'd had his way, he'd have done a fuck of a lot more damage.

"If he goes off-book, I'll shoot him myself." Roz glanced at James who nodded his understanding. "Good, when we have Bebe back safe and Atticus secured, we'll do what we can to keep the auction on track and under our control. Mercy and the others need more time to dig in on their own situations. I understand we want The Collector, but this won't be a short operation. We need to play smart, not fast."

Leo agreed, and if he wasn't so invested personally would've thought the same thing. But right now, all he could think about was Bebe. He knew she was capable and smart, strong and resilient but she was also human, and humans got hurt and felt pain and he could hardly bear it. "Fine."

"Where is your armoury?"

"I'll show you."

Leo led the way toward the armoury, the palace deserted except for a few members of staff cleaning the wood on the large double banister.

Kanan walked beside him shoulder to shoulder, Alex on his other side. "I get it, man. Loving a woman like the ones we do is tough. Having them in danger, no matter the fact they could outgun, outfight, and outmanoeuvre us, goes against every instinct we have as protectors. Let me say this from experience though. If you love Bebe like I suspect you do, then don't crowd her. Let her be proud of who she's fought to be and don't stifle her. She won't thank you for it."

"What if I can't accept that?"

They stopped at the door to the armoury and Alex lifted a hand to scratch at the back of his neck. "Then you need to let her go. You love all of her or walk away, man, because it will poison what you have if you force her into a box she doesn't fit into."

Leo nodded knowing he and Bebe had a lot to discuss. "Let's get her back so we can decide together."

Roz patted his shoulder. "Now you're talking."

Twenty-Three

Bebe jumped as the sound of shouting came from outside her cabin door. It was pitch dark outside, the afternoon light having faded hours ago. The gentle bobbing of the boat had her body lulled into an almost dream state until the sounds of gunfire followed the shouting.

Sitting up, she abandoned the façade of still being bound and readied herself to strike whoever came into the room next. Whoever was firing on the yacht would give her an advantage, whether they were here for her or not.

Opening the door a pinch, she peeked out and saw a man from earlier racing away from her. Stepping out of the room, she ran on bare feet toward the bow where she knew the bridge was located. If she was Atticus, that was where she'd be with the yacht under attack.

Rounding the corner, she came face to face with Denis. He sneered, lifting his gun. Bebe didn't think, just reacted. Dropping low, she struck out with a blow to the groin. He screamed, losing his grip on the gun. It fell just out of her reach but she didn't need it.

Denis grabbed her, using his strength to try and hold her arms at her sides and get control of her. In such a small space it was a mistake he'd regret. Using her feet, she placed them on the railing and pushed off, sending them both flying backwards.

Denis fell and she jumped up, delivering a kick to the head with the heel of her foot, which knocked him out. Dragging his prone body into the nearest cabin, she thanked her lucky stars that it was empty. Quickly securing him, she lifted her head, the smell of burning tickling her senses.

The yacht was on fire.

Heading out, she grabbed the gun from the floor, checked the clip, and kept moving. Coming to the bottom of the stairs that led to the bridge, she listened, hearing gunfire coming from the aft of the yacht, the engines a low hum beneath the fight going on.

The smell of smoke was thicker here, the air a fuzzy film over her eyes making her cough. Lifting an arm over her mouth, she tried to control her breaths as she coughed again. A sound from behind her had her spinning and levelling the weapon at a large dark figure hurrying her way.

"Bebe."

She almost sagged with relief at hearing his voice. "Leo."

He moved to her, grasping her face, and pulling her close for a short, heated kiss before letting her go. "Are you okay?"

"Yes."

"We need to go. The engine room is on fire."

"Atticus is behind this. We need to find him."

"Roz and Kanan have him on the top deck. We're waiting for the helo to extract us."

A thousand questions were going through her mind, but she hushed them all, knowing now wasn't the time. "Let's go."

Leo took her hand and they ran back onto the deck, following the curve of the boat. A man stepped out, firing a gun, and Leo took him down before she could. He fell and she jumped over his body, recognising him as the man from Proenia.

An explosion rocked the boat beneath her feet, and she reached for Leo as they were both thrown into the cold darkness of the ocean. Their hands lost contact as the water swallowed them up.

Bebe felt the shock of the cold water tighten her chest and fought the urge to try and take a breath. The silence of the inky blackness made it disorientating as she swam for the surface. Her head broke free, and she dragged in deep lungsful of air, her head swivelling as she looked for Leo. Treading water, she spun in a full circle looking for him and spotted him not ten feet away, floating and lifeless.

"Leo." Her scream felt muted under the sounds of the yacht burning. The blaze took hold as a helo came into view above her, the light casting around her and allowing her to swim to Leo with ease.

Blood covered his head and face, and she placed an ear to his chest to hear the beautiful sound of his heart beating steadily. Relief flooded her that he was breathing but they needed to get out of this water before the yacht blew.

A rope fell to the side of her, and she looked up to see a man descending the line. As he landed in the water beside her, she recognised Mitch and could've cried with relief.

"Here, help me get this on him so I can get you both winched up."

The wind blew her hair across her face as she used numb fingers to wrap the loops of the rope around Leo before clipping herself to him and then Mitch. Her friend gave the thumbs up, and they began to lift from the water, the view of the burning boat that much more terrifying seeing it from above.

As Waggs leaned out to haul them into the helo, she fell to her knees beside Leo as he coughed and looked like he was coming around. "Leo."

"Bebe."

"I'm here."

Her hand brushed his forehead as Waggs checked him over; the Eidolon team were all fully qualified in field medicine because of the work they did for the Queen. Zenobi and Eidolon worked some missions together, but this hadn't been the original plan for this operation. At least not to her knowledge. She had no clue why they were there and had no energy to ask right now. She was just grateful they were.

"Looks like a concussion, but he seems fine. Maybe a few bruises."

Her heart finally began to steady at the news Leo was okay. "Thank God."

"Let me check you out."

Bebe attempted to brush off the concern with a wave of her hand. "I'm fine."

Leo squeezed her knee and groaned as he moved to sit up.

Bebe pushed him back down. "You stay down. You must have hit your head pretty hard if it knocked you out."

"Let him check you over."

"Fine."

Bebe knew better than to argue with Leo or her friend, allowing him to check her over as she kept a very close eye on the man next to her.

"You should get an x-ray on those ribs to rule out a break, but I suspect it's just bruising."

Bebe had no intention of wasting her time on an x-ray when she trusted Waggs when he said it was just bruising.

"Don't worry, I'll make sure she does."

Bebe attempted to glare at Leo, but it fell flat when he brought her palm to his lips and kissed her tenderly, making her belly turn to goo.

Offering him a gentle smile, she knew she needed to tell him how she felt. This had stopped being a pretend relationship days ago. If she was honest, she wasn't sure it ever had been. It was a blow from left field, but Cupid had hit her right in the heart when she met Prince León of Soflye. Whether he felt the same she didn't dare guess, but she had to lay her truth on him and let the chips fall because she couldn't live her life with what-ifs. She'd spent years doing that very thing and it had got her nowhere fast.

Mitch threw the rope ladder down and the helo quickly filled with Roz, Kanan, who was carrying a bound and gagged Atticus over his shoulder, and finally Brody James. Bebe leaned her head back against the metal of the helo as Gunner flew them out of there and back to dry land. She had so many questions but right now all she needed was a few minutes alone with the man she loved.

Twenty-Four

A HAND CURLED OVER HER BREAST AS THE WARM WATER CASCADED over her skin. Bebe leaned back into hard muscle and let Leo take her lips in a kiss that was languorous and full of passion. Sliding a hand down the flat of her belly, his fingers found her wet sex. Lifting her arm, Bebe wrapped it around his neck, ignoring the pinch of pain in her ribs. This was what she needed, this connection with him to restore the balance of the last twenty-four hours of hell.

The emotion they shared, the intimacy of having him inside her made her soften against the steely strength of her feelings for him. Releasing her, Leo spun her to face him, gently lifting her so her legs wrapped around his hips, his hard length rubbing against her clit until she was delirious with need for him.

"I thought I'd lost you."

His words, whispered against her breast as he lavished her with attention, went straight to her heart. His mouth and hands worked over her skin with fervour as if the drive to touch every inch of her consumed him.

"You won't lose me, Leo. Not if you want me." The stark honesty she offered him made her pulse beat faster.

"I want to make love to you with nothing between us, but only if you want that."

Bebe was lost in a haze of lust, her body screaming at her to beg him to fill her. To claim a part of her body like he had her heart. "I'm not protected."

She knew now wasn't the time to explain her crusade to get pregnant alone and she hated that she had to stop him from something they both craved. If and when they ever got to that point, it would be by his choice too, not a moment of passion that might leave him with regrets. She cared too deeply to ever trap him and take away his choices.

He kissed her upturned mouth, slanting his head and flicking his tongue against hers as he claimed her. That was the only way to describe it, a claiming. Opening the shower door, he walked with her body still wrapped around his to the bed they'd shared and lowered her to the soft duvet.

Her eyes were heavy with lust and love as she watched him reach into the drawer by his bed and retrieve a condom. He stroked his length with a firm grip, teasing her as he held her eyes. Her body burned with the need for him, the ache in her pussy consuming her as she ran her hand down over her sensitive nipples, his gaze hot as he watched her. Her fingertips pressed her clit, and she heaved out a sigh of pleasure before her hand was brushed away and he was there.

Her hands clutched his shoulders as he eased between her thighs, his cock brushing against her clit and making her moan.

"I love you, Bebe. I love you so damn much."

She had no time to react or reply before he was pushing into her body, every inch of him penetrating her soul. They kissed, neither of them seeming to be able to get enough as the pressure inside her built. Her legs began to quiver as his pelvis stimulated her aching clit, his cock rubbing along that secret place inside her, with every stroke.

Leo held himself on one elbow as he lifted her leg higher, driving into her harder as his restraint began to snap. Her hands reached for his biceps as she felt the climax build, her body shaking as she crested the brow of what she knew would be a life-altering orgasm.

Leo slammed into her with a roar as her body shattered and she screamed out in pleasure. The swell of his cock inside her as he came only added to the intensity of the feelings. Bebe's heart rate slowed as her legs fell slack on either side of his hips, his body shivering as the last few pumps of his hips inside her left him spent.

Leo's body sagged against her, but he held his weight off her as he rolled them, so she was lying across his body. It took a few moments for them to get their breathing under control before he kissed her head and rose to deal with the condom.

Bebe watched his tight, muscular ass as he walked away and felt the flicker of desire surge again. This man had turned her into a sex addict, but more than that, he'd stolen her heart. Her mind went to the words he'd spoken, and her belly flipped with the tiniest grain of hope.

As he exited the bathroom, she examined the cut above his brow that Waggs had taped before he and Mitch had left. Eidolon were only there to offer support, and according to the brief conversation she'd had with Roz, had men stationed close to the members of her team in the event they needed an assist like she'd done. A smidgen of guilt washed over her as she thought of her friends and what they might be dealing with while she was falling in love.

Her happiness had always left her feeling like she didn't deserve it. She knew it was a throwback to her childhood and the demons she was yet to fully deal with. Perhaps she should speak to someone like Peyton Lawson, the PTSD councillor that Eidolon used. Maybe she'd be able to help her move on from her less than stellar beginnings in life and get over the guilt she felt when the other therapist she'd seen hadn't.

Leo put a knee in the bed and crawled closer to her, dragging her across his body like a blanket, and pulling her from the dark thoughts. Resting her cheek against his heart, Bebe laid a hand over his abdomen as he put a hand over the top, his thumb stroking over her skin in small relaxing circles.

Taking a leap, she uttered the words she hadn't said to anyone since her sister died. "I love you too."

A rush of air seemed to leave his chest as he rolled her to her back and loomed over her with a grin. "Thank fuck."

Bebe laughed at the look on his face, feeling the joy in her heart ease the weight she'd been carrying for so long. "That's not very princely language, Leo."

"I don't care. I was so worried you wouldn't feel the same."

Bebe touched her fingertips to his lips, feeling the softness as he kissed them, and then held her hand against his heart. "I do, I think I have from the start. I didn't expect to fall in love at first sight. I wasn't even sure I still believed it existed for me, yet here we are."

"I felt the same. It was like being drugged or bewitched in some way. I couldn't keep my hands off you and then you revealed more of yourself with every conversation, and I fell in love with every part of you."

Bebe frowned. "I still don't see how this can work, Leo. You're a Crown Prince and I'm an assassin."

"You're a warrior. The world needs more people like you. And if that's what you want to do, I'll support you."

"You would?"

"I've seen how good you are, Bebe. We need people like you to defend against evil and stand up for the innocent, and if I get to be by your side then I'm one lucky bastard. I can't say it won't take restraint not to jump in and rescue you, but that has nothing to do with your ability and everything to do with me not being able to bear it if something happened to you."

Bebe stroked his stubble roughened cheek in awe that this man could love her and offer her everything she'd ever wanted. A niggle of fear worked its way in as she waited for the other shoe to drop and all of this to be taken away from her.

Caution made her ask. "You'd give this up?"

She saw the pain it caused him to say it, but he did. "I'd give everything up for you."

Bebe shook her head, knowing she'd never make him walk away from his birthright, not when he was born to lead. "I'd never ask it. This is your legacy, your life."

"You're not asking."

"I know but I respect your father and he needs you. I think I'd like to find a compromise."

Bebe bit her lip and Leo got distracted, his eyes becoming hooded, his cock twitching against her thigh. Lust coursed through her veins, and she hoped it would always be that way between them. Wriggling, she laughed at the growl that vibrated through his chest as his hands wandered over her skin.

"Behave a second."

He buried his head in her neck. "I can't. You consume me."

"I have to tell you something."

He must have heard the serious note in her tone because he raised his head, worried eyes finding hers. "What is it?"

Bebe saw the look of love she was still in awe of on his face as he waited for her to continue, not rushing her as she tried to find the words.

Taking a deep breath, she went for it. "Before I met you, I'd decided I wanted a family. I'd had no luck with love, but I had this urge to make a family. Perhaps I was trying to create what I never had, but I had good friends, so I decided to go it alone. For the last year or so I've been undergoing IVF. The last two attempts failed but I have the funds to continue, and I'm going to do so."

Leo released her and sat up, leaving her feeling cold at the loss of his touch. Fear at the rejection she guessed was coming like a knife in her gut. He pushed his hair back from his face and her mouth watered at the sight of his biceps bunching. Even as she was paralysed with doubt, she still wanted him.

"I hate your parents for treating you as they did. They should be whipped for ever making you believe you'd failed. You were innocent and alone and my heart breaks for that little girl who felt her only choice was to run." He angled his body toward her, taking her hands in his and watching her reactions. A tiny flicker of hope worked its way to the surface as he spoke with such vehement defence of the child she'd been.

His eyes on hers, she felt like she was drowning in the stormy green depths that changed colour with the emotion he was feeling.

"But I believe everything happens for a reason. Without you running away, you'd never have met Roz or joined Zenobi. If not for that, we'd never have met, and I'd never have known there was a woman out there who understood me. Who could open her palm and have me gladly laying my heart in it. Don't do IVF, Bebe. Have a child with me. Let's do this together."

Bebe thought her heart might pound out of her chest at his words. Tears pricked her eyelids, and she felt her throat choke with emotion. "You want to have a baby with me?"

"I want it all. I want you beside me one day as I sit on the throne as King. Be my Queen, Bebe."

Her voice wobbled as she let the tears fall. "What about your dad?"

"He loves you. He told me he hoped to call you daughter one day."

Tears dripped from her face onto their joined hands, as Leo released her to swipe his thumbs over her cheeks to clear them, love clear as a crystal blue sea on his face. "Okay, yes. Yes, please."

Leo pulled her in for a kiss full of promise, and love, the future in front of them marred by only one thing. "First, we have a job to do."

"Then let's get it done so we can get on with our life together."

As she jumped from the bed, with renewed energy, Leo captured her for a toe-curling kiss, that had her wanting to ignore the threats they still faced and fall back into bed with him. "I love you, Bebe."

"I love you too. Now, let's go join the team and see what the next move is."

Twenty-Five

His hand firmly in hers, Leo walked tall as they headed for the King's private quarters. His father had taken control and designated his rooms that were clear of any bugs or cameras as mission control for the foreseeable future. To say he felt ten feet tall despite the pounding headache from the header he'd taken off the yacht would be an understatement.

When they'd been blown from the yacht by the explosion, he'd seen his life flash before him. Not the one he'd already lived but the one he could've had with the woman he loved if only he was brave enough to grasp it with both hands and claim it.

Regret had been the last emotion he felt before he'd been lights out and he never intended to live his life that way again. When he died, God willing at least fifty years from now, he'd do it looking back at a life full of love and not a single regret in sight. Laying his heart on the line after that had been an easy decision. Kanan had warned him to walk away if he couldn't accept who Bebe really was, and it had made him wonder if he could be the man to let his woman face danger.

As he saw her covered in dirt and smoke, having faced the dangers she had, and still fight to save him, he knew he'd be a fool to walk away from a woman like her because of his own fears. Asking her to take a chance on him was a risk for her, but he hadn't lied when he said he wanted it all and he'd spend every day trying to be worthy of her. The thought of a family with her filled him with so much warmth he wanted to shout it from the rooftops.

He stopped her before they went into the King's quarters. "Just so you know, that wasn't a proposal back there. When I propose, you'll know about it."

Her lips tipped into a smile, making his heart beat faster and he gave in to the need to kiss her, wondering how he'd ever managed to curb it or if he even cared to. He released her and love filled him for this warrior.

"I look forward to it."

The door opened and Roz stood smirking at them before she stepped back. "Sorry to interrupt but we have a plan we'd like to run by you both."

He and Bebe swept inside, and he let her hand go, as she began speaking with Roz and Evelyn, to move to his father. The King had changed and was now wearing a different two-piece suit, this one darker and perhaps mirroring his feelings. Today must have been hard for him, and Leo wondered if it might be a good idea to get him checked by a doctor.

"Father, how are you feeling?"

"I'm fine, son. You're the one who got the bump on the head."

Leo's hand went to the cut in his hairline which had knocked him out and he touched it lightly, feeling the small lump. Waggs, who he'd been determined to dislike for purely selfish reasons, had turned out to be a great guy. He'd shown him pictures of his wife and son, the love evident for anyone to witness. "I'm fine, I have a thick head."

Leo followed his father's line of sight and saw Bebe hugging Evelyn, her expression so open and alive, it was hard for him to tolerate even this small space between them.

"She looks happy and well despite what she's been through."

Leo shoved his hands in his pockets as he studied the interaction between the women. There was no doubt about the intense bond between them. The affection was clear as day to see, and from Alex and Kanan too. They were a family; one she'd built for herself from the ashes of her childhood.

"We talked and she's a little banged up, but she's a fighter."

His father turned his focus back to him, his smile wide. "Does this mean I might get a daughter one day?"

Leo placed his arm around his father's shoulder in a rare display of affection. "Perhaps even a grandchild or two one day."

Joy wreathed his father's face as he hugged him. "Oh, you've no idea how happy this makes me."

Leo didn't say but he suspected he might.

"Sorry to interrupt but can we discuss the next steps?"

Bebe moved to his side, and he pulled her close to his hip, her arm going around his back and resting on his hip.

The King motioned toward his private dining area where they'd eaten just a few days ago and they followed. "Of course. Please sit."

Leo bent to whisper in Bebe's ear. "My father is over the moon we talked and worked things out."

"I adore your father."

Leo looked up at the man who'd raised him and who was now leading a country from a nightmare he'd only just learned about and felt a wealth of pride. He was so lucky to have a parent such as his father, even when he hadn't deserved or appreciated it. "Me too."

Seated beside the King and Bebe, Leo waited for Roz to begin.

"As you know, the first auction triggers the second, in a series of five. I know from communications with Mercy that she hasn't found the buyer in Proenia yet. So, we need our auction here to go ahead. Atticus has given us nothing of worth. It seems he never spoke with The Collector and has no idea of their identity. What works in our favour is that The Collector doesn't know Atticus's identity either."

Leo leaned forward on the table, his elbows resting on the polished wood. "How did he manage to get access to the auction then? Surely The Collector would be cautious and would vet any potential buyers to make sure it wasn't a set-up?"

"Yes, that's true. From what Atticus said, bringing Alwyn and Alain on board, making them the scapegoats, and blowing up *The Grace* was his proof."

Leo frowned not convinced by that. Anyone could've staged those things.

Roz cocked her head to the left. "I can see you're not convinced."

Leo shrugged. "Both those things are easily staged."

"True but handing over the Tanzanite Tears is further proof. No government or Monarch would freely hand over the gemstone with that kind of value."

"So, handing over the gem before the auction is the final demand for entry?" Bebe asked.

"According to Atticus, yes."

Leo shook his head, steepling his fingers. "How can we trust him?"

Kanan smirked. "Believe me, Atticus is a pretentious asshole with no morals but a hardened criminal he's not. Let's just say he gave it up easily and he was telling the truth."

Leo had forgotten while he was making love to Bebe these people were interrogating Atticus. He should feel a modicum of sympathy for the man, but the second he'd put Bebe in danger any hope of forgiveness from Leo was long gone.

He trusted these people. He knew tier-one operators. being one himself, and he easily recognised the skills they had at reading people. So if they trusted Atticus was telling the truth, then he would too.

"We have Atticus's phone where the details of the auction will be sent. I propose we have someone pose as Atticus and enter the auction. We buy the program Atticus was after and kill two birds with one stone by getting dangerous software out of the hands of a maniac and triggering the second auction, buying Mercy and the others some time."

Bebe rubbed her hands along her thighs, momentarily distracting him from the conversation, before she spoke. "Won't that mean handing over the gemstone?"

Roz paused and her eyes came to him and then the King. "Yes. Of course we'd get it back for you once The Collector is taken down."

Leo looked to his father, a silent conversation going on between them as he nodded.

The King pinned Roz with the look of a leader willing to do anything to keep his people safe. "I'm willing to do this. I trust you to deliver it back safely."

Bebe touched his thigh, making him look down at her. "Thank you."

"Of course."

"Now, the next obstacle is the auction. They're expecting a man. I could send either Alex or Kanan in."

"No, I'll do it." Leo knew he needed to end his country's part in it.

"No." Bebe and the King exclaimed at the same time.

Ignoring his parent, he addressed the woman he loved. "Bebe, this is my country. I need to extract us from this mess my family has made. Plus, I do resemble Atticus in height and build, so if for some reason Atticus has been identified as the buyer, I can hopefully pass myself off as him."

"And if you can't? They'll kill you, Leo."

"Bebe is right, son. Listen to her."

"Not to pick sides, but Prince León is right. He's our best bet for this, and I'd rather not take a chance our cover gets completely blown. With four other girls out in the field with similar cover stories, we don't want to tip The Collector off that we're in any way on to him. It will completely compromise them and leave them wide open."

Bebe crossed her arms over her chest, and he knew he had to let her come around to this idea on her own.

Blowing out a breath, she sighed. "Fine, but I'm going with him."

"We can handle that." Roz motioned to herself, Kanan, Evelyn, and Alex.

Bebe stood her ground. "It's not a request, Roz. He goes, so do I."

Leo desperately wanted to go all alpha and demand she stay put, safe in the Palace, but he knew he couldn't clip her wings like that. "She should come. I trust her to have my back."

Roz lifted her perfectly arched brow and crossed her arms before she smiled, and he wondered if he'd just passed some imaginary test. "You'll do."

Bebe shook her head in exasperation and grinned. "Looks like we're heading to Proenia."

Twenty-Six

Proenia was very different to Soflye. Where Soflye was luxurious, with wealthy and beautifully sculpted models and actors around every corner, Proenia was magical. The weather was warm, the sun not as powerful, and Bebe was glad for the reprieve. They drove to the safehouse Roz had procured along narrow streets, with high buildings on either side. Some had the national flag of Proenia hanging proudly from the window and some had colourful bunting strung from one house to the other in a diagonal direction. It reminded her of some of the Italian villages she'd visited.

Sitting beside Leo in the back of the blacked-out jeep, she felt the comfort of his presence even as her belly flipped with nerves over the upcoming auction that night. A week had seemed like enough time to strategize every eventuality, but she knew there would never be enough time to consider every scenario when a maniac was at the helm, and that was exactly what The Collector was.

Kanan drove, Roz beside him, and she was glad to have her friends there as backup for this mission. Alex and Evelyn were two cars behind, making sure they didn't have a tail, as a further precaution. The King had handed over the Tanzanite Tears to her and told her to keep his son safe.

The tenderness and love in his voice, coupled with his belief in her to do as he'd asked, had brought tears to her eyes. The kiss on the head he'd given her as he wished her a safe trip, gave her heart the strength to do what she knew she had to do.

Brody James had proved useful when he'd shown up later that night after the details of how they'd approach the auction were ironed out. Using nanotechnology he'd given them, they were able to attach it to the gemstone so it could be tracked. That might give them the lead they needed to find The Collector because right now, they had nothing of value.

Roz had vetoed Brody's plan to be involved in the op, saying he could be in the van close by with Alex and Evelyn and watch, but no involvement. Bebe knew he hadn't liked that but given he wasn't supposed to be there, he'd taken it. She still didn't trust the spook, but he'd proven at least some of his words were true when he'd helped them rescue her from the yacht.

Leo had yet to forgive him for allowing her to be taken, but he hadn't broken anything else on the man since his nose and that was a bonus.

Stopping outside a stone building nestled into the heart of the quiet street, she glanced around before exiting the car, finding nothing of note to put her on guard or further on edge. Leo held his hand out for her to proceed him as Roz opened the door.

The space was small, with the front door opening directly into the living room. A small kitchen was directly behind and a staircase leading up to the second floor on her left. The décor was simple but clean with a touch of Italian chic giving the place a homey feel.

"Why don't you two get some sleep? I know none of us have slept in days."

Roz motioned toward the upstairs as she began setting up her laptop on the kitchen table. Most likely so she could work or face time with her kids. She knew the separation from them must be hard. As a woman so focused on saving the world, Roz had almost lost her chance at love, but Kanan had never given up on them. His love for her had begun over fifteen years before when he'd saved Roz from a cruel man who'd broken her in ways that were almost unimaginable.

"Are you sure you don't need me to stay and help out?"

Roz gave her a kind smile, one of the rare times she showed her caring side. "Go, we're going to speak to the kids and get some shut-eye. Alex and Evelyn are on overwatch until we leave for the auction."

"Okay."

Roz turned to the screen as Kanan stepped up behind her to lay his hand on his wife's nape, an easy affectionate move, which showed how far they'd come.

"Roz?"

Her cool blue eyes met Bebe. "Yes?"

"Thank you for coming."

A small twitch of her lips was her only response, and it was enough. Leo took her hand, and they headed upstairs to find a double bed waiting in the first bedroom they came to. "This place is so pretty."

Leo placed their bags, one filled with clothes for the auction, the other with weapons and her wigs and disguise make-up inside. She was going as Chelsea tonight. Not something she relished but added a further layer of deceit to back up their claims. The woman herself was still being held without charge as was the law for treason in Soflye. They had sixty days to charge her, and Bebe knew it would never get that far. The shallow woman would plead guilty and ask for an incapacity plea.

Not wanting to think of her anymore, she joined Leo by the window, the shutters obscuring them from view while still letting in the sights below. Her hand on his back, he turned to her, his eyes going to her mouth and desire bloomed between her legs.

"Have you been here before?"

"A long time ago, yes. Prince Luca Buccio and I spent a summer at the same prep school. He's a good guy. I find it difficult to believe he'd be involved with any of this. But then again, I haven't seen him in a long time, and I didn't see what was right in front of my face, so who knows."

"If anyone can get to the truth, it's Mercy."

"You worry about her?"

She wasn't usually such an open book, but it seemed Leo could read her easily. "She went through something beyond awful while doing this job and it took her a long time to recover. If you can really recover from what happened to her. She has this vulnerability about her now that makes us all very protective."

"I'm sorry to hear that."

"Yeah, me too."

Leo cupped her cheeks and brought his lips to hers as she basked in the feel of his mouth on hers. It wasn't a wild, passionate kiss, but a gentle heat filled with love and compassion.

Lifting his head, he brushed her hair back from her neck. "We should get a few hours' rest. Tonight will be crazy and we need to be sharp."

"Thanks for having my back when I wanted to come. I'm not sure Roz would've backed down otherwise."

Leo sat on the bed and pulled her down until she was cradled with her back to his front, his arms tight around her body holding her close. "I think it was a test from Roz to see if I'd support you and I do. I always will."

A sigh of contentment flowed through her, and she wished they had the luxury of getting undressed and allowing their skin to touch, but they had to be ready in case there was an attack. "Leo?"

"Yes, my love?"

"If something goes wrong...."

His hand lifted to turn her head toward him. "Nothing will go wrong."

"But if it does...."

"No, I won't accept that. We're going to go in, buy that bloody program, and get ourselves out of there and back home."

She would've argued but he kissed her, and she lost her train of thought.

"Now get some rest."

"Okay."

She wanted to fight it, but the last few days had dragged every ounce of energy reserves she had out of her and now she was on empty. To ensure she was at her best she needed to recharge so she could have her man's back.

Three hours later, she woke when a tap on the door had her sitting up straight.

"Hey, we need you downstairs."

Groggy from sleep, Bebe watched Leo sit up looking much the same way.

"We'll be down in a few minutes, Roz." Rubbing her hands down her face, she blinked a few times and then turned to León. "You ready?"

"As I'll ever be." He kissed her slowly, taking her mouth in a languid dance before he moved back, muttering, 'like a drug' as he headed to the small bathroom.

Bebe laughed and headed down the stairs, finding fresh coffee and turkey, brie, and pear sandwiches laid out on the table.

Her belly rumbled and Kanan smirked. "Help yourself. I made enough for everyone."

Bebe dug in, sitting on the kitchen chair, her leg tucked beneath her as she waited for news.

"You know these are my favourite." Bebe sighed as she took a bite, realising she hadn't eaten since yesterday morning. Leo walked in and came straight to her, sitting beside her and stealing her coffee.

"Hey."

He smirked and her belly fluttered with nerves and lust and all the delicious things associated with new love.

"Here," Kanan passed Leo a mug and a plate so he could help himself to a sandwich, "before she decides to bury your body somewhere cold for stealing the goods."

"Nah, she loves me, she'd never."

Reaching out, he caressed her calf and she winked at him.

"Your funeral, man."

Kanan disappeared back into the kitchen and Leo helped himself to a sandwich, inspecting the content before taking a cautious bite.

"What?"

"Pear in a sandwich is weird."

Bebe pursed her lips and shook her head. "I guess it was fun while it lasted, but I can't be with a man who doesn't appreciate the culinary genius of a turkey, brie, and pear sandwich."

"Is that so?"

"Mmhmm." She inclined her head toward him a look of fake sadness on her face.

Leo chewed the mouthful he had and swallowed before he placed it on the plate before him. "I guess I can see the appeal."

Having finished her own, she sat forward and draped her arms over his shoulders, leaning close to his face. "Good because I really like you."

"Yeah?"

"Yup."

"Good."

Roz swept into the room, looking as wide awake and gorgeous as ever. "Sorry to break up this love fest, but I have the details of the auction."

Bebe sat forward, dropping her feet to the floor, the atmosphere in the room turning serious. "Tell me."

"It will be held at the sight of the old Rose Garden Psychiatric Hospital. At eleven tonight. As we expected the dress code is evening wear."

"A psych hospital? That's not creepy at all." Bebe stood, energy buzzing through her veins now the game was on, yet the nerves she experienced knowing Leo would be there were new. "What else?" She paced the small space, tapping her hands together as adrenalin began to ooze into her bloodstream.

"We have to deposit five million dollars into an account before the auction starts to ensure no payments fall through after the bid ends."

Bebe eyed Roz. "And to make sure it isn't a sting. No government is going to risk that kind of money."

"Exactly, but we can."

"What else? Because I know there's something."

"Pax found evidence that might link this auction to one five years ago. It wasn't traced to The Collector back then, but it now looks like it might have been. Do you remember when the CIA asked for help because three of their black sites had been compromised and they suspected an insider was leaking the details?"

Bebe's jaw tightened. "Yes, the one where Laverne nearly got killed by a damn missile strike from a rogue officer."

"Yes. Well, it looks like the officer in question wasn't just leaking information, he was giving the details to The Collector who then auctioned them. Unfortunately, that officer died before he could be questioned, which in itself is suspect."

"How does it link to The Collector?" Bebe glanced at Leo who was leaning forward, elbows on his knees.

"They were later auctioned off. That was how we managed to find the terror group who bought them. What we didn't know until Pax checked was that the terror group used two panels from the Amber Room as payment to enter."

Bebe gaped at Roz. "Are you kidding me? The Amber Room, commissioned by King Frederick I of Prussia and lost after the second world war?"

"One and the same."

"How do we know?"

"Two years ago, the terror cell was caught by a drone strike but one of the leaders survived. He told the CIA in exchange for a lighter sentence."

Bebe paused her pacing and glared at Roz. "Tell me he didn't get it?"

Roz shook her head. "No, he was killed in a car accident on his way to a black site holding facility."

Leo rolled his eyes. "Convenient."

"Exactly."

Bebe chewed a nail as a thought ping-ponged around her brain, looking for something tangible to hold onto.

Leo stood and came to her, pulling the nail she hadn't realised she was chewing from her lips. "What is it?"

Her eyes came to him in triumph. "I think The Collector is a woman!"

Roz stepped past Kanan who was watching them all with an intense focus only former spooks had. "What makes you say that?"

"Think about it. Every item is not only collectable but it's beautiful in a way men don't always desire. If The Collector was purely after a rare item, you might see other things. I bet if you check back to all the items linked to The Collector, you'll find they're gems, art, jewels, and the like."

Roz nodded. "I'll get Pax on it right away and have her reach out to her contacts too."

Roz gripped her hands and smiled. "This is good work, Bebe. I think you're onto something here. It could change the way we hunt this person down. The psychology of a woman is so different from a man. Luckily for us, we have women hunting her."

"If I'm right."

Leo squeezed her hip, bringing her focus to him. "You are, I can feel it."

Roz glanced at her watch. "You two need to get ready and I need to share what we have with the others."

Bebe nodded, for the first time since this mission began feeling that perhaps they were making some headway.

Twenty-Seven

Leo took a step back when Bebe entered the room. Her blonde wig styled in loose waves mimicked Chelsea so much it was disconcerting. Her beautiful brown eyes which he loved were now blue from contacts. She wore a long navy gown with a sequined bodice revealing the creamy tops of her breasts, the satin skirt fitted to her hips with a split up the side. He guessed it was in case she needed to move quickly. She had navy satin heels on her feet which, he was sure after seeing her array of weapons, probably had a blade in the heel. She was breathtaking, and yet, he hated it. He wanted her, not this horrible facsimile of a woman he now hated.

"I know it's hard, but this will be over soon. I promise no more dressing up. Unless you want me to, that is." She winked and he saw his Bebe, hidden inside the disguise, her full lips a deep berry red. She was trying to distract him, and it was working.

He led her to the long limousine that would drive them to the venue and held her hand as she stepped inside. Leo followed and caught Kanan's eye in the mirror. He'd be driving them while Roz, Alex, Evelyn, and Brody set up as close as they could get to the psych hospital.

There was a myriad of things that could go wrong. They had no real knowledge of the inside of the hospital apart from a decades-old blueprint on the internet. They had state-of-the-art comms though, and although he wouldn't be strapped going in per the instructions, he did know how to handle himself in a fight better than most. But not even he could stop bullets.

Glancing at Bebe, he saw she was calm, her face turned to the window as they were driven south of the city. The stunning villages gave way to taller skyscrapers as they hit the main capital of Proenia, Torez. A glittering jewel with lights and energy much like London or New York, Proenia was bigger than his Soflye and different in so many ways. Leo's eyes caught on the rising glass tower owned by Buccio Industries, the very company that Luca Buccio ran. A billionaire prince with a head for business and a reputation as a ruthless advocate in the boardroom.

He couldn't believe that the man he'd met and spent a summer with was involved in this mess. It went against his instincts but then he'd been wrong before.

"Hey, where did you go?"

Leo blinked and found Bebe's gaze on him, the blue startling him once more. Her hand covered his and he twined their fingers together, wishing he could just grab her and run to a place where they weren't hunting bad guys. "I was just wishing we could run away to a beach somewhere and hang for a while with no responsibilities, no worries. Just you, me, and the beach."

Her lips hitched in a sexy smile that stole his breath. "No clothes?"

"Definitely no clothes."

"Where would I hide my weapons?"

Leo kissed her palm, the movement making her breath hitch, her scent the one she always wore grounding him to the moment. "You won't need weapons or clothes."

"Sounds idyllic."

"It will be."

Before long the limo was pulling up to a huge, angular building made of concrete and stone, which resembled a mausoleum rather than a psychiatric hospital. Grand columns on either side of the iron gates stood like sentries. As they drove closer to the main building, he could see the moss and ivy growing inside the cracks of the stone structure. Small windows with artfully crafted bars on the outside tried to make it seem less like a jail and failed horribly. Gardens, which would've once been filled with flowers and greenery, were now filled with dead grass. Lights over the door gave him a view of four heavily armed men. Their limo pulled in behind another and they waited while a man he recognised as an oil billionaire got out. He was ushered inside and then it was their turn.

"Comms check."

"Copy."

"Copy."

Came the replies before the door was opened and he exited the vehicle buttoning his jacket before offering his hand to Bebe.

A burly guard wearing a semi-automatic weapon on a sling over his shoulder stopped them. "Password?"

"Tanzanite."

"Please place the product in the bag."

He held out a black silk bag while another man checked a tablet in his hand, most likely checking the payment was made.

Leo took the gemstone, and with some regret, placed it in the bag before looking the man in the eye.

"Please proceed to the main room following the directions on the floor. Don't deviate or you'll be removed forcibly."

Leo had no doubt that *forcibly* meant in a body bag. He took Bebe's hand and placed it in the crook of his elbow, and they did as they were told.

A broken wheelchair was off to the side, torn curtains and smashed cabinets were evidence of what this used to be.

"This place is giving me the heeby-jeebies."

Leo felt his lips tip up in a smile despite the situation. "Do you think the main attraction will show their face?"

Bebe shook her head. "No, but I suspect we all have eyes on us. That's why we were made to dress up."

Leo kept his counsel on that and instead looked around the main room, which, by the high windows and large open area, had been the common room before it was closed fifteen years earlier. A musty, damp smell mixed with the remnants of bleach and cleaning products gave the place a nauseating scent.

A wealth of riches filled the room, from mafia dons, terrorists, charitable benefactors, and government officials. It disgusted him to see people charged with caring for the countries they represented here more than the terrorists. At least they owned what they were and didn't try and hide behind a façade of respectability.

A podium at the front caught his eye and he motioned to Bebe with a squeeze of her arm and a glance. A man was stepping up as the doors behind them began to close, locking them inside. Leo felt his heart rate skip up a beat knowing that Bebe was with him and facing this danger among these vultures only made it worse.

A hand on his chest made him turn to her. "It's fine."

Leo dipped his head, not trusting himself to answer when his whole body screamed for him to take her and run. Every instinct he had was on fire telling him that something was amiss here in a big way. Could Atticus have played them and set them up? Had The Collector figured out they were onto her? So many things could go wrong, and he had the woman he loved in the middle of it.

"Just concentrate on winning the auction and I'll cover our backs."

A man with a moustache and glasses stepped up to the podium and a hush came over the room as anticipation built.

He pressed something to his ear and seemed to nod, evidence he was being fed instructions. "Ladies and gentlemen, we'll shortly begin the auction for item seven-nine-three. Please take your seats and we'll begin."

Leo led Bebe to a seat on the outside of the room near the back. He wanted them close to an exit if the shit hit the fan.

He found himself seated next to a Chinese billionaire he knew from his appearance in multiple issues of Vanity Fair. Neither man made small talk, only one task on their minds but for very different reasons.

"Let us begin."

The auctioneer went on to describe in detail what the program for sale could do. With every word out of his mouth, Leo was more determined to win. If this got into the hands of any of the people here it could cause a global catastrophe costing millions of lives.

"Shall we start the bidding at two million dollars?"

Leo watched a hand go up but kept himself out of the bidding war between the mafia don and the Chinese billionaire beside him. As the price rose to near on six million dollars, other bidders came in and some dropped out. As it hit seven million only two men were left. Leo held off, holding his nerve and waiting for one to drop out of the race before he came in and scooped the prize.

When the man beside him dropped out, Leo placed his bid. A man he recognised as an Egyptian he'd done business with turned to him and blinked in surprise. His heart rate rocketed as he realised he'd been recognised.

Turning back to the auctioneer, he focused on winning. His identity coming out would be a concern for after they got out of here.

At eight point five million the Egyptian conceded, and Leo won the bid.

"Congratulations. Will you please make your way to the exit to the back left? Everyone else, please remain in your seats until you're told you may leave."

Leo felt some relief, but he wouldn't truly relax until they were back home in Soflye, and this nightmare was over.

The auctioneer left using a door behind him, and Leo and Bebe followed the man with the tablet who'd ushered them inside. As the doors closed behind them, five men began sealing them with chains.

Leo looked at Bebe who seemed as alarmed as he did by the new development.

"This way."

Leo tried to get a closer look as he was ushered away and saw masking tape and large rolls of plastic being fitted over the doors. "What's happening?"

The man, who was of average height with a Fabergé egg tattooed on the side of his neck, scowled. "I suggest you stop asking questions and follow me."

He motioned with the semi-automatic in the direction of the front office they'd passed on the way inside. A laptop and a ratty desk with a broken office chair were the only things inside.

"Please complete the payment."

"I want to see the program first?"

"It's coming, just make the payment."

With the goon waving the gun around he had no choice but to do as he was told. The last thing he needed was to get Bebe hurt because he was being mouthy.

Logging in he made the payment and was handed a USB Drive.

"The only copy of the program is on that drive."

"How do I know you haven't copied it?"

The man smirked. "You don't."

Then he bent and picked up what looked like two World War II gas masks from the floor and handed them to Leo. "Wait ten minutes before you leave."

With that, he left, closing the front door as he and the men he was with jumped into a van.

Glancing at the mask in his hand a horrid realisation came to him. "They're going to kill them all."

Bebe had clearly come to the same conclusion and gave Roz the details. The sounds of people screaming and shouting hit their ears.

"Get out of there," Roz yelled through the comms, and she sounded like she was running.

Bebe shook her head. "We can't just let them all die."

"You have one minute to see if you can help and then I'm coming for you," Roz yelled into the comms.

Leo was torn, his first instinct was to protect the woman he loved. Right on top of that came the urge to help people. They might be criminals, but they were still human beings.

Bebe looked at him waiting for his reaction. Grabbing her face, he positioned the mask and hoped like hell the seals weren't compromised.

"One minute."

He put his mask on, ignoring the foul smell and headed back down the hallway where the sounds of furniture hitting walls echoed into the night. A yellow, green aura inside the common room was the first sign of what they were dealing with. He peered inside and saw more than half the people they'd been sitting with not minutes ago rolling on the floor fighting for breath.

"We need to get these doors open."

Bebe had lifted a fire extinguisher off the wall and began hitting the metal chain to try and break the lock.

A whiff of chlorine hit his nose burning his eyes and his fear that the masks were compromised came true. The sounds were growing less and less as he took over hitting the lock with everything he had.

"Hurry, they're dying."

As the lock gave, Bebe quickly began unwinding the chain from the doors and ripping the seal away. He grasped her hand, stopping her from opening the door. "You won't be able to save them all. We don't have time."

"I can try. Please." Her need to save people, even those not worthy, was part of what he loved about her and also part of her deep-seated need to make up for something she'd never been to blame for.

"Is your mask secure?"

Bebe nodded and he wished he had time to tell her he loved her before he followed her into hell. "Let's go."

Yellow gas erupted as he pulled the door open. He grabbed the arms of the closest person, dragging them to the exit, as Bebe did the same in front of him. They found Kanan, Roz, Alex, Evelyn, and Brody at the main door waiting to help.

His lungs burned, eyes running with tears as he began to cough, passing Bebe as she handed off a second victim to Alex and ran back inside. With at least a dozen more inside he knew they'd never get them all out before the fumes overtook them both.

"Bebe, we need to go."

"One more." She rushed back in, and he followed even as his vision became blurred, his legs growing weak from lack of oxygen.

"Everyone out. We have a missile incoming."

Bebe glanced at him as his legs gave way, a hacking cough consuming his body. "Leo."

Anguish covered her face as he tried to wave her away, but his vision was almost black now, the sting from the chlorine gas burning his skin.

An arm came around him and then another and he was hauled to his feet and dragged until the cold night air slapped his skin.

His mask was wrenched off and he took his first deep pull of fresh air as the building behind them exploded into the quiet of the night, sending him and his saviours to their knees.

Flames and smoke hit the night sky as the ringing in his ears muffled the sound of the nightmare around him. Looking around desperately, he found Bebe a few feet from him, probably blown by the blast. Her wig had fallen off in the melee, her hair dark around her shoulders as she ran to him.

He caught her as she fell into him taking them both to the ground.

"Oh my God, I thought I'd lost you."

"Never. You'll never lose me, Bebe, not ever."

Twenty-Eight

"Mercy, I'm so happy to see you." Bebe wrapped her friend in her arms before stepping back to get a better look at her. She looked well, happy even. Bebe wondered if it had anything to do with the insanely hot Prince Luca Buccio standing close behind her looking like he might step in and strangle anyone who said a cross word to Mercy.

"I heard what happened. I'm so glad you're safe. That must have been horrific."

Bebe glanced at Leo, who moved closer, wrapping his arm around her back, and pulling her close. "It was awful but at least some of the objectives were achieved and we all got out safely if a little banged up."

Bebe was still miffed that Leo hadn't told her his mask was leaking, but she figured he'd suffered enough and she'd eventually get over it.

They were meeting with Mercy and her contact Prince Luca here in Proenia to hand over all the information they had, before heading back to Soflye where they'd remain on hand to help out Mercy should she need it. Roz, K, Alex, and Evelyn had gone back to the UK to dig up as much as they could on The Collector now they were sure it was a woman. Releasing poison at the auction was another confirmation for them that it was a female.

Luca eyed her before dipping his head at Leo. "I'll have people I've hand-picked clear the site and go through the evidence."

"Be careful, Luca. I found that even those closest to you can stab you in the back."

Luca was a cool customer, with an air of austere reservation and devastatingly handsome. Not as handsome as her man, but Bebe could recognise she was biased.

"I'm aware and will be on my guard." Luca glanced at Mercy who blushed under his gaze. "There's too much at stake for me to take any risks."

Bebe raised her eyes at her friend but didn't voice her suspicions that there was way more going on here than the investigation. How could she when she'd met and fallen in love with the man of her dreams on this mission?

"Roz and the team, with the help of Brody James, are tracking down whoever stole the program in the first place to see if we can dig up any leads there. Do you have any idea who's involved in the plot to steal the Blood Ruby from the vault?"

Mercy, who was wearing a black pencil skirt and cream blouse with red stiletto heels and a red belt Bebe knew contained a garrotte, shook her head. "Not yet, but we have a few leads to follow."

Mercy cast a look at Luca who was watching her, and Bebe could practically feel the sexual tension between the two of them. She just hoped this man didn't play with her friend's heart. She'd been through far too much to have her heart put through the wringer.

"Have you heard from Laverne, Lily, or Lorna?" Mercy bit her bottom lip, a sign she was worried.

"No, but Roz has and she says they're fine." Bebe motioned toward the vacant space. "Can I talk to you in private a second?"

Mercy nodded and led her a few feet away from the men to the side of an abandoned building. They'd chosen to meet in this disused industrial park over fear of bugs and cameras catching their conversation.

Bebe glanced at Leo who was speaking with Luca, both imposing in their own right. Leo with his green eyes, brown hair, and muscular build had the dangerous air of a warrior. Luca, by contrast, was equally compelling in a refined, dominant way. He had dark hair and blue eyes against his tall, muscular build. He looked exactly like the playboy and powerful businessman he was, and she knew, like Leo, he had a reputation. He might be a prince but if he hurt Mercy, he'd be a dead prince, that was for sure.

"You and Prince León?"

Mercy's smile was wide as Bebe dragged her gaze away from the two princes. "I know. It was unexpected, to say the least."

"You look happy."

"I am. I didn't know love like this existed in real life."

Mercy looked away and Bebe followed her gaze toward the man now staring back at her as if he'd burn down the world for her. "I'm happy for you."

"Looks like Luca has a thing for you."

Mercy laughed but it was nervous and unsure, her confidence in herself since the attack was obliterated. She'd been a lively, outgoing girl with confidence in abundance but now Mercy Quintrell was a different woman. "What? No. He's just protective because he feels responsible for this nightmare."

Bebe disagreed but didn't say so. Luca was looking at her like a man who wanted to usher her away and keep her safe from the world while ravishing her body. Mercy would need to work this out for herself.

"Is there anything else I should know about this case?"

"We had CIA undercover on our case without our knowledge so watch out for that. Also, expect the unexpected. You'll need to find a new way to get the third auction to stay on track because there's no way Roz will send one of us again after what went down."

"I don't blame her. Can you believe The Collector had all those losing bidders killed?"

"Luckily, we managed to save a few and they're being interrogated by the teams. The other bodies were destroyed by the missile strike and fire, and I think their deaths are being kept a secret for now."

Mercy smoothed her hands down her skirt, her tiny frame accentuating her small curves. "That makes sense."

"I understand you have Liam Hayes and Kirk Reid from Eidolon as backup if you need it. Leo and I are only an island hop away as well if you need us."

"Yes, I didn't know they'd be on this operation, but honestly, it's nice to know we have them as backup."

"I don't think Roz was comfortable with us being here alone, so she brought Jack and his team in as backup in case we needed it."

"Well, I, for one, am happy about it."

Bebe gripped her friend's hands, studying her and finding she looked stronger, more of her old self showing from the dust of her life, at least professionally. Personally, she knew it would take a very special person for Mercy to ever trust enough to be vulnerable again. "Be safe, my friend."

Luca, who'd walked closer, laid his hand against Mercy's lower back in a possessive and deeply intimate way. "You have my word that I won't let anything happen to her on my watch."

Mercy frowned and stepped away from him, putting distance between them. "I don't need saving. I'm not some weak child. I'm capable and smart, so stop treating me as if I'll break."

Bebe was taken aback by her friend's outburst but also glad to see her spirit rising again. Yes, indeed. It would take a very special man.

Luca winked at Mercy who ignored it and faced Bebe. Mercy had this, of that she had no doubt.

Leo took her hand and faced Luca and Mercy. "We'll leave you to it, but if you need anything, please call. A phone call between us wouldn't seem out of the realms of possibility and shouldn't raise suspicion."

Leo offered his hand to Luca who shook it and then did the same to Mercy. Bebe gave her friend a hug and shook Luca's hand.

"Be safe."

With that, they got into the black jeep with blacked-out windows and headed back to Soflye. Two hours later, as their private jet took off, Bebe looked down at the blue sea and sighed.

Warm skin touched her as she felt Leo's hand cover hers. "What is it?"

Her gaze locked on his green eyes, and she wondered how she'd gotten so lucky. "You could've died."

His eyes softened and he scooted closer to draw her over the seat across his lap. His hands and arms wrapped around her tightly, and he brushed his nose along her jaw. "I didn't though."

"You should have told me your mask wasn't working properly." This had been playing on her mind since the previous night when they'd barely escaped with their lives.

"You needed to try and save those people."

"Not more than I wanted you safe."

His lips peppered her skin with kisses, and she sighed into him, her body becoming pliant as she let go of her anger at him. "I know you wanted to do what was right and save the people you could. I never want you to feel like you've failed because no matter what, you're the best, most selfless person I know, and I love you more than I can ever express."

"I'm going to speak to someone I know about getting some counselling so I can let go of my past hang-ups. I also thought I might track down my parents and have a face-to-face and tell them how they made me feel but I'm not sure about that yet."

"Whatever you need, I'm here for all of it. You have a family, Bebe. With me and my father as soon as I can get a ring on that gorgeous finger, and with Zenobi and the friends you have there. They love and adore you. They see your value. Your parents don't deserve you, but if you want to find them, I'll be with you, standing beside you as you let them have it."

"I love you, Leo."

"And I love you, my Queen."

Bebe laughed. "Not yet."

"Now and always you'll be my Queen and I'll humbly thank the gods that I found you."

Epilogue

Leo rolled over in bed, his hand reaching for smooth soft skin and found the sheets empty. Sitting up, he looked around his luxury villa in Guadeloupe for a sign of where Bebe might be and found the home they'd shared for the last two weeks silent.

Rising from the bed, he pulled on some board shorts and ran a hand through his hair, trying to tame it where her hands had tugged as he'd gone down on her, lapping up her sweetness with the flat of his tongue.

His morning wood, already perked up, was now rock hard as he remembered the way she'd screamed his name as her body contracted around his cock. Ambling to the bi-fold doors that led from the bedroom out onto the private terrace and infinity pool, Leo scanned the area looking for the woman he loved more with each day that had passed.

Spotting her alone on the beach, her back to him as she watched the sun begin to crest over the horizon, he made a decision. Grabbing what he needed, he jogged down to the secluded beach and stopped for just a moment to take in the breathtaking view. The sky turning from inky blue to purple, Bebe with her face tipped to the sun, he felt his heart quicken with nerves.

He'd faced untold enemies in combat and held his own the last six months as betrayals had been exposed, and still, the thought of her rejection was more terrifying than all of it. He might be a prince, but she was everything to him.

Walking up behind her, he smiled when she cocked her head as he sat down behind her and pulled her warm pliant body into the shelter of his spread legs, his arms wrapping around her. "I missed you."

Her cheek brushed his as she turned her head, her soft hair tickling his nose. "I wanted to see the sunrise."

Leo nuzzled her cheeks with his nose. "You should have woken me."

"You looked so peaceful. I didn't want to disturb you."

"You could never disturb me."

Her lips tipped up and he took them, his tongue teasing her slowly before releasing her and smiling. Her return grin was lost as they both turned to watch the sun make her magnificent entrance for another day. The beauty and splendour of the cacophony of colours were magical, but what took his breath away was watching it with her.

"I never get tired of watching this."

"Me either."

Leo reached into his pocket and produced the box containing his mother's engagement ring. Opening the box with a flick of his fingers, he held it in front of her as the sun bloomed on the horizon. He hoped her gasp as she twisted to look at him was a good sign.

Bebe spun, her legs straddling him now, her fingers trembling as she held them to her lips.

His hand shook with nerves as he brought the ring between them. "Never in my wildest dreams could I have predicted our love story. I never imagined I'd meet the woman who owned every part of me, body and soul, and fall so hard that I couldn't imagine my life without them. You're strong, kind, giving, and beautiful on the inside and out. It would be the greatest gift of my life if you'd agree to be my wife. To stand beside me as my Queen one day. Will you marry me?"

Taking the third finger of her left hand, he placed the ring at the tip, waiting with his stomach in a knot for her answer.

A hiccupped sob tore from her as tears cascaded down her perfect cheeks, a smile brighter than anything the sun could produce spread across her face as she nodded. "Yes. Yes, I'll marry you."

Leo felt elation like he never had before, joy making him feel light and carefree for the first time since before he'd lost his mother. Pushing the ring firmly onto her finger, he wrapped his arms around her and kissed her, revelling in the passion they shared. Pulling away, he swiped the tears from her face and kissed the trail they left.

Her eyes fell to the ring his father had given him. "This is so beautiful."

Leo looked at the oval-shaped yellow sapphire with two tear-drop diamonds on either side, surrounded by two diamond-studded bands. It had been worn by his mother and, after learning of the true love between her and his father, he'd asked if he could have it for Bebe.

"It was my mother's engagement ring. If you don't want it, I understand."

Bebe's hand rested over his heart. "I love it. It's perfect."

"My father said the day he gave it to my mother was the happiest day of his life because he'd found the missing piece of his puzzle. That's how I felt when I met you for the first time. I didn't know it back then, but my heart did."

"Oh, Leo, I love you so much."

Her arms came around him and he crushed her to him as he rolled them to the white sand. Her laugh was pure delight, unabashed pleasure, tinkling the early morning quiet. His lips found hers and he quickly divested her of the gold bikini she'd been wearing. Kissing his way down her collar bone, he sucked on the flesh of her breast, marking her as his for all the world to see.

Her legs came around his hips as she arched her body, making his dick almost punch through the fabric of his shorts. "Fuck me, Leo."

He growled into her skin before sucking her taut nipple into his mouth, teasing and torturing her as she ground against him. Pushing his own needs to the back of his mind he made her come from just nipple play. His woman was so responsive to his touch, and it was a huge fucking turn on.

As she came down from her first climax, he quickly divested the other barriers between them and knelt between her thighs. The sun beat down on his back as she lay before him like a banquet he couldn't wait to dive into.

Running his hand from her cheek down her chest, over her belly, he skimmed her smooth pussy and grasped her thighs, lifting her towards him. Her pussy glistened with how much she wanted him, the evidence of her climax on her thighs. Swiping his thumb through the wetness, he lifted it to his lips and sucked the sweetness of her into his mouth. "So fucking sweet."

"Fuck me, Leo."

"Dirty girl."

Bebe responded to his words by arching her back, her hands squeezing her nipples as she moaned. She loved dirty talk as much as he did, another reason in the thousands why she was so perfect for him.

He couldn't hold back any longer and positioned the tip of his cock at her entrance, coating himself in her slick arousal before he plunged into her, filling her to the hilt, making her cry out as she clenched around his cock.

A hiss of pleasure slipped past his lips as he gripped her ass, rocking into her in smooth fluid strokes as he watched her gorgeous face. Her body fluttered against him, building as he went up onto his knees, changing the angle so he was hitting her g-spot.

Bebe's hands clasped at his forearms, seeking relief as she gripped him. "Leo, God, Leo."

"You gonna come for me, beautiful?"

"Yes, oh God. Yes."

Her sex convulsed around him, pulsing as her orgasm overtook her and she cried out. Her fingernails scratching at his arms only added to the pleasure. As she came down from her second climax, he saw her languid eyes move over him. Pulling out, he flipped her so she was facing the ocean on her knees.

The sand was harsh against his legs as he stroked her ass, the lush curves one of the things he loved the most about her body. She wasn't skin and bones, but soft pliant flesh he could adore and cherish.

Gripping her hips, he impaled her with his cock. "Play with your tits, Bebe. Squeeze those gorgeous nipples for me."

Her moan as she lifted, driving him deeper inside, and palmed her tits, made him close his eyes, every sensation and feeling overwhelming him. Intoxicated by her, he opened them again to see her fingers plucking at her nipples. Moving his hand from her hip, he trailed it up her torso until he was gripping her throat in his hands, her pulse pounding against him as a flood of her juices dripped down his cock.

A whimper vibrated on his hand as he felt her getting close again. Her hands holding those glorious tits, she turned to him. "Kiss me."

Leo bent close but didn't give her his mouth. Teasing her with light brushes over her cheek instead. A moan of frustration had him on the edge of sanity as he worshipped her body until she was shivering and shaking.

Only when he felt that first clench of her pussy around his cock, did he kiss her, losing himself in her as he found his own climax. His cock pulsed inside her as his seed washed over her womb.

Panting, he held her around the waist as she settled back into his embrace.

"Can we do that again?"

He laughed, joy filling him as he wondered how he'd ever gotten so lucky.

It was their last day in Guadeloupe and while Bebe was happy to get back to the Palace and begin planning the wedding she thought she'd never get, she'd miss this little slice of paradise.

She and Leo were sitting at a candlelit table for two on the private beach, a meal of cold meats, cheeses, fruits and nuts the perfect backdrop to a wonderful evening.

"Penny for your thoughts? You've been off the last couple of days."

His thumb caressed her hand before bringing it to his lips. He was such a good man, loyal, kind, protective, supportive, and an alpha animal in the bedroom or anywhere else he could make love to her. That he'd read her so easily should be disconcerting, but it wasn't. Having a man know her so well was a blessing.

Like he'd known when they travelled to Pakistan to meet with her parents that she needed to leave before the first excuses had left their mouths. That he'd given her the space she needed to cry and grieve that relationship she'd never have with them. Then he held her while she came to terms with that and helped her find peace in that.

Leo had been her rock, helping her secure her past where it belonged and get over her guilt for the things she wasn't responsible for.

She'd stood beside him as Atticus and Wojcik were sentenced to life in prison for their crimes. As Chelsea was stripped of her social status and banned from entering Soflye ever again. She'd also helped him recruit a new butler when Hans had admitted to being blackmailed by Alain for an affair with a younger woman. Alain and Alwyn had escaped prosecution much to her annoyance, but the King had banished them and stripped them of their wealth and titles. They now lived in France with a mediocre income, and the public knowledge of what they had done made them pariahs, which the King felt was enough. Bebe didn't agree but it wasn't her place and she had grown to love the King over the last six months as a father figure she had never had. She'd held Leo's hand as he worried about the toll the last six months had taken on the King and helped him through the mire of guilt he had for his treatment of his father.

Together they'd come through it all. The King was stronger than ever, and he treated her like the daughter he'd never had. In exchange, he was becoming the father she wished she'd had growing up.

Life was good and as she laid a hand on her fluttering, nervous tummy, she hoped it was about to get even better. "I was just wondering how quickly we can get married."

Leo cocked his head his lips twitching. "I'd marry you tomorrow if that's what you want."

"No, I want your father to get the wedding he wants for us."

Leo shook his head a smile covering his face. "This isn't about my father."

Bebe cupped his hand between her palms. "I know, but I want him to have it and I want the big dress. I just want it soon."

A slight frown crossed his handsome features, and she rolled her lips to stop herself from blurting out. "Any reason?"

"Well, I don't want to walk down the aisle with a big belly."

Leo froze, his whole body and face turning to stone for the briefest of seconds and nausea from that morning gripped her again but for a different reason this time.

He stood abruptly knocking the chair to the sand and grabbed her pulling her up into his arms. His voice broke as he ran his palm over her flat belly. "Are you saying what I think you're saying?"

Tears stung her eyes as she nodded, too choked up to say the words.

"We're having a baby?"

"Yes. I found out this morning."

Bebe found herself up in the air as Leo swung her around, burying his head in her neck and yelling out his joy to the world.

Suddenly he stopped and placed her on the ground as he dropped to his knees, his hand on her tummy as he looked up at her. "This, you, the baby, are the best things to ever happen to me."

Bebe cupped his cheeks in her hands and felt a love like no other as she looked at him. "No, Leo, that's my line."

As he hugged her waist, pressing a kiss to her belly, she ran her fingers through his hair and looked to the sky hoping her sister could see how beautiful her life was. She'd vowed to live for them both on the day she'd died. Bebe was keeping that promise and would every day for the rest of her life.

A shooting star shot across the night sky, and she smiled as her life was made perfect from the ashes of her beginning. Far from being a saviour, she'd met and fallen in love with her very own.

This might be the happy ever after for Bebe and Prince León, but for a sneak peek of Mercy and Prince Luca's story, read on.

Sneak Peek: Crown of Deceit

PROLOGUE

MERCY HOLLAND LICKED HER WRIST, RAISED HER TEQUILA TO HER reflection in the mirror behind the bar, downed the shot, and popped the wedge of lemon into her mouth. Today was a milestone she never thought she'd see and, in the beginning, had no desire to either. Yet here she was, alive and if not thriving, at least she was contributing again. None of it would have happened without a shit tonne of help, support, and most of all love from her friends who were the only family she had.

Today her therapist had signed her off and said she didn't need to see her again unless Mercy felt she needed it. Motioning to the bartender, she ordered another shot and smiled when he handed it over with a flirty wink. He was cute, but not her type. Although she had no clue if she even had a type now.

Repeating the process, she slammed back the shot wincing as the alcohol burned her throat and warmed her belly. Shaking her head, she put the glass down and glanced back up, blinking. Sudden awareness prickled down her spine. Not from fear, although up until this year it would have been her instant reaction. No, this was more a feeling of being watched, studied, like a butterfly under a microscope.

Her eyes moved over the etched glass of the bar until she found the source of the feeling. A hitch caught the back of her throat as her breath stuttered in and out before levelling again, even as her heart beat faster in her chest. A handsome man watching her. No, not handsome that description was too banal for the man whose eyes skimmed her skin like a lover's touch. Tall, easily over six feet, with dark hair that had just a slight wave as it swept back from a strikingly handsome face. A square jaw which her fingertips itched to touch and high cheekbones, that would make a sculptor crave the feel of clay to try and recreate such beauty. Mercy couldn't see his eyes but if she had to guess, she'd say blue or maybe grey, something bright and contrasting with his dark forbidding looks.

Yet it was the full lips pulled into an almost cruel smirk as he lifted his crystal glass to her in a silent salute that had her thinking of hot, sweaty sex. Wondering how they would feel. Would they be warm, firm, soft, or cold? She didn't know. He was an exotic mystery she wanted to untangle.

Intrigued by a man for the first time since her attack and feeling emboldened by her win today, Mercy turned in her seat toward him, crossing her legs as she faced him and watched as he sauntered toward her like a predatory cat. A panther, sleek and muscular, but a threat she figured most never saw until he wanted them to.

Yet she didn't feel like prey, she felt strong, confident, powerful for the first time in years. Lust swam in her belly like smooth brandy as he moved close enough for her to smell the evocative scent he wore. It moved around her, filling her senses and making her body pulse with a need she thought long dead.

"May I buy you a drink?"

His accent held the merest hint of what she thought was Proenian or Soflye. "No, you may not." She could see her words surprised him, but he didn't seem offended, merely acknowledged her answer. He was confident, that in itself was sexy as hell and had her wanting to squeeze her thighs together to ease the ache that bloomed there. "May I buy you a drink?"

A twitch of his lips told her he was trying hard to keep his smile hidden and she wondered why a man like this would try and hide something she knew would be magnificent if it was allowed free rein.

"I would never turn down a drink from a beautiful woman."

Mercy signalled the bar tender. "A cola for me and whatever this gentleman is having. Please put it on my tab."

"Yes, ma'am."

Turning, she uncrossed her legs, the fabric of her skirt, riding up her thighs, not so it was indecent, just a hint of warm tanned flesh. Lifting her head, she caught him watching her legs but when he raised his eyes which were a cool ice blue, he didn't try and hide it, letting his appreciation show in his hungry gaze.

He was honest and open in his interest of her, and she liked that. The games and deceptive plays that people engaged in weren't for her. Mercy needed to know where she stood with people, and players weren't attractive to her in the least. As their drinks were placed on the polished bar, the man took his and raised his glass to her, cocking his head.

"What are we celebrating?"

Mercy tipped her head in question.

"You were toasting something earlier, it looked like a celebration. Perhaps we can do it again? Something worth celebrating should never be done alone."

Mercy had no intention of telling this man her life story or revealing the true nature of why she was here in a luxury hotel bar drinking alone. "Life. I was celebrating life in all its powerful, dangerous, cruel beauty."

A slight nod came from the mystery man, which held an almost imperiousness to it, before he clinked his glass to hers and they both sipped. "So, what is a woman who looks like you do, doing in a bar alone?"

Mercy almost smiled at the cheesy line, and when she looked, he was shaking his head.

"Scratch that, I'm aware of how bad that sounded. I promise you I have more game than that."

Mercy laughed and it was husky, a side effect of the damage done to her vocal cords during her attack. "I have no interest in games."

Her eyes moved to his throat, where the white shirt he wore open gave a glimpse of tanned skin. The fitted style pulled across broad shoulders and muscular arms and as she let her gaze wander over him, she saw powerful thighs that ended with a hard evident ridge in his groin area. Lust pooled inside her at the sight of such masculine desire aimed her way.

When her eyes finally came to his she saw heat bloom, dark and potent, behind the cool gaze.

"You are not what you seem are you, Miss?"

Looking into the face of the sexiest man she'd ever met, Mercy felt like she was on a precipice of something monumental, with a choice to make. Could she jump or did she live in this isolated bubble of fear and regret for the rest of her life?

As he held her eyes without flinching, she made her choice.

"Are you an honest man?"

He seemed unconcerned by her change in subject. "I like to think so, yes. Although there will be some who disagree with that statement."

"Are you married or in a relationship?"

"No to both. I do not approach women in bars when I'm committed in any small way to another."

Again, he was honest, and it made her feel like she could take the leap and trust her instincts again. "No names, one night?"

His nostrils flared but he showed no other signs of surprise at her words. As he turned away she thought he was going to reject her offer and the sting to her fragile ego was sharp, but he merely nodded at the bar tender in some kind of unspoken conversation, before he stood and offered his hand.

Pushing away the last of her nerves she vowed to have this night and kiss goodbye to the woman who everyone saw as damaged and become everything she was meant to be. Slipping her hand in his, she felt electricity zip up her arm, causing goosebumps to break out all over her body.

As he walked at her pace toward the bank of elevators in the main reception, which was much brighter and lighter than the bar, she got a sense of how tall he was compared to her five feet five inches. Her head only came to his shoulder even in the four-inch heels she wore and yet he let her set the pace, happy to follow her.

As her mystery man held the door of the elevator open, she stepped in first and hit the button for the ninth floor.

Nerves attacked her belly as the doors closed and it was just the two of them. A moment of panic seized her, and she wondered what the hell she was doing sleeping with a man she didn't know from Adam.

A shadow appeared in front of her as he stepped closer, lifting her chin so she could meet his eyes.

"We do not have to do this, little one. If you have changed your mind, rest assured we can go back to the bar and drink cola until the sun comes up. But if you decide to give me this, I will treat you with the care you deserve."

His touch was firm yet gentle, his words enough to slay the doubt trying to weaken her. "I want you."

Mercy didn't wait as they came together, lips crashing into one another in a frenzied kiss that had her blood rushing in her ears. His hand cupped the back of her neck as he crowded her against the back wall of the lift. Lips and teeth competed for dominance as each tried to control the kiss until he backed away, leaving her gasping and flushed with desire.

His cheeks were high with colour but it was the need that was barely contained behind the façade of control he wore that really made her body ache for him.

Lifting his hand, he swept her long, wavy blonde hair away from her neck before running a finger along her bottom lip, eyes riveted on her mouth. Mercy held still as if paralyzed in the moment her breath trapped in her chest, and then it was gone as the doors swished open behind him breaking the spell. He stepped aside so she could exit first, his hand warm on the base of her spine as she led him toward her room and sending sparks over her skin.

His body warmed her as she accessed her key in her bag, and with shaky fingers opened the door.

Throwing her bag and the key on the side, she barely had time to turn before he was backing her up against the wall, his lips on the pulse in her neck. Mercy felt her nipples peak as his hands gripped her ass and lifted her, urging her to wrap her legs around him.

"I've been imagining this all night. Your sweet thighs wrapped around me as I fuck you and make you come so hard you see stars."

A moan slipped out of her mouth at his dirty talk, desire soaking her underwear as his fingers flexed into the bare flesh of her ass where he held her. Passion raged between them as her fingers tunnelled through his thick dark hair. "You have?"

"Fuck yes."

"What else?"

Her teeth nipped his at her throat as she flicked her tongue over the lobe of his ear and bit down, making him flex his hips into her on a growl, his hard arousal causing a delicious friction against her clit which made her arch into his touch.

"I imagined my tongue teasing and tasting you until you can hardly breathe. I'd build you higher and higher until all you could think of is how it feels to have my mouth between your legs."

His hand moved over her hip and up to the edge of her pale pink blouse, his fingers pushing the buttons open and popping a few in his haste to touch her. Using his thumb, he hooked her bra under her breasts and rubbed the tight nipple with his thumb, causing her pussy to pulse. Lost in the moment, she yanked at his shirt needing to see him, exposing the hard flesh she could feel driving her crazy.

Buttons flew and he growled.

"Fuck."

Suddenly he let her go. Bewildered and shaking she stood against the wall, her skirt shucked around her waist, blouse open and breasts exposed but still dressed. Stepping back he dragged his eyes over her from top to bottom, and she could feel the heat of his gaze like a caress.

"Do you have any idea of the fucking picture you make standing there looking like sin, waiting for me to fuck you?"

He gave her no chance to answer before dropping to his knees, his fingers ripping the flimsy G-string from her body. His eyes feasted on her smooth flesh causing heat to burn through her skin. "Perfect."

He locked eyes with hers and she couldn't look away as he lifted her leg and hooked it over his shoulder as she grasped onto his shoulder to hold herself up.

"Watch me eat your pussy, little one."

His words caused a surge of moisture and she groaned but held his gaze.

Dipping his head, she felt the sweep of his tongue over her slit, the flat of his tongue driving her crazy before he flicked her clit, and her hips bucked into him. Mercy's head hit the wall as she gasped from the pleasure, the sounds he was making adding to the madness she could feel building.

"Eyes on me, and only me, little one."

Mercy lifted her head, seeing the evidence of her desire on his chin and he smirked, his hooded gaze masculine and beautiful. Mercy watched as he licked, nipped, and sucked like it was his full-time job to make her come. Waves of pleasure rolled over her like the waters of the sea during a storm, wild and untamed as he drank her in before thrusting two fingers inside her wet channel.

The feeling of his fingers inside her made her pause for a second as memories begin to flit across her vision. Men, too many for her brain to comprehend, pawing at her, attacking her, hurting her. Panic raced down her spine and she felt her throat close as bitter disappointment crowded her and she fought the onslaught of shame. Panicked breaths see-sawed in her lungs as she tried to stay in the moment and block the past from ruining this moment.

Her foot hit the floor as gentle, strong arms swept her up and she was carried to the couch, her face buried into warm solid flesh that smelled like sweet spice. Sitting on the couch he kept her in his lap as he held her, his long fingers brushing the wetness from her cheeks.

"Come back to me, little one."

Mortified by her reaction, Mercy tried to scramble away but he held her gently. "Hey, talk to me. I'm not going to hurt you."

"I need to get up."

He immediately released her, and she paced away, wanting to run from the shame and pain. She'd thought she was ready, she felt ready and yet here she was, a mess in front of the first man she'd desired. Straightening her clothes, she felt her shoulders slump in defeat as her nostrils flared and tears burned the back of her throat.

"Do you want me to leave?"

Her eyes shot up and she looked at the man who'd shown her nothing but respect and kindness and even now, the kernel of desire sang through her blood. Mercy bit at her fingernail as doubt and regret assailed her.

She knew she should send him away; she was nothing to him but as she went to say the words, she realised she wanted him there. His calm authority had, up until that moment when he'd entered her, given her freedom to just enjoy. "No."

"Thank fuck, because I don't believe I could leave you like this."

Mercy stopped her pacing to see he was leaning forward with his elbows on his knees as he watched her. "I'm sorry."

He stood and as he approached, she had to bend her neck back to look at him and fight the instinct to step back. Firm, but gentle, fingers pinched her chin so he could capture her eyes.

"Never apologise for how you feel. It's real and honest and anyone who tells you differently is an asshole."

He was a good man. She didn't know him but everything in her told her he was good to his core where it counted most. Perfect? Probably not but then that also made him better than most, because he didn't try to hide.

"Can we try again?"

His sexy smirk had need replacing the fear. "Whatever you need, little one."

He didn't lean in this time but when she went up on tiptoes to reach him, he met her halfway, allowing her to take the lead and set the pace.

As their lips touched, she realised he had given her what she needed without her having to voice it.

Control.

This kiss was more controlled. He was holding back, letting her dictate the pace as she walked him backward until his legs hit the bed and he stopped like a solid wall of muscle.

Pulling away, she could see the need and desire in his eyes as he worshipped her body with his gaze.

"You're so beautiful."

Pleasure washed over her at his words as her hands went to her blouse and she discarded it and her skirt. Her hands shook slightly but she kept her focus on the man in front of her who was clenching his fists at his side, the tension in his body a sign of how he was holding himself back from taking control away from her. His eyes told the story of how much he wanted her and how difficult this was for him, yet he still did it.

Lifting her arm, she unhooked her bra and let it fall down her arms to the floor. Dark stormy eyes widened as they traced over her skin and she hooked her thumbs in her panties and drew them down her thighs before stepping out. Nerves fluttered in her belly, and she lifted a hand to her flat stomach to calm the feeling.

His hand covered hers on her belly before he linked his fingers through hers and drew her hand to his chest, the skin warm under her touch.

"Come here, little one."

She hesitated only a second before complying, moving into him so her breasts pressed against his open shirt.

When she looked up, he cupped her face in his big hands and brought his lips close. "Tell me what you need."

"Make me feel again."

His brow dropped as he frowned, not knowing the origin behind her question, but he didn't ask and she was thankful for that.

"I can make you feel again, little one."

Sitting on the end of the bed, he pulled her until she was standing between his muscular thighs. His fingers twined with hers as he lifted each hand to his mouth and kissed her palms, before placing them on his chest. Mercy's breath stuttered in her chest at the tenderness he was showing her.

As her hands began to explore, she felt the ripple of flesh and sinew as she slid his shirt from his shoulders and explored the plains of his abdomen. Pushing him back on the bed, she crawled so she was sitting on his hips, the hardness of his erection beneath her core. Leaning forward she feathered kisses over his chest as his hands clamped down on her thighs, squeezing as he fought to keep himself still.

"Touch me."

She felt the shuddered breath go through him as he ran his hands up her ribcage and over the sides of her breasts, thumbs catching on her nipples.

"You're so beautiful, little one."

His words could feel patronising, but they didn't, they made her feel cherished and desired.

As she kissed her way down his body she waited for the panic to come again but it didn't. Dropping to her knees on the floor, she looked up to see hooded eyes watching her as he rested on his elbows. A silent moment of understanding crossed between them as she ran her hands up his thighs to his belt buckle. The sound of the metal as she undid it and flicked the button open the only sound in the room. The zipper on his trousers slid down smoothly and he tipped his head back on a hiss as she ran her palm over the hard ridge of his erection under the black cotton of his tight boxers.

The feeling of power over him was heady and freeing as he raised his head to watch her lower the rim of his pants to reveal the red, engorged head of his cock. Letting her hand tighten around the warm steel of him, she pumped once, watching a bead of precum slip from the slit.

Dipping her head, Mercy caught it on her tongue, allowing his salty savoury taste to explode on her tongue. Looking up she saw his palm curl toward her neck, grasping the back of her head, but he didn't try to force her down or control her, just held her as his gaze wandered over her skin heating it.

A seductive smile curled the corner of her mouth as she took him into her mouth and bobbed her head, letting the feel of him wash over her. Eyes never leaving his dark stare, she let her tongue flatten over the underside of his cock and felt the ache in her body begin to build as her own desire woke from a long, dormant sleep.

As his cock hit the back of her throat she gagged, and his grip tightened as his hips bucked and the fear from before melted away. She had the power here, he was giving it to her. She sensed that it was unusual for him to do so and took the gift he was giving so freely.

Letting his cock fall from her lips she rose. "You're overdressed."

A sexy smirk quirked his lips before he stood, his chest brushing her nipples and making her hum with need. "I believe you're right, little one."

He dropped his trousers and she watched with rapt attention as he shucked his boxers until they were both naked. Mercy let her eyes wander from proud tilt of his jaw, over his chiselled chest and abs, to the tendons at his hips that made her mouth water, and over the proud jut of his erect cock. He was a stunning masterpiece, with a body and face which would make angels weep and he was waiting for her to make the next move.

It was enough to have her handing back some of the control he'd given her. "Tell me what you want to do to me."

His hand lifted and his knuckles rubbed softly over her straining nipples making her head fall back. "I want to make you come with my mouth on your hungry pussy and I want to lap up all that desire until you know nothing but my name on your lips and the feel of me touching you."

"Then what would you do?"

Her hand reached for his cock and she stroked him, watching his jaw tick and growl rumble in his chest.

"Then I'd make you mine in every way."

"Do it."

Her words were like a starter pistol going off loudly in the room and the next second she was in his arms as he laid her on the bed and crawled between her legs. His teeth and tongue toyed and teased her nipples until she was squirming. He kissed his way down her body, over her hip and the tattoo of a wolf that symbolised the family that was Zenobi. As his teeth nipped the soft flesh in the dip between her hip and thigh she threaded her hands into his hair, trying to force him where she needed him.

"Patience, little one."

Her moan of frustration only made the chuckle she heard that much sexier. He didn't make her suffer, bending his head and placing his lips over her clit before making all the shadows and darkness that crowded her on a daily basis disappear. Pleasure, slow and steady built in her belly as he licked and sucked until she felt herself on the edge of something big, something freeing. Her hands fisted in his hair as she teetered before he nipped his teeth at her clit and she fell, hurtling into a chasm of light and colour as her climax overtook every other feeling.

No pain, no control, only the sweet torture of pleasure so intense she thought she might die from it. As her orgasm ebbed, she lifted her head from the bed where she had thrown it back and looked at him. Evidence of her pleasure coated his chin and lips as he cuffed his hand across it and then licked his lips, closing his eyes at the taste of her.

"Make me yours."

Her hands reached for him and he stood, grabbing his trousers and she worried that he had changed his mind, that she had done something wrong.

He seemed to sense her anxiety and pinned her with a gaze. "Easy, little one."

His fingers ripped the foil off the condom wrapper and she watched as he rolled it down the hard length with a gulp. He wasn't a small man in any part of his body and she feared he'd hurt her, that it would make all the memories and nightmares return. His hand on her ankle made her realise she'd closed her eyes again.

"We can stop right now and I'll leave a happy man, having tasted the sweetest pussy of my life. You're in charge, little one."

Just that small sliver of choice he gave her made her feel safe. She could choose. This was about her and him, nobody else.

Mercy held out her arms to him and she saw the tension slip from his shoulders as he put a knee in the bed and came over her. His lips found hers but his eyes on hers held her captive.

"I don't want to make you mine."

His words take a second to sink in and the rejection is agony as Mercy's muscles tense.

"I want you to make me yours."

With a deft move he spun so she was astride his hips, the hard insistent steel of his cock between her thighs. Relief, sharp and heavy coated her before she felt the slide of his cock against her centre. His dark eyes were on her face as he waited.

Lifting her hips she grasped him in her hand and positioned him at her entrance, the slickness from her desire and climax making him slide the tip of his cock inside her easily. A groan make her look down at him as his hands sweep up to cup her aching breasts. His body was practically humming with tension and she knew deep in her bones that he was giving her something rare. It was exhilarating and terrifying as she realised she might be swapping one prison for another. Before it was barren and cold with only her nightmares, this one would be filled with such perfection that she knew in her heart it was once in a lifetime.

Sinking slowly onto his cock and feeling the stretch before settling against him, his dick inside her pulsing with heat, Mercy knew it was a choice she wouldn't regret.

Lifting, she felt the slide of flesh against flesh as she found her rhythm, riding him as he let her set the pace. His hands didn't still as they toyed with her breasts, running over her ribs, her hips, squeezing her ass and as she felt the pulse of her climax build, her walls fluttering against him, he pressed his thumb hard against her clit and she was soaring.

"Fuck."

"Luca. Say it. Say my name."

His demand forced a keening sound from her and then his name as her climax hit hard and fast, making the everything feel far away. "Luca."

Only the feel of him and this mattered. As she came down he grasped her hips, his beautiful blue eyes, which were no longer ice blue but a deep stormy grey, holding her as he thrust up, chasing his own release.

A deep primal growl came from within him as he filled her with his release. His forehead was sweaty as he cupped her neck and pulled her in for a deep kiss, their bodies settling against one another spent.

True to his word he did. He made her feel it all that night, cherished, desired, wanted. He gave her back a part of herself that had been missing for so long. As the sun touched the horizon she quietly dressed and grabbed her already packed bag from the closet. On the bed, the messy sheets evidence of a night she knew she'd never forget, he slept peacefully. His long dark lashes fanned against his cheeks, the square unforgiving jaw covered in stubble but the full lips relaxed and pure.

Mercy left her hotel room and she knew she'd never forget the stranger who'd given her back her sensuality, and more, her trust of her own self, which had been missing for so long. Regret tinged her heart as she thought of never seeing him again, but it was better this way. Her body might be healed but she knew she could never give a man like him what he needed, that part of her would always be broken.

One

Mercy finished typing her report for Roz on her last case and hit send on the secure server. This had been an easy job for her. Find the leak at the Ministry of Defence department.

She hadn't been shocked to find out the MP who handled that was having an affair, nor that his mistress was the one selling his pillow talk to foreign agencies. It should have shocked her but men and their egos were a law unto themselves. The fact he thought a woman of twenty-five would be interested in his nearly sixty flabby body and balding head, made her shake her head. He and the woman got what they deserved and Roz would handle it from here on out.

She went to close her laptop but stopped, going to the social media platform she used under a fake persona and checked for the latest notifications from her mystery man. It had been almost two years since she'd seen him, since he'd given her a gift he'd never know the importance of.

Finding out who he was had been easy once she'd come home and given in to the urge to look. Had she known at the time she never would've gone near him, but she was glad they had kept things secret. The mystery had allowed them freedom to just be together in a base way which even now, when she thought of that night, found herself smiling and wanting.

Taking one last lingering look she closed the lid on the laptop and stood, stretching her body before heading to the kitchen of her small one-bedroom cottage. The house had been a special find and she'd carefully renovated it and replanted the garden, giving herself a haven that had helped heal her mind and spirit.

As she twirled microwave noodles around her fork, a text came through from Roz.

Roz: Meeting at Athena tonight. Usual time.

Meetings were rare but always held late at night and they usually meant a big case. Intrigued, Mercy finished her snack and went out into the garden to check her tomato plants in the greenhouse. In her wildest dreams she never would've imagined herself here, in this house doing the job she did, and growing plants and vegetables for her own pleasure. But nurturing the seeds and watching things grow gave her peace.

The rest of the afternoon went by quickly and before she knew it the sun was waning and she was hungry again. Grabbing some leftover lasagne from the fridge, she nuked it and ate before deciding to grab a nap. It would likely be a long night and she wanted to be fresh, so she didn't have her friends worrying about her again.

Since the attack they'd all been wonderful, but sometimes it felt like they were too overprotective. They worried about her eating enough, if she was okay mentally and she loved them for it but sometimes she just wished they would see her as not broken but strong, like they were.

When he alarm went off a few hours later, Mercy dressed in jeans and t-shirt and shoved her feet into trainers before shrugging on a black bomber jacket with silver zips. Tying her wavy hair into a pony tail, she headed to her car, a VW Beetle which she adored.

When she pulled into the car park at the front, the lights were out in the building. They must be using the room at the back. With no windows or access other than the front, it was secure, confirming this mission was a big one. It gave her a thrill to be included, to know that Roz thought she was capable.

Mercy grinned as she heard laughter ring through the building. Closing the door and reactivating the alarms, she made sure Athena was the fortress it was supposed to be. The sound of Lili laughing made her grin, a sense of warmth and love for her friend filling her heart. Lili was the eldest of them after Roz, and had been a prosecuting lawyer, working for the Crown Prosecution service before Roz had recruited her. Seeing one to many evil men get off because they had a good lawyer to find the technicalities had been enough.

Zenobi had given her second chance to avenge the victims she felt she'd failed, but Mercy had a feeling that like her, there was more the story behind Lili's drive for justice. Lili had been the one to get through to her when she'd wanted so badly to leave this world. She knew her friends hated how close they'd come to losing her. First physically from the wounds she'd received, then from the mental torture she'd been through at the hands of monsters. But now she was out the other side.

"Hey, sweetie."

Mercy smiled, her honey blonde hair swinging in the ponytail she wore. "Lils." Mercy hugged her friend before pulling back and letting her look at her.

"Peachy?"

Mercy nodded. "Peachy."

After getting annoyed with everyone tiptoeing around and constantly asking if she was okay she'd agreed that if they said peachy she'd reply peachy if she was truly okay and if not, she'd say carrots. It was crazy and silly but it worked to reassure them and they'd given her some space, but only some. They still hovered and while she loved them for it, she also hated it.

"Good.

The door opened and Bebe walked in the room. She was a true beauty, with thick, long dark hair, copper skin inherited from her Pakistani parents, and lush full lips which always smiled.

"Mercy."

Mercy hugged her and they exchanged greetings. "It feels like forever since we've caught up."

Bebe pulled back to look at her and get a feel for how she was doing and Mercy let her, until she was satisfied all was well. "Yeah, we've crossed over a bit, but it's good to see you now."

Mercy shrugged. "Nature of the job."

"Bebe!"

Mercy looked up to see Lorna and Laverne walk into the room and stand behind Lili. The three women were all wildly different to look at but all stunningly beautiful. Lili was medium height with dark hair and big blue eyes and looked as innocent as the purest snow. Laverne was blonde, with long hair and hazel eyes with long lashes, and at nearly six feet in height was model tall for a woman. Then there was Lorna, who looked like she ran an empire and dripped class from every pore with her sleek blonde hair and intelligent hazel eyes.

Lastly, there was Roz, who was the epitome of badass. She had short dark hair, full lips, wide, pale green eyes, and a body men had, and would, die for if she were still in the field.

Mercy always felt like the plain Jane in the room when they got together. In the past it would have bothered her but now she was relieved she could sink into the background.

Honey blonde hair, brown eyes, and a naturally slim build with just the hint of curves, she was the shorted in the group and the youngest. Yet she often felt like she'd lived a thousand lives already.

"Hey, boss lady."

Roz cocked her head, her hard gaze revealing nothing as she assessed her, trying to take in her mental state. Mercy had gotten good at hiding her feelings and Roz tipped her lips up in respect before giving her a short nod.

Mercy grabbed a coffee from the machine as Roz caught up with Bebe and Lili about their most recent job. Taking her coffee, she stirred in the milk and sugar and went to take a seat. Seeing the handful of files in Roz's hand as she moved behind her desk and sat gave Mercy a buzz. This was big, she could feel it.

The meeting room was large, leaving plenty of room for them to sit in the easy chairs or on the couch as the meeting got under way.

Leaning forward, Roz clasped her hands, and the anticipation in the room rose, each woman could feel it as Mercy glanced around at her friends. No, not friends. They were sisters to her. There was an electric current in the air increasing the feeling that something big was about to happen.

"I know I don't have to say this, but I want to reiterate that the job I'm about to give you is top secret. Nobody but the people I'm talking with and those of us in this room are to know about it unless I say so. Do you all understand?"

Mercy felt her body begin to hum with excitement. Her interest piqued at the serious tone. "Yes, of course."

Murmurs of agreement came from the others, and she cast a glance at Bebe, wondering if she had any clue what the job was but judging by her expression, she was in the dark too.

"Good." Roz nodded and opened the file on the top. "We have reason to believe that five underground auctions will take place over the next six months. We don't know where, or exactly when, or what the product will be, but we do know that the buy-in for even entering the auction is a priceless object."

"Do we know who?" Bebe asked, making Mercy look her way.

"We believe The Collector is behind it."

Laverne crossed her long legs. "Damn, no wonder they called us. The entire world has been hunting that bastard for years and hasn't had any luck."

Mercy had heard of The Collector. Who hadn't. Nobody had3 been able to catch him, but then Zenobi had never tried.

"Which is why they brought us in to handle this. We believe the items for auction are projects stolen by The Collector and his people from different government agencies around the world. Not just projects but software and hardware that, if allowed into the hands of terrorists or even garden variety assholes, could bring the world to its very knees. The agencies involved haven't come up with anything, and as they don't trust each other not to lie, they decided as a group to bring in an independent to chase this down."

Bebe cocked her head, a frown marring her brow as her lips pursed in thought. "I agree it's a good solution. Although I'm shocked they went for it. Multiple government agencies agreeing is almost unheard of, but why us? Surely Shadow would be the obvious choice."

Shadow Elite was a secret group that handled this kind of thing, and although they were just as good, Zenobi was more independent. Shadow answered indirectly to the Queen of England and came under Eidolon as their parent company.

"I'm glad you asked." Roz flipped the folder and spread out five pictures on the desk in front of her.

Mercy leaned in and had to muffle the gasp that almost shot from her lips with her cup. Lined up were five images of priceless gemstones. The Blue Water Diamond, the Blood Ruby, the Tanzanite Tears, the Mystic Alexandrite, and the Evergreen Emerald. All were unique and invaluable pieces.

Her eyes shot to Roz before looking around to see similar looks of surprise on the faces of her friends. "The Collector wants them?"

"Yes, and they've been pledged as bids for entry into the auctions. These gemstones were gifts to the monarchs of these five countries by Queen Lydia. As you can imagine, we don't want them falling into the hands of this thief."

"So, what's the mission?"

"Each of you will go undercover in the Palaces of these countries and find out who's entering the bid. The ultimate goal is to find each auction location and bid item and stop whatever it is from falling into the wrong hands. Identify the person involved and find The Collector. Each auction will trigger the next one. Bebe, that means you have the least amount of time."

Bebe shrugged. "How long?"

"We think a month, six weeks tops. Here, read your dossiers and if you have any questions, ask them now or see me later."

Mercy took the file handed to her and hesitated a fraction of a second before opening the file. The breath left her lungs as if she'd been punched when she saw the arrogant, handsome man staring back at her. How could this be? How had her world collided on itself like this? As she read the details in the file, her instinct was to tell Roz she couldn't do it, but this was the first big job she'd been offered since the attack and she wanted so badly to prove she was still good enough to belong with these elite women.

She was so lost in thought she didn't realise Bebe had left until Roz was standing in front of her.

"Are you good?" Roz didn't suffer fools or bullshit and lies weren't forgiven.

"Yes and no. I have a history with this man."

"I'm aware."

Mercy blinked in shock. "You are?"

Roz took her hands and held them. "Mercy, you may think we're overprotective because we don't believe in you, but that's not true. I'm especially overprotective because until my dying day, I'll blame myself for what happened to you."

Mercy went to deny that, but Roz held up a hand. "I know, but you're all mine to protect and that time I failed and that will forever be a stain on my heart. So, yes, I watch you all like hawks now because I'll never let it happen to any of you again. Now, I ask again, are you good to do this job?"

"What's my cover?"

"Prince Luca Buccio is your contact, and you'll be going into the Buccio Industries as his replacement PA. You'll work alongside him to uncover the truth and stop the threat."

Mercy bit her lip as she considered working with him, seeing him again, and she couldn't help the thrill that went through her. "Does he know it's me?"

Roz shook her head. "No, although he's had his security team looking for you since the night you left him sleeping in your bed."

"How do you know he was sleeping?"

A teasing smile radiated off Roz. "Mercy, I saw the joy radiating from you when you came back and the secret smiles you let slip when you thought nobody was watching. If that man wasn't worn out sleeping after that, then I need to get him to give Kanan some tips.

Mercy laughed but couldn't deny the truth of the words. Kanan was Roz' husband and the love and chemistry between them was enough to make a nun jealous. To hear Luca had been looking for her, that she'd made such an impression was wild to her and gave her the confidence that she could do this and make everyone proud.

"Well, looks like Luca is about to get one heck of a surprise."

"That he is, Mercy."

"When do I leave?"

"You have a meeting the day after tomorrow in his offices at the Buccio Industries building in Proenia. Everything you need to know is in the file, but if you need anything else ask Pax. Also, give her a list of clothing and weapons you might need. Remember, you may have to go the Palace so take a few formal gowns too."

Mercy glanced down at the handsome man in the image and felt her body warm as butterflies flew in her belly. "I take it he's the only one we've cleared as he's helping us?"

"He is, yes, but only him. He's very unhappy about the situation as you can imagine. Although I think seeing you might lift his royal spirits."

Mercy blushed at the double meaning and Roz laughed loudly.

"Will you or Pax be my handler on this?"

"I'll be available to all of you, day or night, and so will Pax. Back-up is available when and if we get actionable intelligence, but you can't break cover unless it's irrefutable. You also can't contact each other unless I authorise it or it will compromise the others."

Mercy took a deep breath to ease the nerves.

Roz wrapped an arm around her shoulders. "You've got this, Mercy. You're ready and I'm only a call away. Plus, we'll have Eidolon on the island if you need them. They'll be watching as well."

"I thought it was just us?"

"We're running point but they'll act as hired muscle if we need them to clean up after us."

The competitiveness between Roz and Jack, the leader of Eidolon, was legendary but it was more for fun now than actual hostility. Especially as three of the Zenobi girls had married Eidolon men, including Jack who'd married Astrid.

"Good to know."

Mercy gave the others a hug and wished them well, before sending a text to Bebe with the same love and encouragement and went home to prepare. She was back and she wouldn't fail and maybe, just maybe, she could find the woman she'd been that night with Luca, because while he'd given her the gift of sensual pleasure, he'd spoiled her for other men.

Want a Free Short Story?

Sign up for Maddie's Newsletter using the link below and receive a free copy of the short story, Fortis: Where it all Began.

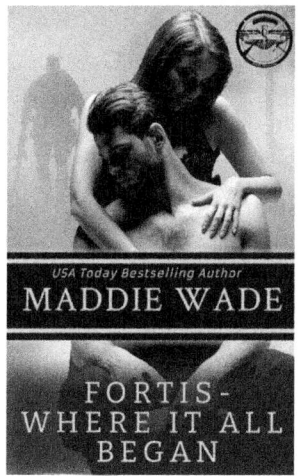

When hard-nosed SAS operator, Zack Cunningham is forced to work a mission with the fiery daughter of the American General, sparks fly. As those heated looks turn into scorching hot stolen kisses, a forbidden love affair begins that neither had expected.

Just as life is looking perfect disaster strikes and Ava Drake is left wondering if she will ever see the man she loves again.

https://dl.bookfunnel.com/cyrjtv3tta

Books by Maddie Wade

FORTIS SECURITY

Healing Danger (Dane and Lauren)

Stolen Dreams (Nate and Skye)

Love Divided (Jace and Lucy)

Secret Redemption (Zack and Ava)

Broken Butterfly (Zin and Celeste)

Arctic Fire (Kanan and Roz)

Phoenix Rising (Daniel and Megan)

Nate & Skye Wedding Novella

Digital Desire (Will and Aubrey)

Paradise Ties: A Fortis Wedding Novella (Jace and Lucy & Dane and Lauren)

Wounded Hearts (Drew and Mara)

Scarred Sunrise (Smithy and Lizzie)

Zin and Celeste: A Fortis Family Christmas

Fortis Boxset 1 (Books 1-3)

Fortis Boxset 2 (Books 4-7.5

EIDOLON

Alex

Blake

Reid

Liam

Mitch

Gunner

Waggs

Jack

Lopez

Decker

SHADOW ELITE

Guarding Salvation

Innocent Salvation

Royal Salvation

Stolen Salvation

Lethal Salvation

WOMEN OF DECEPTION (ZENOBI)

Palace of Betrayal

ALLIANCE AGENCY SERIES (CO-WRITTEN WITH INDIA KELLS)

Deadly Alliance

Knight Watch

Hidden Obsession

Lethal Justice

Innocent Target

Power Play

Until Forever (Shane and Emme Wedding Novella)

RYOSHI DELTA (PART OF SUSAN STOKER'S POLICE AND FIRE: OPERATION ALPHA WORLD)

Condor's Vow

Sandstorm's Promise

Hawk's Honor

Omega's Oath

Lyric's Truth

TIGHTROPE DUET

Tightrope One

Tightrope Two

ANGELS OF THE TRIAD

01 Sariel

OTHER WORLDS

Keeping Her Secrets *Suspenseful Seduction World* (Samantha A. Cole's World)

Finding English P*olice and Fire: Operation Alpha* (Susan Stoker's world)

About the Author

Contact Me

If stalking an author is your thing and I sure hope it is then here are the links to my social media pages.

If you prefer your stalking to be more intimate, then my group Maddie's Minxes will welcome you with open arms.

General Email: info.maddiewade@gmail.com
Email: maddie@maddiewadeauthor.co.uk
Website: http://www.maddiewadeauthor.co.uk
Facebook page: https://www.facebook.com/maddieuk/
Facebook group: https://www.facebook.com/groups/546325035557882/
Goodreads: https://www.goodreads.com/author/show/14854265.Maddie_Wade
Bookbub: https://partners.bookbub.com/authors/3711690/edit
Twitter: @mwadeauthor
Pinterest: @maddie_wade
Instagram: Maddie Author

Printed in Great Britain
by Amazon